AMANDA WASHINGTON
LIBERTY'S HOPE
PERSEVERANCE BOOK 2

*Terry,
Looking forward to your feedback on this one. Thanks bunches!
A. Wash*

Sale of this book without a front cover may be unauthorized. If this book is coverless, it may have been reported to the publisher as "unsold or destroyed" and neither the author nor the publisher may have received payment for it.

Rescuing Liberty is a work of fiction. Names, characters, places, and incidents are the products of the author's imagination and are used fictitiously. Any resemblance to actual events, locales, or persons, living or dead, is entirely coincidental.

ISBN: 978-1495491429
2014 Amanda Washington
Copyright © 2014 by Amanda Washington
All rights reserved.

Published in the United States

*This one's for the Liberty and Connor fans
who wouldn't let me give up.
Thank you for keeping the dream alive.*

ACKNOWLEDGEMENTS

First and foremost I thank God—for just being, blessing, and forgiving.

Special thanks to my family, especially Meltarrus and our boys, who sacrificed daily so I had time to work on this manuscript. Mel, thanks for letting me read aloud to you! I love you!

To my editors—Benjamin Spurlock, Tracey Jackson, Mykle Lee, and George Hill who never shied away from pointing out my numerous mistakes—thank you! Each of you has contributed so much, and I am eternally thankful.

I'm greatly indebted to the talented creative team who developed my cover. Cover design: Jackson and Tracey Jackson. Cover models: Jessica Yonko and Caleb Kauffman.

Sincere thanks to Zak Amodt for his sharing his expertise on Special Forces, and to the many people who encouraged, prodded, and even threatened me during the creation and editing of this book. I seriously don't think I would have ever gotten it done without you. Your faith in me has been humbling, and your friendships, worth more than gold. There are too many of you to list, but you know who you are. Thank you for keeping me from giving up. I love and appreciate each one of you!

CHAPTER ONE

Liberty

"Darkness cannot drive out darkness; only light can do that. Hate cannot drive out hate; only love can do that." —Martin Luther King, Jr.

~July 7

THE INTENSE JULY sun beat down on my head as I sat in the middle of Highway 530, contemplating the stretch of road before me. It wound and curved, clinging to the side of the Skagit River, with only a narrow line of trees separating it from the water. A thriving forest grew on the opposite side of the road, with evergreen trees so lush and thick I could barely see past the first row. Green foliage blanketed the forest floor, concealing all sorts of ankle-twisting and bruise-producing hazards. I knew those hazards firsthand, and had the beaten and battered body to prove it.

I leaned forward and slid a map of Washington state out of my back pocket. Unfolding the map, I traced a line, starting at Mount Baker National Forest and going west to my approximate location. Highway 20 was maybe five miles to the north of where I sat. If I followed that road to the east, then Highway 9 North would almost take me to Canada. My map showed me just a smidgeon of southwestern Canada, so I'd have to filch a Canadian map once I hit the border. From there I'd travel to Kamloops, the last known location of my best friend, Michelle.

I had believed life would be different in Canada. I'd clung to unfounded hope the roads wouldn't be deserted and the kids wouldn't be trying to kill us. I could stay with Michelle's family while I searched for a job. Then I'd find a cute little apartment, rescue another dog from the pound and rebuild my life. At least, that had been the plan.

It had seemed like such a simple and realistic plan, too, but now there were complications. One such complication appeared while I traced Highway 9 with my fingertip. Out of the corner of my eye, I watched him step out of the forest and slink toward me. When his boots reached the road I slid my Smith and Wesson Sigma free from its holster and aimed it above his head.

"Good," Connor Dunstan said with an infuriatingly handsome lopsided grin. His perfect, stubborn jaw was two days past a five o'clock shadow which managed to increase the mystery in his intense dark eyes. His solid athletic build—accustomed to running long distances and breaking down doors to save the day—was hidden under fatigues. He moved with the grace and confidence of a trained killer, because that's exactly what he was. "But I could have shot you from the trees."

I shrugged, knowing no amount of caution could prevent the inevitable bullet with my name on it once it came for me. "Death, I can handle." I holstered my gun, and then smiled at him.

His grin turned to a grimace as he eased closer. In the month that we had known each other, we'd been hunted, captured, and tortured, barely escaping with our lives. We both knew there were fates much worse than death, and since he wore 'overprotective alpha-male' like a badge of honor, he quickly changed the subject.

"What are you doing?" he asked.

I didn't think he could see the map from his angle, so I folded it and slid it under my leg. "Just thinking."

"I see." Connor sounded apprehensive. He walked over and offered me his hand, as if to heft me to my feet.

I didn't want him to know I'd been studying the map, so I shook my head. "I'm good. Just want to sit a bit. Legs are tired.

Where's Ashley?" I asked, in my own pathetic attempt at a subject change.

Ashley filled the role of the other complication keeping me from my Canadian destination. Connor's beautiful daughter shared his dark, fathomless eyes and his brunette hair, and I loved her like she was my own. I couldn't leave the girl any more than I could leave her overbearing, tenacious father. Feeling his eyes boring into my skull, I tugged on one of my shoestrings, and then retied it.

"She's with Jeff," he finally replied. "She found out that he's some sort of karate expert and pestered him until he agreed to show her the beginner moves."

"You're okay with that?"

"Not really." Connor shrugged. "But I trust the camp security to keep her safe."

"Connor, I know Jeff's made mistakes, but he's not the bad guy you keep making him out to be. Yeah, he's got some baggage, but he's trying to cut free of it."

"Libby, his dad and sister both want you dead."

"But Jeff's not like them. Once you get to know him, he's pretty sweet and adorable."

Connor cocked his head to the side, and a vein started throbbing in his forehead. "Must you refer to him as adorable?"

"Aww, you're jealous? Although, I'm not sure why. I'm twenty-eight, Connor. Adorable isn't exactly a quality I'm looking for in a man."

Connor sat on the road in front of me, mirroring my crossed leg position. Our knees touched and he leaned his upper body toward mine.

"So, tell me, what qualities are you looking for in a man?"

Taken aback by his flirtatious tone, my mouth snapped shut. I wanted to fire back some sort of witty retort, but the musky scent of metal, earth, and man that made up Connor invaded my senses, making it impossible to think. His presence invaded my personal space, and, although terrified of his proximity, I didn't hate it. Refusing to lean back and show him how uncomfortable he'd made me, I squared my shoulders and raised an eyebrow at him, trying to look contemplative.

Connor grinned and asked, "Are you getting a sunburn or blushing? I can't tell."

I gripped the bottom hem of my jeans, in order to keep myself from hiding my face from his gaze, and shrugged nonchalantly. "It's sunny, I'm a redhead ... you're smart. You'll figure it out. Is there something I can help you with?"

"Just surprised you're out here sitting alone in the sun." He seemed to consider me for a moment. Then he held out his closed fist in the space between us, opened it, and presented me with a beat-up, dirty penny. "A penny for your thoughts?"

I smiled in spite of myself and closed his fingers back around the coin, trying to ignore the way my heart sped up at the contact with his skin. It felt a lot like playing with fire: exciting and warm, but I knew it would burn me if I got too close.

"You might want to keep that," I said. "Probably don't want to know what I'm thinking about."

"The funny thing is—," he returned my smile, grabbed my hands, pulled me into him, and then reached under my leg and swiped my map, "I already know."

"Hey!" I yelled, pushing myself back from his chest. "Give me that back!"

Holding the map out of my reach, he unfolded it and looked it over. "You're still planning that trip to Canada, huh? Were you intending to tell me about it, or would I have had to follow you?" Seemingly satisfied with himself, he refolded the map and offered it to me.

I grabbed for it, but he only tightened his grip. Annoyed, I glared up at him. His dark pupils were like tar pits, and I knew that if I stared into them too long I'd be stuck for good. Like my own personal groupie, he promised to give up his life and follow me to Canada. My stomach flipped over the idea, terrifying and exciting me. Finally, he released the map, and I took it and secured it back under my leg, like I could make believe he hadn't called me out on it.

"That sounds pretty stalkerish," I countered, hoping I sounded more put-off than I felt. "I heard you had finesse and skills with the ladies. Following me wherever I go? That's kinda creeper territory, there. Whatever happened to the wine and dine approach?"

"Oh, my mistake. I didn't peg you for one of *those* girls. Want to be wined and dined?" he asked. The smile that stretched across his lips looked so delicious it sent goose bumps up my spine. "I'm on it. In fact, that's the very reason I came to find you."

Oops. "It is?" My voice cracked and I coughed to cover it up.

Connor's smile widened. "Yep. Come now, the limo will be here momentarily." He grabbed my hand and stood, pulling me up with him.

I barely had time to grab the map off the road before being hefted to my feet. I stuffed it back into my pocket and eyed him suspiciously. "A limo, huh? And exactly where will it be taking us?"

"Seattle. Close your eyes so you can see it with me."

I hesitated and his fingertips landed on my eyelids, gently lowering until they closed.

"Better. Now imagine the Space Needle. The limo will pull up to the curb and the driver will open your door. You'll be wearing something stunning, yet classy. Maybe a dark green dress to bring out your eyes. Thin straps, fitted waist, long layered skirt. Something from Valentino or Dolce and Gabbana."

"I had no idea you were so into fashion."

"What can I say? I'm a man of many talents." He tugged at the pony tail holder securing my braid and gently ran his fingers through my hair, separating it.

I chewed on my lip as electricity shot through me at his touch.

"You'll wear your hair down, leaving it curly. I'll meet you on the curb in front of the Space Needle and take your hand in the crook of my elbow. We'll make our way to the famous spinning restaurant, where we'll be seated immediately and our server will pop the cork on a hearty red wine ... something from the chef's private cellar. Then they'll bring us baby spinach and raspberry salads, followed by crab cakes. For the main course, we'll get lightly seared ahi tuna and tenderloin so tender it will fall apart the moment it touches our tongues."

I tried to avoid getting swept away in Connor's imagery, even reminding myself that Connor "playboy" Dunstan had once been labeled as 'Washington's Most Eligible Bachelor.' Still, I couldn't resist his charm. I wanted to go where he was taking me, to escape reality and just dream about what our lives could be like if the world hadn't changed. I clung to the fantasy until my mouth watered and my stomach rumbled. He put his hand on the small of my back and leaned closer to me, drawing me further in.

"We'll hold hands and watch the lights of the city spin around us, enjoying the company as well as the view for hours. Next, we'll exit the Space Needle and walk the few blocks over—"

"Walk?" I interrupted. "After that huge meal, you may have to roll me down the street."

He ignored me and continued, "To this little Italian dive that serves the best gelato in the U.S."

"Gelato?" I asked, opening my eyes. "Do you have any idea what I would do for gelato right now?"

Connor leaned closer and gave me a butterfly-inducing grin. "No. Do tell."

Little bells and whistles went off in my brain, screaming at me that he'd crept too close with eyes too hungry. I leaned back and looked around, saying, "Yeah, so where's that limo? Shouldn't it be here by now?"

Connor laughed.

In truth, no limo would be coming for us. There were no more fancy restaurants or little Italian dives. The last time Seattle graced my television screen, the city was on fire, its ashes packed with rioters. I didn't even know if the Space Needle still stood. The country had changed in the blink of an eye, and we'd probably never get it back.

"Okay, you called my bluff." Connor grabbed my hand and tugged me off the road. "But they are cooking up the last of the venison. We should probably get back there if we want any of it."

"Mmm, venison," I replied, letting him tow me toward the camp. It wasn't exactly crab cakes and tenderloin, but to be honest, I wasn't that picky.

We walked for a bit, and then Connor paused and squeezed my hand. He whistled our approach and another bird call answered. He gave me one of his arrogant half-smiles that made me want to punch and kiss him at the same time. "Admit it. I had you. If I could wine and dine you like that, you'd be putty in my hands. You almost kissed me back there."

I rolled my eyes and tugged my hand away from him. Just like the date he'd just created, Connor's affections for me drifted somewhere beyond reality. He swore he loved me, but I feared he only loved the chase. Like a dog after its tail, he'd have no idea what to do with me if he ever caught me.

"Connor, if I had a bottle of wine right now, I'd dump it on your head." I turned and stomped off.

"What if I rubbed gelato on my lips?" he asked.

CHAPTER TWO

Connor

CONNOR LEANED AGAINST a tree and watched Liberty walk away. He'd grown accustomed to the sight, but this time it was different. Rather than scowling and fuming, this time she tried to hide her smile as she left. He drew hope from that observation as he followed her past the barely-visible white rock that served as a range marker and into a dense patch of evergreens.

Movement called Connor's attention to the northwest. The black barrel of a machine gun mounted on a bipod, pointed in Connor's general direction, brought him back to reality. It had been several years since he'd retired from the Army, but now, it needed him back. And, how could he say no? Not only was the country in trouble, but when he, Liberty, and Ashley had been trapped in the clutches of the Progression and facing death or worse, the Army rescued them. The captain of the Army platoon—Carlos Ortega, known by his friends as 'Boom'—had served on Connor's Operation Detachment Alpha team back when Connor commanded a Special Forces team. Boom's platoon consisted of mostly green soldiers, refugees of the war the Progression waged against the country. Connor was a welcome asset, so Boom asked him to act as his first sergeant until they reached Fort Lewis. Then, the leaders who were trying to bring order to the chaos of the states would most likely force him back into a Special Forces Team Commander position. Connor didn't want to be back in command, but he'd do it, if it meant keeping Liberty and Ashley tucked behind the security of the Army.

Corporal Patrick Shortridge stood in a chest-high hole in the ground, pulling security behind the southwest machine gun. He gave Connor a quick nod before looking past him to watch the trees. Connor scanned the forest floor to the east until he saw another black barrel, behind which, Private Tyrone James kept watch.

The third and forth machine guns were positioned further to the north, but trees blocked Connor's view of them. He stepped between Shortridge and James, avoiding the other partially-covered holes that served as individual fighting positions, and walked toward the scattering of one- and two-man combat tents that housed eighteen soldiers in addition to him, Liberty and Ashley. The three-foot-high tents were tucked behind trees and bushes, making them almost impossible to see until he was upon them. Northeast of the small camouflage domes, stood a hastily-constructed corral that caged the platoon's eleven horses. To the west of the corral, the main tent stood nestled against the sheer side of a mountain. The mountain served as both a blessing and a curse, reducing the number of sides the platoon had to secure, and consequently limiting their avenues of escape. Though not the best campsite Connor had constructed, It would be good enough for the few days they occupied it. Then they'd resume their journey to Fort Lewis.

Connor heard a whistle and paused to see Private Anthony Stein step out from behind a tree, followed by Private Noah Warren. Warren split off and headed north as Stein made a beeline straight for Connor. Although Connor didn't know much about Warren, he knew Stein had owned and operated a small taxidermy business in Snohomish before the economy collapsed.

When the riots began, Stein and his wife and kids retreated to their hunting cabin, where they managed to escape from the reality of the situation until about a month ago. Stein had come back from a hunting trip to find his house in flames. He busted through the door to find his wife with her neck snapped and their ten-year-old sons missing.

A proficient tracker, Stein hunted down the butchers who'd done the deed, but not before they killed his sons. When the platoon came across Stein, he was single-handedly mowing down a camp of rogue soldiers who called themselves the Progression. The Army jumped to his aid, supplying him with bullets and backup as he unleashed vengeance on murderers, and afterward, Stein enlisted.

"Private Stein." Connor greeted with a nod.

Stein was in his mid-thirties, but stress and grief had aged his face by at least ten years. With a grim expression, he approached Connor.

"Excuse me, First Sergeant, but have you seen Captain Ortega recently?" Stein asked. Then as an afterthought, he saluted and apologized.

Connor shook his head. "I haven't seen him since this morning. Is everything okay?"

Stein hesitated and glanced around, clearly still unsure of protocol.

Smiling, Connor reassured the soldier, "I was a Special Forces ODA commander. Trust me, I rank high enough to receive whatever intel you have."

"Right." Stein frowned. He seemed to consider Connor for a moment before bowing his head. "My apologies, First Sergeant. Private Warren and I were out checking the game traps to the east. On the way back we found a few sets of boot tracks heading south. They're new."

"How new?"

"Today. Early this morning. I believe we just missed the intruders."

"How close did they get to the camp?"

"About a hundred yards, but they know we're here."

Connor scratched the stubble on his chin. "How can you be so sure?"

"They broke the trap."

"They left us a message." Connor frowned. "And they didn't even stop in for a cup of coffee. Imagine that. Yes, you should definitely find the captain and tell him what you've found. I'll be in the main tent, ready and awaiting his orders."

"Yes, First Sergeant!" Stein saluted again and then jogged off.

Connor scanned the surrounding trees, wondering what sort of play the Progression was making. *Only a few? So they know where our camp is. Now what?*

Just outside of the main tent, Connor greeted Sergeant Kai Soseki, who headed toward the northeast machine gun position. Now in his mid-twenties, Soseki had joined the military fresh out of high school. He stood about five and half feet tall, his body all lean muscle. Boom had hand-picked Soseki for their current mission because of his skill in stealth and hand-to-hand combat. He was one of the few trained soldiers the platoon could boast of.

The smell of cooking meat tantalized Connor's taste buds and made his mouth water. Deciding to wait for Boom behind a plate of warm venison, he followed his nose and slipped into the largest tent in the camp.

The "main tent," as they called it, was a green rectangle about 650 square feet in size. Two flaps allowed entrance; one on either side of the eating area. The first, Connor had entered through. The second led to a Dakota fire hole—a smokeless fire pit dug about a foot into the ground with a second hole to ventilate it—with a giant cast-iron pot balanced on metal stakes above it. The front three quarters of the "main tent" held three utilitarian folding tables, surrounded by collapsible chairs, about half of which were currently full of soldiers. Beyond the tables, a canvas divider separated the front from the back quarter of the tent. Behind that divider, another table stood, covered by the maps, schedules, and paperwork Boom used to run the camp.

Connor slipped through the tent and peered into the cast-iron pot. Chunks of venison, potatoes, carrots, and onions swam in a thick, brown broth. Deciding it looked edible enough, he grabbed a bowl and ladled himself some stew.

When Connor stepped back into the main tent, he found Liberty sitting toward the end of the middle table, talking to a man sitting across from her. Dark hair, scruffy beard, pockmarked face with bags under his eyes. If Connor had to guess, he'd place the man in his mid forties, but time had pulled no punches with this one.

Connor paused in front of the empty chair beside Liberty and asked, "This seat taken?"

"No," she said between bites. "Sit and meet my new friend, Tyler."

Connor put his bowl down and the new recruit stood and offered his hand, clearly ignorant of protocol.

"Name's Private Tyler Noke. Pleasure to meet you, First Sergeant."

Connor decided to ignore protocol as well and shook the recruit's hand before settling into his seat. "How long have you been with the platoon, Private Noke?" he asked.

"I joined about a week before the two of you showed up. Used to drive log trucks out of Sedro-Wooley before the country went all to hell. Was holed up in my house with a rifle and a shotgun, surrounded by a bunch of kids who promised to shoot me if I didn't turn over my weapons and join them. When the captain and his men came through town they ran off the kids and invited me to enlist." Noke shrugged. "I didn't have nuthin' better to do and I've never been good at stayin' in one place too long. Figured I might as well join the good guys."

"Lucky you were home, and not on the road, when everything happened," Liberty observed.

Noke nodded. "Yes, ma'am. I was scheduled to head to Boise later that week. I saw what Boise looked like before the T.V. went dark. Thank the good Lord I wasn't in that mess."

A heavy silence settled over the trio at the mention of the riots. Connor stirred his stew, searching for chunks of meat through the mush of over-boiled vegetables as his mind drifted back to the riots.

He parked in front of his brother's store as Jacob waved frantically for him to hurry into the store's walk-in safe. Connor grabbed the box of food he'd salvaged from his house and opened his car door. Alarms and sirens greeted him, blaring from the strip mall on the next block. Shots were fired. Clutching the box, he sprinted toward his brother's store.

"You okay?" Liberty asked, interrupting Connor's thoughts.

He looked up. Noke had disappeared. Liberty's bowl sat empty and concern creased her forehead as she stared at him.

"Connor?" she prompted.

"Yeah. Just ... remembering."

She nodded. "That's dangerous. You should eat before your stew gets cold. I mean it's not ahi and tenderloin, but it's not bad."

Thankful that she'd rescued him from his memories, he took a bite. "Nope. Not bad at all. Not as good as that quail you cooked for us, though. Now that was some tasty meat."

Being quite possibly the worst person in the world at taking a compliment, the slightest hint of pink colored her cheeks before she broke eye contact.

"I can't wait to see what else you can cook."

She glanced up at him, and he got the feeling she was trying to decide if he was just poking fun at her. He wanted to reassure her of his honest curiosity, but Boom entered the tent and made a beeline for Connor. Connor smiled and squeezed her hand before standing to greet his friend and commanding officer.

"Good afternoon, Connor. Libby." Boom nodded to each.

"Hello Boom." Liberty stood. "Is everything okay?"

"It will be. I apologize for interrupting, but I need a few words with Connor. Will you please excuse us?"

"Yes, of course," Liberty replied.

Connor followed Boom to the back of the tent where they went through the flap and straight to the table.

Always one to get to the point, Boom uncovered the largest map, spread it across the table, and placed a marker to the east of the campsite. "This is where the tracks begin. Stein said that they go to the southeast. You'll take five men with you and find out if the tracks lead to a camp or not. We need to know how far away the camp is and whether or not they have mobilized their forces to come for us yet."

Connor nodded. "Yessir."

"Stein will be your tracker. Who else do you want to take?"

Connor looked at the map and considered his options. "Soseki for stealth. We'll need a medic just in case. Maybe the veterinarian. What did you say his name was again?"

"Magee." Boom rubbed the stubble on his chin. "Yes, that leaves Osberg here. What about Thompson?"

"Jeff?" Connor let out a breath. "I'd rather not."

"You still don't trust him?" Boom asked.

Connor shook his head. "I'd rather keep him here under surveillance."

Boom nodded. "Alright, Jeff stays behind. Who else do you want to take?"

"You have some pretty green recruits. Met one by the name of Noke today. Does he have any combat training at all?"

Boom chuckled. "No, but don't let him fool you, he's excellent with a rifle and his sense of direction is spot on. If you need to communicate with the camp, he can be your runner. He's faster than he looks. You should take Mark Teran as well. He's been with us since right after we left the fort. He used to be a department store manager in Tacoma, and I caught him trying to steal food from the wagon. He's got guts, but desperately needs training. That will round out your team."

Connor nodded. "I'll get started on the op order. How soon do you want us to head out?"

"Within the hour. It'll be a good training exercise for the recruits."

CHAPTER THREE

Liberty

MY STEW BOWL sat empty, and I had nothing to do but wait for Connor and Boom to return from the back of the tent. Determined to make myself useful, I collected empty bowls from the soldiers who were finished eating and washed the dishes in the buckets of water beside the fire. While I cleaned, someone filled my vacated seat, so I homed in on the empty seat beside a man reading a tattered John Grisham paperback.

He had short blonde hair and didn't even spare me a glance as I slid into the chair beside him. Since he didn't seem open to conversation, I watched the back of the tent, wondering what took Connor and Boom so long to return.

After what seemed like forever, Connor pushed through the divider and headed toward me. Halting directly behind my chair, he handed a sheet of paper to the soldier beside me.

"Corporal Marr, deliver this warning order to Stein, Soseki, Magee, Noke, and Teran. Relieve Soseki on the northeast machine gun."

Pocketing his paperback, Marr stood and saluted. Then he hurried out of the tent.

"A warning order?" I asked. "That sounds pretty serious. They're not in trouble, are they?"

Connor sat in the chair that Marr had vacated and turned toward me. "No. It's just a heads up to help them prepare for a little adventure we're planning."

"You're leaving," I said.

It wasn't a question, but he nodded anyway. "We had some curious visitors checking out our camp this morning. We're going to go say 'hi.' Maybe even take them a fruit basket."

He joked about it to set me at ease, but in truth, his humor did the opposite. Goosebumps rose from my skin. I glanced toward the door of the tent, wanting to run out, find Ashley, and reassure myself of her safety. "What do you mean by visitors? They were in the camp? Watching us?"

He grabbed my hands and held them in his. "We have constant security. There is no way they could come into this camp unannounced. I don't think they even know where it is yet. They were just trying to figure out our general location. I'm not telling you this to freak you out, but I do need you to be careful. Look after Ashley and please don't leave the camp while I'm gone."

I nodded. "How long will you be?"

"My team is just going to gather intel. We'll find out how many of them there are and what they're up to. We should be back before dark."

With the mid-summer days stretching into the night, dark was a long way away. A thousand protests formed on my tongue, but I didn't have the courage to voice a single one. I wanted to ask him not to go—no, I wanted to beg him to stay—but I couldn't. Even if I could, Connor's sense of duty would torment him until it ripped him from my side and flung him into combat.

"I'll be careful," he replied to my unasked request.

I nodded, not trusting myself to speak without sounding like a codependent idiot.

He leaned forward and kissed my forehead.

"I love you," he whispered, then stood. Without waiting for me to return the words we both knew I couldn't, he said "I'll be back."

Then he walked away.

A sense of dread crept up my spine as I watched Connor walk out of the tent.

"No need to worry about that one," said a voice tinted with a slight Hispanic accent.

I hadn't heard Boom approach, and his sudden appearance made me jump. I looked over my shoulder at him. "Would you stop that already? I swear I'm going to put bells on your boots or something."

Boom laughed and sat in the seat beside me. The Army captain was made up of five and a half feet of Latino Catholic faith and wielded explosives with a level of ease that most people used to operate a remote control. He and Connor had a past, and though I didn't know all the details, I knew Connor trusted the man more than anyone else alive. It would be difficult not to trust Boom, though. He had a smile that lit up his eyes and created crinkles around the edges.

"How are you?" he asked, resting his hands on his knees and leaning toward me.

I wanted to lie and reassure him of my wellbeing, but the concern in Boom's voice demanded honesty.

"Worried," I admitted. Since the ground didn't open and swallow me up for admitting my weakness, I continued, "Tired, sad, confused. How are you?"

He chuckled. "Better than you apparently." He rested his hand on my shoulder and asked, "Anything you want to talk about?"

"Have you ever been to Canada?" I asked.

"Yes."

"Which part?"

Boom rubbed his chin and looked up at the ceiling.

"Is this one of those things that if you told me about it, you'd have to kill me?" I asked.

Boom chuckled and shook his head. "You know we don't actually say that, right? Anyway, my business in Canada was more of a personal nature. I flew to Whistler for a friend's wedding. Why do you ask?"

"I have a friend who lives in Kamloops. That's where I was heading before … well before I ran into Ashley and Connor. I had an incredible plan to start a new life in Kamloops."

Boom chuckled again. "Yep. I'd imagine you did. I had a friend who used to say 'Man plans, God laughs.' I believe that's pretty accurate."

I frowned. "Well, that's rude."

"Indeed."

Boom watched me for a few moments, and I got the feeling he wanted to tell me something, but held back.

"What is it?" I asked. "Just give it to me straight and don't pull your punches."

"Did you ever play a sport?" he asked.

I shrugged, wondering where he was going with his question. "A little volleyball and basketball, but I was never very good. Too clumsy."

"I played baseball and I was very good," Boom grinned. "I was a solid base hitter, but first base was my sweet spot. My whole family made it to every game, and we all knew that baseball would be my future ... my ticket to a better life."

He paused and stared off into space for a moment.

"What happened?" I prompted.

"We got a new coach my senior year." Boom chuckled and shook his head. "And man, did he hate me. I don't know what I did to him, but he seemed determined to hold me down. Stuck me out in right field and kept me there for the entire season."

"Ouch. That's rough." I replied. "I played right field in little league. It's where they stuck me to keep me out of the way of the action."

Boom nodded. "My pride was hurt, and after the new coach told me he had no intention of returning me to first base, I quit the team and walked away from baseball. I used to spend a lot of time wondering what would have happened if I'd only stuck it out. Maybe if I'd shown him how well I played right field, he would have changed his mind and given me back my base. But now I understand. That coach was the best thing that ever happened to me."

Confused, I raised an eyebrow at him. "Why would you say that? Do you have any idea how much professional baseball players make? You could have done a lot of good with that money."

Boom laughed. "I was a selfish young man. The only good I would have done was for myself. But where do you think those professional baseball players are now? What good is all their millions doing for them in this?"

"Good point."

"My plan was ripped out of my hands, and I went into the Army because I didn't know what else to do. I followed God's plan, and He has been using me to help people and rescue them from the oppressive hand of the Progression. Look around you. Each of these men is worth more millions than I ever could have made playing ball."

He gestured, and I glanced around. Only five soldiers remained in the main tent. They had gathered around the table by the entrance, playing poker. They looked like a family, with how they joked around and poked fun at each other.

I nodded.

"What we tend to forget is that God is our ultimate coach. But unlike flawed human coaches, His motives are driven by love as He tries to save not only our team, but the people from the opposing team as well."

I rubbed at the goose bumps that sprouted on my arms. "Wow, that's deep. I never thought of it that way."

"He's going to move you into the position He needs you in to have the greatest impact. The question is, are you willing to give up your plan for His?"

I considered the invitation in Boom's words for a moment before asking, "Do you think I'm supposed to join the Army? I won't kill again. I can't, Boom." I hadn't meant to blurt out that last little tidbit of information. I swallowed back the lump in my throat and rubbed my hands on my pants, as if that would wipe off the blood stains I couldn't seem to forget were there.

Boom stared at me. I felt him watching me as I rested my hands on the table. "You killed someone?"

"Once. One of my neighbors, a creep named Rodney, broke into my apartment and threatened me with this." I pulled the Sigma out of its holster and studied it. It felt like death and security, such an odd combination. "I don't know what happened. He threatened me with the gun, and then this spirit just came over me. I wasn't myself. The gun went off, and then Rodney died on my floor."

"You disarmed him?" Boom's eyebrows rose in question.

"I guess, but it wasn't me. It was like I had no control. I just moved out of instinct, and I didn't even mean to shoot him."

Boom continued to watch me. "What did you do next?"

"Threw up. Seriously, it was the worst feeling ever. I'd been hunting before, but this … it wasn't the same." My sadistic mind served me up an image of Rodney.

A red flower blossomed from his chest. Strangled sounds came from his dying body as he fell to the floor. Blood pooled around him as his eyes watched me until his life drained away.

I shuddered at the memory.

"He would have killed you," Boom observed, trying to be reassuring, but his words just irritated me for some reason.

"I know." I shrugged and stuffed the gun back into its holster. "But that doesn't change anything."

Boom looked up at the sky and I got the feeling he prayed. Probably for me, since I clearly needed it. After a moment his attention returned to me. "Do you know what the motto of the Green Berets is, Libby?"

Thrown off by his question, I shook my head no.

"*De oppresso liber.* To liberate the oppressed. With that as our objective, Connor and I trained for years to become the best. Not because we chased glory, fame or riches, but because we believed in the mission."

Boom looked away, and his eyes unfocused as he smiled. "Connor was a ... resourceful and determined leader. It was my honor to serve our country beside him."

We sat in silence for a moment while Boom seemed lost in memories. Finally I asked, "What happened?"

Boom shook himself out of his trance and asked, "What do you mean?"

"Well, you stayed in the Army and he didn't. Why not?"

"That is not my story to tell," Boom replied. "But I can tell that you're not a killer, and that's okay, Libby. *De oppresso liber* doesn't always come through weapons. Often we liberate through negotiations, making people understand the value of their freedom and encouraging them to fight for it. Our world already has more than enough killers. Maybe it's time for something different."

'Yes.'

I felt the "call" seep into my conscience, settling my nerves and calming my doubts and worries with a peace that passed understanding. *Something different.* It sounded so farfetched and yet so perfect. Exactly what we needed.

"I think you're right," I said.

He smiled. "Of course I'm right. In fact, I have need of your very different set of skills right now."

CHAPTER FOUR

Connor

An unnatural creaking noise caught Connor's attention as he came to a break in the giant evergreens. He paused at the tree line and motioned for the soldiers behind him to do the same. Approximately a hundred and fifty feet in front of them stood a two story wooden barn. Empty corrals surrounded the barn and one of the wide double doors creaked back and forth in the breeze, providing the sound he'd heard. The barn doors continued to creak, giving the place an eerie, not-quite-abandoned feel.

The tracks the crew had been following continued to bend the knee-high grass, leading to a single lane dirt road that skirted the barn and continued on. Connor circled around the tree line, remaining hidden as he moved to get a better view.

About two hundred feet on the other side of the barn sat a ranch-style farm house, detached garage and a shed. The dirt road curved in front of the house, then circled back to connect with itself and lead out through a narrow gap in the trees. Connor rejoined his team to report his findings.

"The tracks end at the road," he said. "There's a house to the west, and I'm betting if we follow this road to the east it will take us back to the highway."

"If I could get to the road, I could most likely tell you which way they went," Stein said. At Connor's nod, Stein crept forward.

"Soseki," Connor motioned the soldier over. "You and Teran, go with Stein. We'll cover you."

Soseki nodded and, with Teran on his heels, followed Stein. Teran held his assault rifle away from his body, like he was terrified of the weapon. Connor stopped him and repositioned the soldier's hands.

"Pay attention to how you're holding it. I know Boom has showed you the basics, and now you have to remember what you learned and do it." Connor tugged the gun upward and showed Teran the correct firing position. "You've got this."

"Yes, First Sergeant," Teran thanked him, and then scurried off to catch up to Soseki and Stein.

On alert beside Connor, Tyler Noke and Vincent Magee scanned the tree line. Connor raised his own weapon and kept his eyes on his three soldiers on the road.

Stein stared at the ground for a few minutes, and then jogged back to Connor. "They took the road and headed for the house."

"Alright." Connor adjusted his grip on his weapon. "Noke, Boom said you'd be able to find your way back to the camp."

Noke nodded. "Yes, First Sergeant."

"Good. We were just supposed to gather intel on their camp. But, since this definitely isn't their camp, we're going to go find out who's home. This could be a trap. I need you to wait here and watch as we enter. If anyone shows up or anything happens to us while we're in there, do *not* engage. Instead, I need you to hightail it back to the camp and report whatever you see to Boom. Understood?"

"Yes, First Sergeant." Noke saluted.

The rest of the team crept out of the trees and skulked down the road without incident. They paused when they reached the house, and Stein crouched to study the ground again.

"They split up," Stein declared. "Two went in the house, two continued on."

The flicker of a curtain caught Connor's eye. He looked at the front window in time to see the outline of a person before the curtain closed.

Leveling his assault rifle at the window, he projected his voice. "There's only two of you and five of us. We all know how this is going to end. Let's make it easy. Come out with your hands up, and no one will get hurt."

No reply.

Not that he expected one, necessarily, but it would be nice if something could go easy, just once, but no such luck. He growled in frustration and motioned for Soseki to take Teran and Magee and circle around to the back door. Soseki nodded and the three disappeared around the corner.

Turning his attention back to the window with the flickering curtain, Connor projected his voice once more. "We're soldiers with the US Army. We're aiding survivors, and we'd like to help you. Just come out with your hands up so we can see that you're not hostile. We can offer protection and food."

He waited for a response, but only silence answered him.

"We can offer proof of our goodwill, and orders showing that we're with the Army. We don't want to hurt anyone. Just open the door so we can talk," Connor shouted.

Still, there was no response.

"Alright," Connor told Stein. "We do this the hard way."

After giving Soseki's team a few more moments to get into position, he motioned Stein to the door and leveled his assault rifle to protect him.

Stein smashed into the wooden door and it flung open. Stein ducked low and Connor covered high as they rushed into the living room. A wide-eyed young boy stood in the center of the room with his hands raised. Soseki's team busted through the back door. As Connor kept his weapon leveled at the boy, the rest of the team split up into groups of two and searched the house.

Connor stared down the kid. "We knocked. Why didn't you answer?" He barked.

"First bedroom, clear!" Soseki shouted.

The boy's shabby black hair slipped forward, covering his face. He glared at Connor and pushed it back behind his ears.

"Empty your pockets, slowly," Connor commanded.

The boy scowled at him. "Or what? You'll shoot me?"

"Nope. But I will treat you like a hostile detainee." Connor lunged at the kid and grabbed his arm. He spun the boy around and toward him, until the kid's back pressed against Connor's chest and Connor had the kid's arm bent behind his back. "I said empty your pockets."

The boy didn't move.

Connor started pulling the kid's arm upward.

"Ouch! Okay, stop and I will." The boy pulled a small switchblade out of his left pocket and tossed on the floor.

"Give the knife a little kick to get it out of your range," Connor said.

The boy barely nudged it with his foot.

Connor frowned. "You're making it really difficult to like you. Now pull your pockets inside out."

The boy didn't move. Connor wanted to shake the defiant attitude out of him. Instead, he calmly pulled up on the boy's arm again until the boy cried out in pain.

"I don't think you understand the situation here," Connor told the kid. "So, let me tell you how this works. You do what you're told, or I'm going to have to hurt you. Got it?"

The boy nodded. With his one free hand he awkwardly turned his pockets inside out.

Relieved, Connor thanked him for complying.

"We didn't find anyone," Soseki reported as he stepped into the living room, followed by the rest of the team.

Teran whistled. "This here's just a pup. Can we keep him, First Sergeant?"

The boy bared his teeth at Teran.

"On second thought, he might be rabid." Teran replied.

"That's okay. I have a rabies shot back at the camp," Magee replied with a wink. "We'll fix him right up."

Connor released his hold on the boy and stepped back. He turned the kid to face him, and haunted eyes exposed secrets of a rough past, and his dry, cracked lips told of dehydration. He considered the kid's scrawny legs and gangly arms, wondering how few and far between his meals had been. He wore jeans and a t-shirt, both so dirty their original colors were a mystery, and the hole worn through the top of his right shoe was big enough to advertise that he wasn't wearing socks.

Connor relaxed his stance, trying to appear less threatening. "Who's here with you?"

The boy dropped his gaze to the ground and didn't respond.

Soseki moved in on the kid. He pivoted left, and then in one swift move, effortlessly pulled the boy into a full nelson.

"Answer the First Sergeant," Soseki commanded, his mouth right beside the kid's ear.

The boy didn't reply Soseki squeezed the kid's arms harder until he cried out for Soseki to stop. Soseki didn't let up.

"I'm waiting for you to talk." Soseki squeezed harder still.

"Okay, okay stop. I'll talk."

Finally, Soseki loosened his hold.

With a scowl the boy answered, "I'm alone, alright? Now let go of me."

"Oh, really?" Connor challenged.

The living room was the only room left for the team to search. He glanced around, searching for possible hiding place. A sofa, two recliners, a modest thirty-six television atop a small wooden stand, and a large wooden coffee table furnished the room. Connor leaned to the left, trying to see if the coffee table could hide a person.

"Uh, yeah," the kid said. Though he kept his scowl in place, his feet shifted.

Curiosity steeped, Connor stepped around the boy. Two doors hid a storage area in the center of the table. Although it wouldn't be comfortable, a child could fit in the space.

Bingo.

"Right." Connor motioned toward the table, drawing his weapon. Soseki and Stein swept forward, one on each side. Once they stood ready, Connor nodded. Each man grabbed a hold of the door closest to them and swung them open. Then they aimed into the small space.

"Don't shoot," said a female voice from inside the coffee table.

"You're alone, huh?" Connor asked the boy.

The kid shrugged.

Connor turned his attention back to the table and ordered, "Come out. Slowly."

Short, slender legs kicked, wiggled, and slid out of the compact space, followed by the rest of a young girl. She looked slightly older than the boy—maybe fifteen—and her wavy, dark hair fell just below her collarbone, elongating her thin face.

Soseki moved in to search the girl as Connor asked the kids who they were.

The boy stayed silent, but the girl seemed all too willing to talk.

"I'm Kylee," she replied. "The idiot you're harassing is my brother, Braden."

"I'm the idiot?" the boy fired back. "I told you they'd find you in the coffee table."

"Yeah, well at least I hid."

"A lot of good it did you. These guys are with the Army. They can't hurt us. They gave their word."

Connor shook his head. "Who gave their word? I promised nothing ..."

Three shots rang out and the living room window shattered. Connor grabbed Braden's wrist and pulled the boy away from the window and to the floor. Connor ducked behind a recliner as Soseki covered Kylee and the rest of the soldiers went prone.

Connor used the armrest of the chair to level his gun and returned fire. Then he paused to address Braden, who curled up behind the chair, cowering in fear.

"Is this who told you we couldn't hurt you?" he asked the boy.

Braden looked away.

"They're shooting blindly into a building that they know you're in." Connor fought the urge to shake the kid into reality. "Do you really think they care if you live or not? Tell me how many there are and we might be able to keep you alive."

Braden still didn't answer.

"He's right," Kylee said, popping out from behind a second recliner. "I told you we couldn't trust them."

"Trust who?" Connor asked. "The Progression? Who are you and what the heck are you doing with the Progression?"

"Kye, don't!" the boy shouted.

"Yeah, 'cause your plan worked so great, right?" She turned to face Connor again. "They put us in here to get your attention. They told us to keep you here for a while. Said we were supposed to be a distraction."

Keep us? Distraction? Connor's chest tightened with understanding. *Away from the camp.* He saw the horror he felt echoed on the faces of the men around him. With his team gone, the camp held fifteen people, one of whom was Connor's twelve year old daughter.

"A trap." Teran aimed his gun at Braden's head.

"No, wait!" Kylee pleaded.

Stein turned his gun on the girl.

"They have our mom." She stifled a sob. "We had to. They promised to release her if we helped them."

Tears began to stream down her face. "Please don't hurt us. We didn't have a choice."

The Progression was the enemy; a brutal army, confined by no laws and no morals. Ruthless in their recruiting, heartless in the atrocities they committed to get what they wanted. Braden and Kylee were just more naïve kids they had manipulated into doing their bidding.

Connor hesitated. "How many of them are there?" he asked Kylee.

"Four," she replied. "Two stayed on the road, two were already in the house. They left through the back."

More gunfire sprayed the front of the house. A whooshing sound preceded the shattering of glass. Then fire engulfed the couch.

"A molotov cocktail?" Teran asked. "You have gotta be kidding me."

"At least it's not a grenade," Noke replied.

Connor nodded in agreement, thankful the Army had stolen or exploded most of the Progression's arsenal during the raid that rescued Connor, Liberty, and Ashley from their clutches. Smoke rapidly filled the living room, forcing Connor's attention onto this battle.

"Time to go," he said, pulling Braden to his feet. "If you run, I *will* shoot you. Got it?"

"Don't do anything stupid, Brae," Kylee told her brother.

"Soseki, take the girl," Connor said. "Out the back. Teran and Stein, you go with him. Make for the tree line, we'll cover you."

Soseki nodded and grabbed Kylee by the wrist. He pulled her to her feet and dragged her toward the back door with Teran and Stein on his heels.

"Stay," Connor told Braden. Braden nodded and huddled behind the chair as Connor knelt and returned fire out the front window.

Shots came from the back of the house, announcing that it was time to move.

Connor stood and turned toward Braden. "Keep up or die," he told the kid.

Braden nodded, looking adequately cowed. "Wait, don't I get a gun or something?" he asked.

"So you can shoot me in the back?" Connor asked. Then he added a curt, "Nope. Just stay alive."

Connor reloaded his assault rifle as they headed for the back door. "We're needed back at camp."

He opened the door and rushed into the chaos.

CHAPTER FIVE

Liberty

M<small>Y TALK WITH</small> Boom had given me a lot to think about, as well as a task to get to. Feeling encouraged and useful for a change, I stepped out of the main tent and looked around the camp. The hot July sun stood high in the sky, baking everything that unprotected by shade. Desperate for something cooler to wear, I stopped by the tent I shared with Ashley long enough to exchange my t-shirt for a tank top, and then headed out to find Ashley and Jeff.

Jeff's tent stood on the east side of the main tent, toward the outside of the camp. As I approached it, I could hear him talking to Ashley on the other side of it. Not wanting to interrupt their training session, I snuck up on them and crouched down, eavesdropping. They practiced on the other side of the tent with their backs toward me. I crept around the side of the tent so I could get a better view.

Ashley had secured her long, dark hair in a pony tail. She wore jeans that drifted above her ankles and a white t-shirt that barely reached her waistband. When she turned, I caught a glimpse of her pale, flat stomach. Her clothes had fit her perfectly when we left Olympia almost a month ago, but she seemed to be in the middle of some sort of crazy growth spurt that had gained her at least two inches in the past few weeks. Since Connor and I were first-time guardians, we had no idea whether or not this was normal, and hoped to find her larger clothes before she busted out of hers like the Incredible Hulk.

Her normally soft, sweet face was all hard lines and business as she held out her arm in front of her, and asked, "Like this?"

"Sort of," Jeff replied. "But you gotta bend your elbow. You can't lock it up like that." Jeff kept his dark hair under an inch long. He chose shirts that clung to his muscles and carried weapons like they were an extension of his arms. He had a strong, serious jaw that appeared to have been chiseled from a childhood without smiles. Though only in his early twenties, the hard lines of his face made him look closer to my age. Despite the fact that he didn't want to be in the military, dressed in camouflage pants, a tight blank tank top, and looking deadly, he could have been cast as the lead role in an action movie.

"But then it feels funny and I can't swing it right," Ashley complained.

"Yes you can. Just bend it slightly. Your elbow shouldn't be turned completely in like that." Jeff sounded exasperated, like he'd explained this same thing to her millions of times. He grabbed Ashley's elbow and tried to rotate it, but I could tell she'd locked her arm and he was trying to be gentle with her.

"Relax your arm," Jeff ordered.

"It is relaxed."

"No, it's not! It's completely stiff. If you're not going to listen and do what I say, I can't teach this to you." He let go of her arm and scratched his head. Although I couldn't see his face, I had to stifle my laughter, just imagining the way frustration must be tugging at his features. Ashley stood in an awkward-looking stance, all elbows and knees with absolutely zero grace.

Her back stiffened. "I can learn anything, and I will learn this. You promised you'd teach me, so stop trying to get out of it. When are you going to teach me the fun stuff, like kicks and punches?"

"You have to learn the basics first."

"Why?" she asked.

"Because if you don't learn the stances correctly, you will get hurt."

"Have you ever gotten hurt doing karate?"

Jeff seemed to consider this. "Yes. A couple of times during practice or competitions."

"So you know the stances, but you've still hurt yourself?"

I chuckled. Ashley had inherited her father's impressive argumentative skills. Jeff groaned, and I felt sorry enough for him to step out from my hiding spot and intervene.

Ashley saw me, and frowned. She relaxed her stance, putting both hands on her narrow hips. "You're not supposed to find me until I have some awesome kick-butt moves to show you, but Jeff won't teach me any."

"I heard." I said. "Sounds like the killjoy is trying to teach you the proper stances so you don't hurt yourself. Didn't you tell him you only want to learn the fun moves?"

"Yes!" she exclaimed. "But he won't listen!"

"What a jerk! How dare he be concerned about your safety!"

Finally catching on to my sarcasm, Ashley rolled her eyes at me and crossed her arms. "Figures you'd be on his side."

"The side of you not getting hurt? Yep. I will always be on that side." I messed up her hair, and then smiled at Jeff.

Jeff smiled back, and I couldn't help but laugh at the relief in his bright blue eyes. My laughter may have also been a touch sadistic, because if Jeff thought I was the relief he sought, he had another thing coming. The mission Boom had saddled me with included nagging, whining, and being a general nuisance until Jeff agreed to pull on his big boy pants and accept the promotion Boom offered.

"Hey, stranger," I said, sidling up to Jeff.

"Stranger?" he asked, eying me. "What's that supposed to mean?"

"There's only so many people in this camp, yet I haven't seen much of you in the past couple of days. Barely remembered what you look like. Have you been avoiding me?"

He crossed his arms. "Nope. Boom's been keeping me busy. He's put me through all sorts of tests to gauge my combat readiness."

"Ah-ha. That explains how Ash found out about your karate skills." I eyed her. "Have you been stalking Jeff?"

A dark red crept up her cheeks. "No! Everyone was watching. He looked super cool."

"I bet. How did you do on the rest of the tests?" I asked him.

Jeff shrugged. "All right, I guess."

"Just alright, huh? Is that why Boom wants to promote you to corporal?"

Now came Jeff's turn to blush. The color in his cheeks seemed to restore his youth. He looked at the ground like a child who couldn't take a compliment. "The captain told you about that?"

"Corporal?" Ashley asked. "You made corporal? That's awesome! Right? Isn't that awesome?"

She looked at me with arched eyebrows. "Why isn't he smiling? That *is* good, right?"

"Yep," I replied. "Jeff is just being modest, but Boom was pretty darn impressed with our new corporal here. I'd tell you what he said, but he used a bunch of military terms that went way over my head. I did catch the phrase 'Expert Marksman,' though. Apparently Jeff can dot the 'i' of a Pepsi can from really far away. Like miles away."

Jeff rolled his eyes. "Not miles. It wasn't that far."

"That is so cool!" Ashley said, ignoring his protest. "Next, you can teach me how to shoot!"

Jeff winced, but the girl didn't seem to notice. He sat on a box beside his tent and selected a rifle from the cache. Running an oil rag down the barrel of the gun, he seemed to drift off into his own little world.

Surprised by his peculiar behavior, I suddenly understood why Boom had sent me to talk to Jeff.

"Come on, Jeff," I whined. "You have to be at least a little excited about this promotion."

He didn't take his eyes off the rifle he cleaned. "It's not a big deal. Just another stripe on the arm."

He gently placed the rifle on top of a separate box and selected a small pistol from the cache. After turning it over a couple times, he began running the rag over the pistol.

"Not a big deal? At my old job whenever someone got promoted we'd all go out to lunch at this little Italian restaurant named Mancini's. They had the best ravioli, but their tiramisu …" My stomach growled. "See, even thinking about Mancini's tiramisu is making my tummy talk, and I just ate."

"Speaking of which—" I tugged at Jeff's arm. "They turned the last of the venison into a pretty decent stew. Come on, Ash and I will buy you lunch. It's not ravioli and tiramisu, but it will have to do."

"No can do." Jeff shook me off and returned to cleaning the pistol. "I'm about to pull security, my slacker friend. You'll have to eat without me."

"Slacker? Look, Ash, the corporal is already turning up his nose at us lowly civilians." I jokingly narrowed my eyes at Jeff. "But no, you don't get out of a celebration meal that easily, mister. When I talked to Boom, he said you can start a little late today, so come on. Time's a wastin'."

Jeff's frown deepened. "Rain check?" he asked.

Turning away from the stubborn man, I pulled Ashley aside. "Hey, kiddo, will you please go save us a couple of seats in the main tent?" I asked.

"I know you're just trying to get rid of me so you can *adult talk* with Jeff," she replied.

"And that's why I love you." I smiled and patted her on the head. "You're incredibly observant and intelligent. Now scram so I can whip him into shape without embarrassing him in front of you."

"Fine. Just be nice to him. Don't make him cry or anything."

I glanced at Jeff who would not return my gaze. Focusing back on Ashley, I shrugged. "I can't make any promises."

Ashley giggled. She gave me a quick squeeze around the waist, and then scampered off toward the main tent.

"Man, I love that kid," I said, watching her go. "But thank God there's only one of her."

"Hey!" Ashley stopped and turned to give me an indignant look. "I heard that!"

I shrugged. "Duh."

She rolled her eyes, turned, and then continued on her way.

Once she stepped out of earshot, I turned back to the problem at hand. "Okay, bucko, you need to tell me what's really going on here."

"Nothing." Jeff set the pistol next to the clean rifle and reached into the cache again.

I picked up the pistol and examined it, trying to look like I honestly considered using it. "So help me, Jeff Thompson, I will shoot you with your own gun if you don't tell me what's going on. Right this minute. I mean it."

He waved me off with a hand without bothering to look worried.

Since my bluff had been called, I sat the pistol back on the box and squatted down so I was at eye level with him while he sat. "Please tell me."

"To be honest, I don't feel much like celebrating," he finally admitted. "You don't understand. It's like I'm stuck in this river and I've been fighting the current my whole life. Now I've found this side stream, but it doesn't matter. I'm stuck in the same damn current and I can't fight it anymore."

He glanced at me and I glimpsed the torment hiding behind his eyes. My heart broke, and I reached out and touched his knee. He looked away.

As the son of a Progression major, Jeff had been groomed for military life since birth, but he never chose it. After high school, he had somehow managed to escape his father's grip and enrolled in a liberal arts college, with the dream of becoming a substance abuse counselor. Then the economy tanked, and his unloving father collected him from school and forced him into the Progression, which he promptly ran away from. I'd met Jeff while he was on the road, running from his overbearing alcoholic father.

Jeff could have kept running. He could survive solo, especially after learning that his sister, Gina, was an evil bloodsucker who couldn't be trusted. He'd even had the perfect opportunity to escape and get free of his dad once and for all while Gina busily spun lies, focused on luring Connor into her web. But instead of pursuing his own safety, he chose to stay with us and throw himself in harm's way by rescuing me from his father's grasp. And now here he stood, fighting the same war he'd been running from, but now on the opposite side of it.

"You don't have to fight, Jeff."

"What?" he asked.

I rubbed my head, trying to remember what Boom had just told me. "I'm supposed to tell you something wise and encouraging ... the advice Boom just gave me. It starts with a story about him being good at baseball but getting a coach who hated him, so he didn't get drafted into the pros, but now he's out there saving lives and helping people. Oh, and God is the ultimate coach." I patted him on the shoulder, hoping it would somehow make the botched message more powerful.

"What?" Jeff asked. "God is the ultimate coach who hates Boom? Is that what you just said?"

I tried to put my head in my hands, but since I was still squatting and wobbly, I lost my balance and started falling forward. Jeff reached out and steadied me, and in his arms, I started laughing as I realized what I'd just said. "Yes. That is exactly what I said, but not at all what I meant. Turns out, I'm not so good at wise and encouraging stories. I should probably leave that to Boom." I stood and stretched out my cramping legs.

Jeff nodded. "You should probably stick with what you know. Abrupt, direct, and to the point."

I briefly considered being insulted by what he said, but decided I had no right to be offended by the truth.

"Okay, fine, I'll give it to you straight. This sucks." I pulled my Sigma from its holster. "I don't want to use this any more than you want to use those, and I know that there's a better way. But we have to find that better way, and in the meantime ... we may need these."

I holstered my gun again. "But there's more going on with you, so spill it."

Jeff leaned forward and rested his elbows on his thighs. He laced his fingers and fidgeted with his thumbs. "My dad wasn't always the way he is now. When I was little, he was different. Happier. Then my mom got cancer and he started drinking and talking about strengthening genetics and weeding out weak genes. When she died, he ... well, you've seen what he turned into."

I shuddered. *Monster, psychopath.* I'd only spent about five conscious minutes with Major Thompson, but it had been more than enough to assure me that Jeff's dad was made of the stuff of nightmares. He emanated booze and power in equal parts and his complete and total disregard for human life still gave me nightmares. I had no idea how someone as kind as Jeff could come from someone as horrific as the Progression major.

"Whoa, wait a minute." I held my hand up as a light bulb finally went off in my head. "That's what this is really about, isn't it? You saw your dad change and you're afraid that the same will happen to you."

Jeff neither confirmed nor denied the accusation. Instead he just stared at his hands.

I was an idiot for not seeing it sooner. I smacked myself on the forehead for good measure. "Jeff, using your skills to defend and protect people doesn't turn you into a monster. Something must have snapped inside your father and he took it way beyond defending and protecting."

"Yeah, but if that happened to him, who's to say it can't happen to me too?"

My frustration bubbled to the surface, and I shouted. "Me! I say it can't."

"How could you possibly know that?" he asked.

"You're not the same as he is."

He pushed himself up from the box and stood directly in front of me, with hands clenched into fists at his sides. His eyes were almost level with mine, and I saw desperation and fear when I looked into them.

"Promise me, Libby. Promise me that you'll never let me turn into my father."

I didn't know how to respond, so I put my hands on his shoulders, lowered my head and silently prayed. As I did, I could feel Jeff relaxing.

"I don't know what the future holds," I said, looking at Jeff. "But I do know that a friend loves at all times. You're my friend, Jeff. I'll be here for you no matter what. And if you do start to slip, you better believe that I'll slap the heck out of you."

He cracked a smile.

"Don't think I won't. You might be able to shoot a soda can from ten miles away, but I can backhand you before you can blink. Now come on, Ashley's waiting for us."

He shook his head, chuckling. "It definitely wasn't ten miles away."

"Whatever. Are you coming or not?"

I could tell he wanted to argue, but knew that resistance was futile. "Yeah, I'll come. Just let me put away these guns and—"

A shrill whistle cut through the forest, interrupting him. We paused, waiting to hear another that would reassure us that the coast was clear and Connor's team had returned safe and sound.

Instead, gunfire shattered the morning.

CHAPTER SIX

Connor

CONNOR OPENED THE back door of the farmhouse and peered out. A bullet whizzed by his cheek, so close it felt like a kiss. The shot had come from the southeast side of the house and embedded itself into the siding less than a foot away from Connor's face. He leaned back and watched the trees directly in front of him, where Soseki, Teran, and Stein returned fire.

"Soseki, do you have a visual?" Connor shouted.

More shots were fired, and then Soseki shouted back, "Three enemy plus one down, your nine o'clock, forty-five meters."

Connor scrutinized the twenty feet of open, deadly ground between the house and the relative safety of the tree line. Smoke continued to fill the inside of the farmhouse, but it wasn't intense enough to push Connor and Magee into the line of enemy fire. As if anticipating that result, the Progression gunfire intensified, tearing into the house's siding. Connor slid to the floor, pulling Braden down with him. Magee went prone and watched outside.

Connor felt blind and useless lying face down while his team fought for their lives. He peeked out the bottom corner of the door and looked to the left. Another Progression soldier fell. They hid behind the side of the house, popping out to take shots at the door. Across the clearing, the rest of Connor's team drifted toward the soldiers, firing as they went. Soon the Progression kids would have nowhere to hide. He just had to wait until his men were in position.

The air grew thick with metallic smoke. Braden coughed.

"Get ready to move," Connor said. Then he pushed himself off the floor and hunched over. He ran out the door and paused on the small, partially-demolished wooden back porch, pressing his back against the side of the house. He hopped over the porch railing and regained his position against the wall. Then he gestured for Magee and Braden to follow him.

Magee stood and pulled the kid up with him. Tugging Braden behind him, the medic followed Connor over the side of the porch and froze against the siding.

Connor motioned for the two to stay put, and then ran toward the Progression soldiers, his M4 aimed and waiting for the first sign of movement. Within seconds, a head popped out from behind the house and Connor fired. The body flew back and fell to the ground.

Connor kept moving. He turned the corner and leveled his weapon, expecting to find the last soldier. Instead, four young bodies lay crumpled on the ground before him. He checked each for vitals and shook his head. They were gone, and it was past time for his team to be gone as well.

Weapon in hand, Connor kept scanning the area for more Progression soldiers as he motioned for Magee to bring Braden. Soseki and the rest of the team covered them from the other side of the clearing as they ran across. Reunited, the team slipped back into the safety of the trees.

"Any wounded?" Magee asked.

"Nope. Even managed to keep the girl alive," Teran replied, pulling on Kylee's arm.

She stepped out from behind him and hugged her brother. "You okay?"

Braden nodded and returned the gesture.

"I hate to break up this reunion, but we gotta run," Connor said. "You two, keep up. If you don't, we're going to have to shoot you."

Braden and Kylee nodded.

Connor led his men into a fast jog, stretching out his legs to eat up the miles. As he raced over the uneven forest floor, the pounding of feet behind him served as the only indication that he didn't run alone. His mind ran almost as quickly as his feet, wondering what they'd find back at the camp. Dread crept into his brain, wrapping its tentacles around his thoughts and twisting them into dark nightmares. Images of flames and death flashed, creating his own personal horror flick until he could almost smell smoke and death. Connor forced more speed into his strides.

Desperate to banish the dark thoughts, his mind drifted back to the moments before he'd left camp.

"But he's really good!" Ashley shouted.

She had slipped into Connor's tent and was bouncing on his sleeping bag. Fibers danced through the air, playing in the early morning sunlight of the small, army-issued tent. The day was already warming, and the heat intensified the musty smell of soldiers and soiled clothing; the stench of a military camp. The stuffed bear wedged under Ashley's arm was missing an eye and had a bandage across one arm. Ashley and Liberty both referred to the teddy bear as "Frog," but neither would tell Connor why. He wrote it off as another inside joke the two shared.

Ignoring her pleading tone, he finished lacing up his boots, and then turned toward Ashley. "I don't think it's a good idea for you to spend so much time with him. We don't have much information about him. He could be dangerous."

Ashley's jaw jutted out. "Jeff's a great guy. Boom says without Jeff, Liberty would probably be dead."

Connor felt the proverbial knife slide into his gut and turn. Although happy Liberty was safe, he hated the fact that they owed her safety to Jeff. Too many unanswered questions around the rescue made the whole situation suspect. Furthermore, sometimes he wished he could duct tape Boom's mouth shut.

"Boom doesn't know that for sure." He forced his expression back to neutrality and smiled at Ashley.

"Why don't you like Jeff?" she asked without missing a beat.

"It's not that I don't like him," Connor paused, waiting for a stroke of genius to equip him with a suitable response to give his twelve-year-old daughter. Despite the fact that Jeff had been raised by a psychotic father, the guy had turned out to be a decent soldier. He was an expert marksman and now a black belt, but they knew next to nothing about him. And on top of that, he followed Liberty around like a puppy after a squeaky toy. "I just don't know him, so I don't trust him."

"We'll stay in the camp. How dangerous can it be?" she pressed.

"Has he asked to train you?"

"Not exactly." She smiled. "But I kind of asked him, just in case you were okay with it."

Connor sighed.

"Please? It will keep me busy and I'll learn some self-defense. That'll come in handy, right?"

Knowing she'd never give up, Connor relented. "Fine. You can start after breakfast."

Ashley squealed in delight. "Thank you, thank you, thank you!" She pounced on him and grabbed around his chest, squeezing him tight. "You're the best."

Connor patted her back. "Yeah, yeah, I'm pretty terrific."

Ashley laughed and the memory blurred as the sounds of battle grew.

They neared the camp. Connor glanced back and counted his men. Everyone had kept up, even the kids.

The sun sat in the middle of the sky. The combination of heat and exertion drenched his hair and fatigues in sweat. Connor pressed on, invigorated by the crescendo of battle that seemed to wipe away his weariness and renew his strength.

With weapons in hand, Connor's crew sprinted the last quarter mile, slowing right before they reached camp. They circled around and came in from the northeast side, just shy of the mountain. Connor shouted the running password before they came into view. Gunfire boomed to the south, but he knew whoever controlled the northeast machine gun would hear him.

Someone shouted back, clearing Connor and his team. They ran in and slid behind the machine gun. Ducking, they split up and sought cover behind the numerous evergreens as they added their fire to the platoon's.

Enemy soldiers ran between the trees, coming closer as they fired into the camp. Connor took aim at the closest one and fired. The soldier fell. Connor moved on to the next, and then another. He aimed at a third, but the soldier fell before Connor could pull the trigger. They ran straight into the Army's fire.

So young. They don't even know what they're doing.

Regardless of their youth, they were murderers who needed to be stopped. Connor's arms and heart grew heavy as he mowed down two more soldiers. He swallowed back bile and aimed again. After what seemed like an eternity of bloodshed, the kids lost courage, broke formation, and fled from the camp.

Connor held his position until Boom started barking orders. Then he rushed toward his station to find Liberty and Ashley.

CHAPTER SEVEN

Liberty

GUNSHOTS!

I froze as my mind attempted to process what that meant. It had been a while since we'd been attacked, and I'd enjoyed the reprieve. I wasn't ready to go back to the nightmare of reality just yet.

Jeff started equipping weapons, and then grabbed a bag of ammunition. He paused long enough to give me a good shake. "Libby. Get Ash and get to your station!" he shouted. Then he rushed off toward the sounds of gunfire like the suicidal hero he was.

I dodged the oncoming soldiers who followed Jeff and headed for the main tent, where I found Ashley staring like a zombie at a bowl of stew.

"Ash, come on!" I shouted from the door, gesturing wildly.

She didn't jump up and run toward me, so I went to her. Her small hands trembled as I took them in mine and tugged her away from the table. Connor had dug us some sort of foxhole between where he and Jeff would be stationed, and we needed to get there.

"Come on, you know the drill," I said, dragging Ashley behind me. "Hurry."

She didn't reply, but followed me. As Connor had taught us, we stayed low and crept forward. I glanced at the trees in front of our soldiers, but couldn't see any enemies. One of the machine guns spat out bullets, though, so they must have seen something.

Only Jeff's helmet peeked out of the hole next to ours. I tugged Ashley one more time and we sprinted for our hole. I lowered her into it, and then slid in behind her. The hole had been dug roughly square in shape, measuring about four feet by four feet, and I could barely see over the top of it. Beneath our feet, the ground slanted to the sides, ending in narrow trenches on either side. I'd made the mistake of asking Connor about the purpose of the trenches and he'd launched into some long, detailed explanation, about grenades rolling to the sides. I tried not to think too hard about that, and instead allowed the smell of fresh dirt to clear my head. Suddenly, Connor's what-to-do-in-case-of-a-battle list came back to me.

'As soon as you get into the individual fighting station, gear up.'

Right. Gear was piled in the corner. I grabbed an oversized bulletproof vest and slid it over Ashley's head. It came almost to her knees, but I called that a bonus before shoving earplugs into her ears. Then I balanced a helmet on her head and fastened the chinstrap. Even with the chinstrap pulled as tight as I could get it, the helmet kept trying to slide down over Ashley's eyes.

"Do I have to wear this?" she asked, pushing it back.

Shots rang out and her eyes widened with fear.

"Definitely," I replied.

From the hole beside us, Jeff's rifle barked out a reply to the shots. Ashley sat and pulled her knees to her chest, wrapping her arms around her legs while I geared up. When I finished, she released her knees and motioned for me to come to her. I sat beside her, my legs scrunched up in the small space, and she latched on to me, burying her head under my arm. There we huddled, obeying Connor's second command: *'Stay low and hidden.'*

Life felt surreal as we sat in that hole. Ashley and I clung to each other as the sounds of battle raged on around us, like some deranged earplug-muffled symphony of death. Connor's station remained quiet, and his absence weighed heavily on my heart, making me wonder where he was and why he wasn't back yet.

Ashley must have been wondering the same thing, because she turned and asked, "Do you think my dad's okay?"

My heart leapt into my chest at the Ashley's recognition of Connor's paternity.

"Yeah, of course he's okay." I hoped saying it aloud would reassure us both, but it sure as heck didn't make me feel better. With the way Ashley eyed me, I doubted it helped her, either. I squeezed her shoulders and tried again. "He'll be here."

The gun on my hip felt unusually heavy.

"Stay here." I shook free of Ashley and stood, sliding my Sigma from its holster. Feeling useless, and wanting to help the soldiers, I peeked over the side of the hole. Our men all had their guns leveled at the trees, so I aimed my Sigma in the same direction. A couple of young Progression soldiers ran out of the trees and surged forward. I chose the closest target and breathed out. He paused and aimed his gun directly at me.

No. Not this way.

I couldn't tell if the thoughts were mine, or an order from the "call." Before I could decide, bullets from someone else's gun tore into the kid's chest and he crumpled to the ground like a puppet whose strings had been cut. My legs collapsed and I slunk to the ground.

Ashley gave my leg a squeeze. I'd just added to my ever-growing collection of nightmares. If anyone understood what that felt like, Ashley did. I holstered my Sigma and started to chew my fingernails.

The battle raged on around us as I wondered what to do. Minutes ticked away until suddenly silence filled the camp. Curious, I stood and peeked over the side again.

Another small surge of soldiers rushed from the trees. Out of the corner of my eye, I saw a spray of red. Then the soldier on the other side of Jeff wobbled backward, and then slumped down.

Crap!

On the ground beside Ashley sat a camouflaged first aid kit. I grabbed it and popped it open to make sure it was stocked. Medical supplies greeted me like a beacon of light.

I shot up and glanced around. "I gotta do something, Ash. Will you stay here?"

Her eyebrows shot up into her hairline. "You're leaving me here alone?"

"Yeah. A soldier just got shot. I'm gonna go help him out, but I'll be right back, okay?"

"He got shot? And you're going out there!"

I nodded. "I have to try to help him."

Before she could argue with my questionable logic, I slid the pack over my shoulder and climbed out of the hole. Then I crawled on my stomach to the spot where I'd seen the soldier go down.

"Don't shoot. I'm coming to help," I shouted before peering into the hole.

A camouflage helmet tilted, and then I saw the face of the John Grisham fan from the main tent. "Marr, right?" I asked, sliding into the hole.

He nodded and tucked his legs closer to his body, making room for me in the small space. He had his own medical pack and was trying to keep one hand on his left arm while he opened the thing.

I plopped my first aid kit down beside his and said, "Good. Now tell me what to do."

He released the hold on his left arm, revealing a sleeve dark with blood. More continued to pump out. He winced and returned his hand to his arm and said, "Stop the bleeding. Gauze then pressure bandage. Tight."

Right. I opened the clasp on the first aid kit and unrolled the pockets. Latex gloves caught my eye first. Since they seemed like a good idea, I pulled on a pair. Then regretted the decision as soon as I found the package of gauze. After fumbling to open it for a few valuable minutes, I gave up and ripped the package between my teeth.

While I was busy with the gauze packaging, Marr had rolled up the short sleeve of his t-shirt, exposing the wound. Blood seeped from a sunburst shaped dark circle about five inches down from his shoulder and on the outside of his bicep. Around the wound, his flesh was red and swollen.

"Are there two?" he asked between gritted teeth.

"What?"

"Bullet wounds. Are there two?"

He pulled his hand away and leaned forward, grunting.

I studied the front and back of his arm. "Yes. There are two."

"Good." He let out a breath, and then winced at the pain it caused.

It didn't look good. With the way blood streamed down his arm I worried we'd never get the bleeding stopped. Determined to try anyway, I wadded up two pieces of gauze and stuffed one in each wound. He winced.

I apologized for hurting him and reached for the pressure bandage. My fingers slid over the slick packaging, leaving behind a trail of blood. *Great.* Somehow I'd managed to get the gloves covered in blood. Frustrated by my lack of foresight in not opening the package before I put the gauze in Marr's wounds, I wiped my bloody gloves on the front of my shirt and tried again.

I ripped open the package and barely managed to catch the bandage before it hit the ground. Apologizing again—whether to Marr or to the bandage, I wasn't sure—I unrolled the bandage and gently wrapped it around Marr's arm to secure the gauze in place.

"Tighter!" he snapped.

"Right, sorry!"

I tugged on the bandage and he gritted his teeth. My hands shook. I chewed on my bottom lip and unwrapped the little bit of bandage I'd applied. Then, I tried again, this time stretching the fabric as far as I could. His substantial bicep bulged around the wrap, but he nodded in approval. I tucked the ends into the bandage, and then he thanked me, grabbed his gun and repositioned himself to start firing again. I pulled off the bloody gloves and tossed them aside.

I stood and peeked over the side of the hole at the soldiers further down the line.

"What are you doing?" Mar snapped. "Stay down."

I ducked down to appease him, but not before noticing that the hole two down stood empty. I could have sworn somebody occupied it when I climbed in to help Marr. I tried to ask Marr to confirm, but either he didn't hear me, or he couldn't spare the attention it would have taken to answer my question. Either way, I packed up my first aid kit and climbed out of the hole.

The gunfire seemed to be easing up a little. I glanced in Ashley's direction, but then decided to go check on the missing soldier. Slithering on the ground like a snake, I did just that.

Once I reached the hole, I shouted the same warning that had kept Marr from shooting me, and peered into the hole. A soldier sat on the floor of his shelter, leaning against the wall with his gun at his side. He tugged at the Velcro and snaps that held his bulletproof vest closed.

"You okay?" I asked, lowering myself into the hole.

Pale blue eyes glanced up at me. I'd seen the soldier around, but had never talked to him. As I neared, I saw that the upper left side of his vest was mangled and a crimson stain spread out from his shoulder. Leaning over him, I helped him remove his vest. The t-shirt beneath it was drenched in sweat and blood.

"What do I do?" I asked.

He hesitated. His eyes darted from me to the first aid kit in my hand. Then, he looked down at himself and relaxed against the wall, breathing heavily.

He tugged at the bottom of his shirt. "Cut this off so we can see it."

"Right." I rummaged through the first aid kit until I found a pair of scissors.

He watched me closely as I cut into the hem and gripped his shirt, tearing it up the middle. I then cut a large circle around his wounded shoulder and froze, staring at the bloodied fabric.

"Do it," Marr said. His voice sounded weak and worn. "Fast."

"Okay. Brace yourself." I gripped the sides of the fabric and pulled it hard.

Marr swore, loudly. I backed away and gave him a moment to compose himself. When he finished swearing and spitting, I approached. Beads of sweat covered his skin and he looked like he was about to lose his breakfast. The coppery-sweet scent of blood assaulted my nose as I got a good look at his bare shoulder. Torn skin and mutilated meat gave way to deep gashes that showed white fragments.

Is that bone?

My stomach lurched into my throat. I looked away and swallowed back bile, refusing to throw up. The soldier didn't need some pathetic puking girl. He needed help. Determined to be the help he needed, I rifled through the kit, searching for something to jump out and declare 'use me for excessive blood loss and muscle mutilation!' but nothing did.

"I don't know what to do," I finally admitted, holding the kit up so he could see it.

With his uninjured arm, he pointed to some sort of black strap attached to what looked like a pen with no tip.

"What the heck is that?" I asked.

He muttered a weak reply that I couldn't hear over the gunfire, and then collapsed against the dirt. His blue eyes closed, highlighting the ashy tone of his skin. Blood kept gushing from his wound, and I wondered how much blood a person could lose before they didn't have enough to live.

Not wanting to dwell on that question, I put on a fresh pair of gloves and removed the strap thingy he'd pointed to. The strap expanded, so I pulled on it until it formed a cuff.

A tourniquet? Must be.

I made the cuff as wide as I could, and then carefully slid it up the soldier's left arm and over his wounded shoulder. Positioning the cuff to run diagonally toward his body from his armpit, I pulled the band as tight as I could and affixed it to the Velcro. The pen-type thing had part of the ribbon through the center of it, and when I twisted it, it tightened the band even more. Feeling like a genius for figuring the contraption out so quickly, I twisted the pen as tight as I could then locked it into place using the clamp attached to the band.

The bleeding seemed to be slowing, but that could have been because he'd run out of blood. The wound was exposed and probably needed to be cleaned, but I had no clue what to do about that. Little things I could handle, but I had no idea what to do about this wound. There were probably bullets or fragments or some other foreign objects lodged in his shoulder that I worried about. I would have been tempted to search for them, but thankfully the first aid kit didn't come equipped with tweezers. With nothing more to do, I packed up my bag and climbed out of the hole. I started crawling back toward Ashley. More shots fired, and Jeff slunk down.

I wanted to get to him to make sure he was okay, but suddenly the gunfire increased into a constant stream. It sounded like enemies bore down on us from every direction, overtaking our small platoon. I collapsed on the ground, squeezed my eyes shut, and started praying.

Please, please, please, please.

It was a universal prayer, spawned from fear and distorted by the smell of blood and the sounds of battle.

Please hear me. Please don't take this soldier. Please let Jeff be okay. Please return Connor to us. Please don't let the Progression overrun us.

Suddenly the woods went silent. Inspired by the reprieve, I hastened my crawl toward Jeff. Before I could reach him, he stood, wiped blood from his cheek, and then resumed his position behind his gun.

Since Jeff seemed okay, I altered my course and headed toward Ashley. Boom started yelling, and I crawled faster. Then suddenly a boot appeared, blocking my path. I looked up, and despite everything, I smiled.

Connor.

My heart flipped.

You're okay.

CHAPTER EIGHT

Connor

CONNOR SHOOK HIS head. "What are you doing out of that hole?" he asked, pointing to where Liberty should have been.

She shrugged off the first aid kit and held it toward him. "Helping?" She pushed herself up to a kneeling position, giving Connor a full view of her blood-covered vest.

His heart stopped beating. "What happened?"

Liberty's brows furrowed. Then she looked down, and her eyes widened at the sight. "No. This isn't mine."

Connor didn't know whether to hug her or strangle her. He silently swore she would be the death of him. "Where's Ash?" he asked.

"She's still in the hole," Liberty replied.

"Glad one of you can follow directions."

She smiled. "Me too. Shall we go get her?"

"I can't. I have to report to Boom first." He really just wanted to shake her and ask her why she had no regard for her personal safety. But, since losing his cool wouldn't help the situation, he bit his tongue and turned away before he said something he'd really regret ... again. Pointing out Liberty's borderline suicidal tendencies hadn't exactly benefitted him in the past.

Connor found Boom beside one of the machine guns, assigning security and a cleanup crew. He stood back and watched his friend dish out orders, waiting until Boom signaled for him to approach.

"What did you find?" Boom asked.

"Didn't Noke tell you?" Connor asked.

Boom shook his head. "I haven't seen Noke since he left with you."

Connor swore. He rubbed a hand down his face and glanced around. When his gaze landed on Teran, he was pleased to see that the new recruit still had Braden and Kylee in tow. He waved him over and turned back toward Boom.

"We found a trap." Connor glanced over his shoulder at Braden and Kylee. "And a couple of kids."

Boom's brow furrowed as he considered the children. He directed Teran to take the kids to the main tent and keep them there, and then addressed Connor. "What's their story?"

Connor shrugged. "I don't know. They gave us some sob story about the Progression taking their mother, but ..."

Boom nodded. "You don't buy it."

"No. But on the other hand, they look like they haven't eaten in days. The Progression usually takes better care of their soldiers."

"And, they're still alive," Boom added.

"Yeah. There's that too. It doesn't add up. I didn't know what else to do with them and we couldn't leave them behind, just in case they are Progression."

"I would have made the same call," Boom confirmed.

Magee appeared. "Excuse me, Captain, but I found Osberg. He's unconscious and I'm going to need help pulling him out of his hole."

Boom nodded and sent two soldiers to help Magee attend to the camp's main medic.

"Did we lose any men?" Connor asked the captain.

"One," Boom sighed. "We lost Wallace. Marr took a bullet in the arm. He said Liberty slipped into his position and doctored him up."

Connor shook his head, once again amazed by the woman. "That explains why she didn't stay put where I told her to."

"She doesn't seem much like the 'staying put' kind." Boom chuckled, following Magee's path. "Let's go check on Osberg."

Connor followed his friend to Osberg's position, where two soldiers carefully lifted Osberg's unconscious, but still breathing body out of his hole.

"Will he make it?" Boom asked Magee.

"Hard to tell, Captain. He's lost a lot of blood," Magee replied. "I'm taking him to his tent, and will do what I can."

Boom nodded and looked over Osberg. "At least he got a tourniquet on himself. That's something."

"No, First Sergeant," Jeff said, coming from behind Connor. "Liberty did that. I saw her slide into his position."

"Hmm." Boom looked thoughtful as he turned and asked Connor to debrief him on the operation. While Soldiers moved bodies and broke out shovels, Connor retold the story in full detail. Boom listened until the end, interrupting with questions as Connor spoke.

"Now, Noke." Boom stared at the sky for a moment. "We need everyone who isn't burying bodies to pull security."

Connor watched a soldier drag a young Progression body toward the mass grave being dug. "It makes no sense that they would sacrifice all these lives. For what? What where they hoping to gain?"

"Exactly. We must keep all available men on security. They might be under some delusion that they weakened our forces enough to try again tonight."

"I can go for Noke alone," Connor said.

Boom stared at the sky for a moment before closing his eyes and crossing himself. He looked drained and more exhausted than any thirty-six year old should. "I'd rather not send you alone."

Connor motioned to the lifeless bodies being dragged to their final resting places by the soldiers who'd ended their lives. "We took a pretty big chunk out of their forces here. The woods are probably at their safest right now, since those who escaped are most likely back at camp, licking their wounds."

Boom's hard stare told Connor he knew better. "That would make sense, yes, but as you said, nothing about this makes sense."

Connor straightened. Moments stretched between them as he awaited the permission of his commanding officer.

Finally, Boom nodded.

Suddenly a small mop of dark hair flew through the air toward Connor. He opened his arms and Ashley slammed into his chest, causing him to stumble backwards. She clung to him and he wrapped his arms around her.

"We were so worried," she said. "Thank God you're safe! Libby made me stay in that hole, and I couldn't see anything. There was shooting, and then it stopped, but she said I still couldn't come out."

Connor patted Ashley's back and said, "I'm glad you stayed safe." He pulled her away from him so he could get a good look at her. Then he stole a glance at Liberty, who walked toward him.

"It appears that neither of us can follow directions," Liberty said.

Boom ducked his head, probably to hide his smile. When he straightened, he wore a suspiciously neutral expression. "Libby, thank you for your assistance. That tourniquet gave Osberg a chance. He would most likely be dead now if you hadn't been there to stop the bleeding."

"That's a bit melodramatic. I just stuck a cuff over his shoulder. Not a big deal."

Boom stepped forward and clutched Liberty's shoulders, forcing her focus on him. "Yes, it was. You helped both Osberg and Marr, and we all appreciate that. It's a very big deal."

She nodded, her cheeks reddening. "Anytime. Glad I got the chance to be useful."

Boom turned back to Connor. "Go. Find Noke and hurry back. We have a lot to do here."

"Go?" Ashley's large, dark eyes stared up at Connor. "Where? You just got back. I don't want you to leave. What if the bad guys come back again?"

He knelt in front of her and cupped her face in his hands. "One of our men is still out there. Now that I know you guys are safe, I have to go look for him. It's my responsibility, sweetie. I'll be back before the bad guys even limp back to their camp!"

Pulling her to him, he kissed her forehead and gave her shoulders a squeeze. Her skin felt soft and delicate under his wind-chapped lips, and he savored the fact that she didn't pull away from him like she used to.

Liberty's stare bore into the top of Connor's head. He tried to shrug her off as he lowered Ashley to the ground. He leaned forward and brushed a kiss on Liberty's cheek. "It's nothing. Won't take long at all."

"Cool." She smiled. "'Cause I'm coming with you."

"No, you have to stay at the camp. They may need you here." Connor looked to Boom for help, but his friend shrugged and turned away.

Thanks. Such a pal.

"Can I go too?" Ashley asked.

"Absolutely not." Connor and Liberty said in unison.

Boom paused and turned back toward them. "Ashley, I could really use your help with something. I have a couple of kids to interview, and I'm hoping I won't seem so scary with you by my side. Will you please help me out?"

Ashley wasn't easily fooled. She sighed at Boom, and then eyed Connor and Liberty. "Two hours. That's all you get, then I come and find you."

"Noted," Liberty replied. "We'll be back long before then. Won't we, Connor?"

Connor doubted that Ashley would be able to slip past Boom, but he bet on it. So, instead of calling her bluff, he nodded. "We'll take horses. As long as Libby can keep up, we'll be back in no time."

"Moi?" Liberty asked. "Please, old man. Bengay up, so we can roll."

Connor shook his head. She sure knew how to make the four years between them seem like an eternity.

Boom chuckled. "Come along, Ash, before these two jump into warp speed."

Ashley hesitated. "Are you sure I can't come?"

"Positive," Liberty replied.

Ashley's shoulders slumped. "Fine. But two hours. I mean it." She gave each of them a hug, and then allowed Boom to lead her toward the camp.

* * *

From the Army's supply of horses, Connor selected an appaloosa stud for himself and a black mare for Noke. The appaloosa looked like someone had dumped a bucket of white paint on its backside, so the unimaginative soldiers had named the horse 'Paint.' Connor saddled both horses, and then turned to help Liberty with the sorrel mare she'd selected. Liberty had already tacked up and mounted her horse.

Surprised, Connor asked, "Would you like me to check the saddle for you?" He looked around, wondering who had saddled the horse.

Liberty chuckled. "Thanks, but I think I can manage."

Her tone held more than a little challenge in it. Connor chose to ignore it and mounted, knowing that he'd prove his point when her saddle shifted and she ended up falling off the horse.

Liberty led her horse over to stand beside Connor's and lowered her voice. "Now that Ash is out of earshot, cut the crap and tell me what's really going here. Is Noke alive?"

"I don't know. We sent him back to tell Boom we were pursuing the spies into a building, but he never made it to the camp."

"I like Noke." Liberty tangled her fingers in her horse's mane, and then pulled them out to pat the horse on its neck. "What if they have him?"

He wanted to reassure her that Noke would be okay and that they'd find him, but he couldn't. Instead of making promises he had no way of keeping, he tossed her the first aid kit she'd given him after the battle. She frowned, and then slid it over her shoulder. Connor tied the lead rope for Noke's horse to his saddle horn and pushed Paint into a fast trot.

They rode in silence. Connor watched the trees while Liberty stared ahead like a zombie. He wondered if she was remembering her time at the Progression camp and imagining the truck driver suffering the same fate. Or worse. Throughout the ride, she kept pace with Connor, moving with the horse instead of being jostled all over the place. And, after about fifteen minutes of riding, she broke into a smile.

Connor closed the gap between their two horses and leaned toward Liberty. "You like riding, don't you?" he asked.

She nodded. The wind pushed her red curls out her face and her smile widened.

Encouraged by the smile, Connor asked, "Where did you learn to ride?"

"Why?"

He groaned, wondering why he had to fight for every detail about her. "Because you're good at it, and it's not exactly a skill that the majority possesses anymore."

She nodded. "Thank you. But where I grew up, it's still pretty common."

Reining in Paint, Connor slowed to a walk. "I thought you grew up around Portland?"

"No. What gave you that idea?"

"Probably the way you had your gun stuffed into your waistband when I first met you. Classic city-girl mistake."

She rolled her eyes and tugged on the reins, bringing her horse to a walk beside Connor. Her cheeks flushed and her eyes brightened with excitement. Not only did she know how to ride, but she obviously enjoyed it that it had pulled her out of her dark thoughts. "Where I'm from, we use rifles. I'm not used to handguns."

"Oh? Where is this mysterious place where people ride horses and shoot rifles?"

"I'm sure you've never heard of it. It's a super small town in south-central Oregon. Very secluded. I've been gone for a while, though, and I haven't been on a horse in ages."

"So, was this a rodeo town? Like Pendleton, only smaller?" Connor asked. He forced a country twang into his speech as he said, "Bet you was a purdy rodeo princess."

Liberty snorted. "Hardly a princess. I did rodeo though. I barrel raced and pole raced, but I was a tomboy. I had no desire to get all dolled up and wave at the crowd. No thank you."

A smile tugged at Connor's lips. "I don't believe you. You would have sold out for a crown. Any girl would."

"And that, right there, is exactly why you're single."

Connor chuckled. "Yeah, that's it. Couldn't possibly be the fact that I've spent the past several months in hiding, trying to provide for myself and my daughter while the whole world went crazy."

"Excuses, excuses." Liberty waved him off with a hand. "What about before the insanity? Everyone knows you had lots of relationships, but anything steady?"

The women in Connor's life had been fun, sexy and willing. Not exactly relationship material, but then again, neither was he. Since he knew Liberty wouldn't want to hear those details, he shook his head.

"Nope. What about you?" he asked. "Was there a Mister Liberty in your life?"

She laughed. "Yeah, right."

"Why not?"

"Probably because I wouldn't accept that damn crown."

Connor heard a twig snap in front of them. He held out a hand, silencing Liberty, and then jumped off his horse and aimed his gun into the bushes. Inching forward, he heard Liberty dismount behind him, and turned around to motion for her to stay back.

She shook her head and followed him.

Since he knew nothing shy of shooting her would change her stubborn mind, he ignored her and crept forward.

Someone whistled. It was a weak, breathy sound, but still a whistle that Connor recognized. He whistled an answer, and then Noke stumbled out of the brush. He looked like someone had drained the blood from his face and dumped it down his thigh. Connor looked closer and saw that the old trucker had used a bandana and a stick to fashion a rudimentary tourniquet around his thigh, just above what appeared to be a bullet wound.

As Connor took in the scene, Noke's leg gave out. Connor lunged forward, catching the wounded man right before he hit the ground. Liberty appeared on the other side of Noke, her face drawn tight with worry.

"What happened?" Connor asked. He didn't know how long the soldier had been leaking blood, but doubted Noke could make it the additional ten steps to the horses.

Liberty must have shared his doubts, because she offered to get the horses and took off.

"Ran into a bunch of those kids. I took out a couple of them, but one got me in the leg," Noke replied. "Luckily they were in a hurry, though. Didn't even stop to make sure I was dead. They were heading for the camp."

"They hit it too, but we held them off. Only one dead and a couple wounded."

Noke let out a deep breath. "That's a relief."

Connor agreed.

Liberty angled the black mare to a stop with the left side of the horse directly in front of Noke. "Your carriage awaits, Sir," she said with a bow.

Noke grimaced. "I hope she's got a smooth ride in her."

Connor hoped so as well. Judging by the way Noke sweated, Connor didn't know how he could get the soldier mounted, much less keep him in the saddle. Noke leaned on Connor as the two of them stared at the stirrup.

"What can I do to help?" Liberty asked.

"I'm not sure. Noke, maybe if you put your weight on us and try to put your left foot in the stirrup we can … try to get you up and over?"

Connor glanced around the forest. They needed some sort of pulley system, but he didn't think Noke had the time it would take him to build one.

Noke stiffened. "All right. Let's get it done."

Liberty slid next to Connor, and, as Noke shifted, Connor got under the weight of his body while Liberty held the wounded man steady. Noke leaned against them and jammed his foot into the stirrup. Beads of sweat formed around his hairline and the last drops of color drained from his face. Connor felt Noke's muscles tense, and then they released completely. Two hundred pounds of dead weight crumpled on top of Connor and Liberty.

Connor shifted, shouldering the majority of Noke's weight. "Grab his arms," he told Liberty.

She released her hold on Noke's shoulders and held his arms. "Okay, now what?"

"We're going to lay him on the ground."

With Liberty keeping Noke's arms out of the way, Connor lowered the soldier to the ground and checked his pulse. It was slow, but steady.

"He's alive, but we've got to get him to Magee if we want him to stay that way."

Liberty nodded. "Tell me what to do."

"Hand me the first aid kit and take the saddle off his horse."

As Liberty removed Noke's saddle, Connor checked the tourniquet. It held fast, so he didn't mess with it. Instead, he cleaned and dressed the wound. When he and Liberty finished their individual tasks, they worked together to lift Noke and draped him over the horse's back, leaving his legs and arms dangling over the sides.

"Will he stay like that?" Liberty asked.

"Hope so. Mount up."

As Liberty climbed atop her mare, Connor grabbed Noke's saddle and handed it to her to hold.

"We could leave it behind, but I'd rather not if you can ride with it," he explained.

She accepted the saddle and positioned it in front of her. "I got this."

He knew she had to be scared and worried, but still she put up a brave front. He brushed her cheek with his hand. "I know. I'm going to lead Noke's horse, and I need you to follow it and let me know if he starts to slip off the side."

She nodded and Connor grabbed the black mare's lead rope and went to mount Paint.

* * *

Regardless of how slowly the trio rode, the uneven ground jostled Noke, causing him to slide down one side or the other. Connor lost count of how many times he had to stop and readjust the soldier. As they trekked back to the camp, dusk melted into night. It swept in quickly and blanketed the forest in a thick and heavy darkness. Between the breaks in the trees Connor watched the moon in order to stay on course. By the time they finally reached the camp, the moon stood high in the sky, and Liberty looked exhausted.

Connor whistled the pass code as they rode into the camp. The bodies had all been cleared away, and most of the individual fighting positions were occupied. Blackened guns scanned the forest, and silence enveloped them like they'd been sucked into a sound vacuum.

"Wow," Liberty whispered. "Are we under attack?"

"No. Just prepared. They know where we are now, so we'll stay on high alert." Feeling revitalized by the energy of the camp, Connor slid off Paint and handed the reins to an approaching private.

Magee appeared from the darkness, acting like a mother hen as he clucked over the shoddy tourniquet and checked Noke's pulse.

"Well, he's breathing, at least," the medic declared.

Connor decided to accept that as a good sign. He helped the medic lower Noke from the mare, and two more soldiers appeared to carry the wounded man to his tent. Connor watched them walk away, wondering if he'd ever see Noke alive again.

Liberty rested a comforting hand on his arm. "He'll be alright," she whispered.

Connor didn't know if she was trying to reassure herself or him.

"Yeah," he replied and patted her hand. "I hope so."

He tipped his head over until it rested on her shoulder. Considering that she stood quite a bit shorter than him, the position wasn't at all comfortable, but he didn't care. He grabbed her arm to steady himself.

"Thank you," Connor said.

"For what?"

"For coming."

Liberty chuckled. "You didn't want me to come."

"Sure I didn't."

He closed his eyes and listened to the sounds around them. An owl hooted in the distance, and somewhere closer, a critter skittered through the night. The faint rush of the river sounded like background music to the low hum of conversation coming from the main tent. Regardless of his lack of comfort, Connor could have stood like that forever. Liberty had other plans, though. All too soon she gently pushed his head up and pulled away.

"We should make sure Ashley didn't run off to save us," she said. "She's probably worried."

"She's in the main tent, playing cards. I'll bring her to your tent."

"How could you possibly know that?" Liberty asked.

Connor shrugged. "I'm just good like that."

She slugged him in the arm. It was half-hearted and he laughed it off, holding up his hands.

"Okay, okay. Magee told me."

"I was standing right here. When did he tell you?" she asked.

"We speak in code."

Liberty put her hands on her hips. "I got your code for you."

He smiled. "That sounds promising."

She rolled her eyes. "You are hopeless." Then she turned and headed toward her tent.

Still smiling to himself, Connor drifted through the tents to find Boom and Ashley in the main tent, engaged in what appeared to be an intense card came against Braden and Kylee. Ashley sat facing the entrance and stopped in the middle of her argument with Braden when Connor walked in.

Boom stood and looked at Connor. "Noke's alive."

The captain always could read Connor. For Ashley's sake, Connor nodded like Boom had asked him a question. "He's lost a lot of blood though. Magee is with him now.

Boom set his cards on the table and addressed the children sitting around him. "Thank you for the game, but we should all get some sleep now. Braden, Kylee, a tent has been prepared for the two of you. Private James will take you to it." He gestured toward the soldier standing by the door.

Connor walked to the table, bent down and scooped up Ashley. She protested for an instant, and then dropped her cards on the table and leaned into him.

"Fine. I was losing anyway. See you tomorrow, Boom and Kylee." Then she glared at Braden. "You too, cheater."

Connor clutched her to him, appreciating her fresh, clean scent. For all her ferocity and bravery, Ashley had an innocence and purity about her he'd do anything in his power to protect. He squeezed her tightly as they walked by Wallace's old tent, which would now serve as Braden and Kylee's temporary home. Connor bowed his head and took a moment to remember the soldier who had a slight lisp and a shaky right hand. Thankful for the people still alive, he kissed the top of Ashley's head.

CHAPTER NINE

Liberty

THE STENCH OF rot enveloped me. It tugged at the contents of my stomach, drawing me further into the nightmare with each rancid breath. I stood atop a narrow, broken stone path wedged between two fences. To my right, the fence opened to an inviting meadow, full of beautiful people sitting on white patio furniture. They talked and laughed, and I immediately wanted to be a part of them.

I took a few steps toward the crowd, and the offensive smell worsened. It made me gag, and I covered my nose, watching the people and wondering how they could stomach the stink. They continued to celebrate, seemingly unaffected. But I couldn't handle it, and turned away.

Desperate to escape the foul odor, I ran along the stone path, away from the crowd and toward a familiar wooden door. It stood splintered, faded, and without a handle. Curious, I continued on. The door creaked opened as I drew near.

Beyond the door, a sinister darkness waited for me, watching me. Fear sped my heart, warning me not to enter, but I had to. Light flickered in the distance, calling to me like a shiny trinket lying in the sand. Ignoring my fears and reservations, I stepped through the door, and the darkness embraced me. The slick floor, however, did not. My legs shot out from under me. I reached out, *attempting to catch myself, but felt nothing. I fell. Expecting the inevitable, I closed my eyes and ...*

SMACK!

My backside hurt. I was lying in my sleeping bag, staring through the darkness to the roof of my tent.

A dream. Just a dream.

I rubbed my sore bottom.

How can a dream feel like an ice skating accident?

Since I had no answers, I wrote off the pain to sleeping on the lumpy forest floor. I yawned and tried to stretch, but the tent was cramped and Ashley's sleeping bag lay across my calves. The girl seemed to do gymnastics in her sleep, always flipping and turning and kicking.

"What's wrong?" Connor asked. His husky, sleep-laden voice did weird things to my stomach. Stupid things, even.

"Just some crazy dream," I replied and snuggled back down in my sleeping bag.

Wait, Connor?

I threw back my sleeping bag and sat back up to make sure I wasn't having another crazy dream. "What are you doing in here?"

He slept smushed against the side of our two-man tent with Ashley's head against his chest. He had no mat, nor sleeping bag, and looked incredibly uncomfortable.

"You were already passed out when I brought in Ashley. She asked me to stay until she fell asleep. I must have drifted off." He shifted, gently pushing Ashley away. "I should probably get going."

"You don't have to." I shrugged. "But I'm going back to sleep."

Then I rolled over and did just that.

The next time I awoke, I thought I heard my name. I sat up and looked around. Connor was gone and Ashley snored from the bag now scrunched up at my feet. I took some time to wonder—not for the first time—how she managed to get any rest when she seemed to move all night long. The tent was still dark and cool with the chill of night, and I discounted the noise I'd heard for a dream. Closing my eyes, I tried to drift back to sleep. I heard my name again, so I pulled a sweatshirt over my tank top and unzipped the flap to peek outside.

Boom smiled and held a steaming cup of coffee toward me. "Mornin'."

"Coffee delivery? A girl could get used to this," I said, smiling at Boom as I accepted the cup. "Is everything okay?"

"I was hoping you could spare a few minutes to talk."

I knuckled the sleep out of my eyes. "Now? Uh ... sure. Give me a sec." I handed the cup back to Boom and ducked into the tent to slip out of my pajama bottoms and into jeans. Then I stuffed my unruly curls into a baseball cap and joined Boom in front of the tent.

The morning felt crisp and clean. Dew brightened the grass, glistening in the dawn, and the forest animals sang and chattered in the distance. Several soldiers moved around the camp.

"What's going on?" I asked. "Wait, where's Connor? If he's run off and done something stupid without me, I'm going to kill him."

Boom chuckled. "Nothing that exciting, I'm afraid. He's in the main tent, trying his tactics on the kids." He started walking, and motioned for me to follow him.

We got a few steps from the tent before I woke up enough to understand the meaning behind Boom's words. "He's questioning the kids? Is there a problem?"

"Their reactions are ... inconsistent with their story. Connor has a way of ... well; he was hoping that after a full night's sleep, they'd be more pliable."

I froze. "You guys won't hurt them, will you?"

Boom considered my question for a moment too long before responding. "No point in it unless we're sure they're withholding information. If they are Progression soldiers, they're not following protocol."

"Protocol? Do they have a special handshake or something?"

Boom chuckled. "Something like that."

"But you won't tell me what it is?"

"It's classified. Army personnel only. Are you ready to enlist?"

I held up a hand. "Save it. I don't want to know that bad."

"Ah, well, it was worth a try. Regardless, we enjoy having you and Ashley with us. Speaking of Ashley, she seems to be adjusting to camp life pretty well."

"Yep. She's a trooper." I turned to face him. "But something tells me this conversation wasn't supposed to be about secret handshakes and Ashley's adjustment to camp life."

Boom took a deep breath. He seemed to wrestle with words in his head, which was odd. When Boom opened his mouth, either orders or wisdom spilled out. He normally didn't struggle with getting his point across.

"Libby, you need to understand something about us. We are trained to see the bigger picture. Yes, individual lives and freedoms are important, but not when they have the potential to destroy what we fight for. I do not believe that Braden and Kylee are working with the Progression, but still, we cannot trust them. They are an unknown."

I nodded. "So am I, though. I could just as easily be working with the Progression. I mean, what do any of you really know about me?"

The sides of his lips twitched. "More than you know about yourself, apparently."

Since I couldn't tell whether he meant that as a compliment or an insult, I chose not to reply.

"I understand your affinity for children, but most of our attackers are under the age of sixteen. Regardless, we do not want to hurt Braden and Kylee. Or any children for that matter. I've been doing a lot of thinking about our previous conversation and I ... I would like you to try to talk to the Braden and Kylee as well."

My brow scrunched up. "Like question them?"

"Not necessarily." Boom rubbed his chin. "Actually, I'm not sure what I mean. Something ... different, perhaps?"

I sighed. "That's all the detail you're gonna give me, isn't it?"

Boom chuckled, nodding.

"Fine. I'll see what I can do. Any news about Noke?"

"He's stable," Boom assured me. "The bullet was wedged between muscle and bone. Magee removed it, and as long as the wound doesn't get infected he should recover. It'll be a long time before he can run a marathon, though."

"I'd imagine. And the other guy? What did you say his name was?"

"Osberg," Boom replied. "He's our main medic."

"Man, that sucks."

"Indeed. His wounds are a little more complicated. We need to get him back to Fort Lewis for surgery."

"So we'll be leaving for the fort soon?" I asked.

"Yes. Preparations are being made now, and we'll move soon."

We stood in silence for an awkward moment, and I got the feeling he wanted to say more. "Is there something else I can help you with?" I asked.

"Actually, there is. With Osberg out of commission, Magee could really use an assistant."

Curious, I leaned forward. "What would that entail, exactly?"

"A difficult question, since we never know what may happen."

"Come on, Boom, you have to give me more information than that. Will I be getting him coffee and handing him the scalpel, or will I be doing stuff like holding his sleeves up while he's performing surgery?"

Boom patted me on the shoulder. "Don't worry. Mostly he'll be showing you how to do things like clean and dress wounds. Maybe he'll even teach you how to stitch someone up using dental floss and tampons."

"What? You can do that?"

He chuckled. "Yes, but I'm sure we have more sutures and gauze than we do floss and tampons."

"Yeah, I can see where tampons especially would be an issue."

Boom patted my shoulder. "Libby, none of us can do everything, but we all must do something. Don't worry about what you don't know. Magee will train you."

The idea did have appeal. I could be of assistance without actually shooting anyone. "I'm not promising anything, but I will talk to Magee about it."

Boom smiled. "I knew you would. He's expecting you."

"You think you're so smart, don't you?"

"Mostly, yes." He grinned.

CHAPTER TEN

Connor

CONNOR PAUSED OUTSIDE the main tent long enough to stretch his sore muscles. After yesterday's action, spending the night crowded into the girls' two-person tent hadn't been his wisest decision. But, in hindsight, he would have done the same thing over again, if he'd had the chance, and the reasons why waited for him in the main tent.

He peeked into the entrance and saw Braden and Kylee sitting on chairs in the far corner of the tent. Just as Connor had requested, they sat away from the tables and up against the divider that separated the eating area from Boom's temporary office. They looked every bit like the outsiders they were as they watched the soldiers eat and talk at the tables.

Perfect.

After letting the kids stew in the uncomfortable situation for a little longer, Connor wiped any remaining sleep from his eyes, straightened his back and marched into the tent. He went through the second entrance and over to the pot hanging above the fire. He served up three bowls of oatmeal, and then took them over to the kids and sat down.

"Eat," Connor directed, after handing them each a bowl.

Braden picked up his spoon and dug right in, but Kylee eyed her oatmeal suspiciously.

"What's your name?" she asked.

Connor ignored her question, leaned back in his chair and took a bite of his oatmeal. He chewed, swallowed, and then said, "Not bad. You should eat up while it's hot."

Braden slurped down hot cereal like it was the first meal he'd eaten in weeks. Kylee watched her brother for a moment, and then picked up her own spoon and tasted it. Obviously deciding the cooked oats wouldn't kill her, she devoured her breakfast with the same intensity as her brother. The three ate in silence, watching each other.

Once they finished breakfast, Connor took their bowls and stacked them on top of his own. He set them on the floor and then leaned back in his chair and crossed his arms.

"So," Connor said. "Tell me what happened. From the beginning."

Braden sighed. "We already told that other guy everything there is to tell."

"Which other guy?" Connor asked.

"I don't remember his name." Braden shook his head. "The Mexican."

Connor kept his expression neutral, but remained unimpressed by Braden's all-too-obvious ignorance. Anyone who survived this long past the collapse had to be smarter than the kid let on. Deciding not to call Braden out on his act, Connor asked, "Captain Ortega?"

"Yeah, that's him. We already told him everything."

"Cool. Then it'll be fresh in your mind and you should have no trouble repeating it to me."

Braden looked like he wanted to argue, but Kylee patted his arm, silencing his protests. Then she faced Connor and said, "What do you want to know?"

"Several things, but first ... that house we picked you up from. Why were you there?"

Kylee eyed him. "It was our house. Mom's, Brae's, and mine."

"Just the three of you?"

She nodded.

Wondering how a one-parent home managed to maintain what looked to be a decent sized farm, Connor rubbed the stubble on his chin. "How many acres did your family own?"

"Six," she replied. "The buildings and yard, and then five acres that we leased out to our uncle to hay."

That would make sense, but it brought up another question. "Where's your uncle now?"

"Don't know. He disappeared a few weeks ago."

"So the three of you have just been staying at the house? Nobody's bothered you?" Connor asked.

Braden started to say something, but Kylee jumped in again, cutting him off.

"There's a crawl space under the house," she said. "It has a hidden door. We've spent a lot of time hiding."

Connor nodded, wishing he could check the house out and verify her story. For being so young, she seemed surprisingly composed and quick with her responses. He turned toward her brother and asked, "Braden, what did you guys eat?"

Braden glanced at Kylee for a second before answering. "Mom liked to can food, so we had a lot stored up in the pantry. When we ran out, I started hunting."

Ah-ha. Connor had found a hole in their story. "What did you hunt with?"

"Mom's twenty-two."

Connor's brow scrunched up as he leaned forward, resting his elbows on his legs. "If you had a rifle, why didn't you use it against them?"

"I tried, but there were too many. They took it when they found us."

"The Progression?" Connor asked. When Braden nodded he continued. "How did they find you?"

Again, Braden looked to his sister.

"Braden?" Connor prompted.

"They were waiting right outside the house when I left to go hunting. I didn't know they were there and practically walked right into them."

"Sloppy," Connor observed. "It's amazing you stayed alive this long."

Braden bared his teeth at Connor. "I guess we're just lucky."

"Or ... it could be that you're Progression agents who were planted in that house with this bogus story to get inside our camp."

"Why would we want to do that?" Kylee asked.

Connor leaned back in his chair and studied her. "You tell me."

Boom entered the tent and pulled up a chair beside Connor. "How's it going?" he asked.

Connor shook his head.

"This is stupid," Braden answered. "We told you everything we know. A group of soldiers showed up at our house and took our mom. Then they told us you'd be along shortly, and if we kept you at the house for a while we'd get our mom back."

Braden sounded as frustrated and worn out as Connor felt.

"Why are you guys just sitting here on your butts talking to us?" the boy asked. "Shouldn't you be out there finding our mom?"

Connor considered the story again. Sure, the Progression could very well have busted into their home and taken their mom, demanding that the kids keep Connor and his team busy, but why leave both of them? It made more sense to leave only one child behind to detain the Army. They'd be much more desperate to comply and get their loved ones back if they were completely alone.

"Why'd they leave Kylee?" Connor asked.

Braden shook his head. "What?"

Kylee sat up. "They didn't know about me. I was hidden, remember?"

The girl seemed to have an answer for everything. Either she told the truth—which Connor doubted—or she was a very good liar.

"Mom hid me." Kylee looked away for a moment, and when she refocused on Connor her eyes were moist with unshed tears. "She heard them talking to Braden outside, and knew we wouldn't get to the crawl space entrance in time, so she hid me. She stuffed me in that coffee table and she ... she just gave herself up."

Braden draped an arm over his sister. "We'll get her back. These guys will help us, right?" He looked from Connor to Boom.

Neither of them replied.

"Right? Can't you just take one of 'em captive and torture them until they tell you where our mom is?"

Braden's simplistic plan grated on Connor's nerves.

"Don't you think we've tried that?" he asked. "We've never been able to keep one alive long enough to question them."

"Never?" Braden scoffed. "Sounds like you need better soldiers."

What Connor needed was to backhand the kid's lips clean off his smart mouth. Thankfully, Boom rested his hand on Connor's shoulder and spoke up.

"Thank you for your advice. We'll keep that in mind," Boom said.

In truth, the Army had captured multiple Progression soldiers, but every single one of them poisoned themselves before they could be questioned. Apparently, signing on with the Progression came with all sorts of benefits. Besides the ability to loot and plunder their captives, Progression soldiers were equipped with weapons, gear, and a potassium chloride pill in case they found themselves in situation they couldn't escape from. The Army couldn't figure out how the Progression had convinced all of their soldiers to commit suicide upon capture, but the scary fact remained, they had. Since neither Braden nor Kylee had a potassium chloride pill on them and were still alive, either the game had changed or they weren't with the Progression at all.

"Looks like we can all use a break," Boom announced. Tapping Connor's shoulder he asked, "Can I speak with you outside for a minute?"

Connor stood and turned toward his friend.

"Wait!" Kylee called out. "You never told us who you are."

That's interesting. Connor turned to face the girl. His eyebrows crept up his forehead. "Why do you want to know?"

She swallowed. "In case we remember anything else. Anything that can help you find our mom."

After considering her answer, he replied. "Connor."

"So that's it, Connor?" Braden stood to his feet, fists balled up and face distorting with anger and frustration. "You're not even gonna look for our mom, are you?"

If Braden and Kylee's mother had truly been taken by the Progression, she was probably dead or at least wishing for death by now. But no matter how much Braden grated on Connor's nerves, he didn't have the heart to squash the kids' hopes by voicing the Progression's policy on prisoners.

Boom must have felt the same way. He lowered his head and said, "I'm sorry for your loss, but we cannot spare the man power needed for a rescue mission."

"Fine. If you're too much of a coward, I'll go for her myself." Braden glared at Connor. "I thought you said the Army was the good guys."

"They are the good guys," Liberty said from the doorway. She walked into the tent and stopped beside Connor. "So good that they can't sentence their men to death in order to storm the Progression camp."

"Who the heck are you, and how's this any of your business?" Braden asked.

Connor tensed. Liberty briefly squeezed his arm, and then pushed past him. She knelt on the floor in front of Braden, making herself shorter than the boy.

"I'm sorry about your mother," she told him, her voice shaky and uncertain. "I know if it was my mom, I'd be angry and scared too. I'd want everyone to do something to help her. But honestly, I don't know if anything can be done. The Progression ... not a lot of their hostages survive."

Connor, Liberty, and Ashley had spent less than an hour in a Progression camp and escaped with their lives only because Boom and his team had made a surprise entrance and rescued them. Even with the Army's assistance, Liberty almost died. She'd been beaten beyond recognition and knocked unconscious.

"Boom is great and he likes to help people in need. If there was anything he could do, he would," Liberty continued. "But it's probably ..."

"She's not dead!" Braden shouted. His face reddened and his eyes bulged. "Shut up! You don't know nothing! She's strong. They couldn't have killed her."

Liberty didn't flinch. She stayed on her knees and let the child rage just inches from her face. Connor wanted to step in and move her to safety, but Boom stepped in front of him. The captain clearly wanted to see how the scene played out.

"She's still alive. You just wanna give up on her like everyone. But I know she's not dead. You shut your lyin' mouth!"

Kylee tugged at her brother's arm, but he shrugged her off.

"I'm sorry," Liberty replied. "I'm so sorry."

"No!" Braden shouted. "You didn't even know her. You don't care about her any more than they do. You're a liar and I hate you!"

Liberty's shoulders shook. She opened her arms and Braden rushed into them. He laid his head on her shoulder and let her wrap him up in her arms. His skinny frame heaved with loud sobs. Moments ticked by as Braden mourned in Liberty's embrace.

Feeling like an invader in this very private moment, Connor looked away. He would have walked out of the tent if he thought he could trust the explosive child alone with Liberty.

"I knew it," Braden said after a time. "I knew they'd kill her. I told her not to go. Why'd she go with them?"

Kylee slunk in her chair. "We both know why. She'd do anything to keep us safe. Mom could still be alive, though. She's tough. If anyone could make it, she could."

Braden shook his head. "She's dead, Kye. She died the minute they took her. She knew it, too. You didn't see her face when she said goodbye."

Liberty squeezed him tighter. "I'm so sorry. If I could take her place, I would."

Kylee started tearing up, and Braden released Liberty and retook his seat beside his sister. He draped an arm over her shoulders and squeezed her. "It'll be okay, Kye. We'll get through this."

Liberty stood and turned. Tears streamed from her eyes. She pushed past Connor and slipped out of the tent. He called out to her to wait, but by the time he reached the tent entrance, she was gone.

CHAPTER ELEVEN

Liberty

MY HEART FELT heavy when I left Connor, Boom, and the kids. I searched the camp for Ashley, and found her doing more karate training with Jeff. It looked like she was actually learning a stance, so I didn't want to interrupt their session. But I also didn't want to be alone. I wiped the useless tears from my eyes and let my feet carry me to Osberg's tent. After standing outside of it for what seemed like forever, I finally mustered the courage to tap on the canvas.

"Osberg? You awake?" I asked.

No answer.

I frowned. Boom had reassured me that Osberg still lived, but that was the extent of his medical report. I wanted to see the soldier myself, but I didn't want to wake him if he slept. Turning to leave I heard a weak cough coming from inside the tent.

"Osberg? Can I come in?"

"Yeah. Just give me a sec," he replied. Rustling noises preceded a weak, "Okay. You can come in now."

I unzipped the flap and the smell of antiseptic smacked into me like a wall of sterilization. I fanned the air in front of my face. "Whew. It smells like a hospital in here."

"Yeah, sorry about that. Magee just stopped by to clean and redress the wound," he replied.

Mention of the medic reminded me that I still need to talk to him. I made a mental note to do so and ducked into the tent.

Osberg's small sleeping space was dark, and it took a moment for my eyes to adjust to the change. His sleeping bag was zipped to his left armpit, with his left shoulder and arm sticking out at a twenty degree angle away from his body. The shoulder had been wrapped with what appeared to be a mile's worth of white gauze. His color looked marginally better than the last time I'd seen him, but his skin still looked too pale and his eyes seemed unfocused.

"He cleaned it? That sounds painful," I replied.

"You have no idea. But thankfully, I've got these." He held up a bottle of pills. "Good stuff. Percocet. The breakfast of fallen champions."

"You're surprisingly upbeat for someone with such a bad wound. Speaking of which, how is it?" I asked. Realizing how stupid I sounded, I shook my head and tried again. "I mean, will you recover use of your shoulder?"

He started to shrug, but only raised his right shoulder a fraction of an inch before realizing what a bad idea that was. "Been better. Pretty much destroyed the bone. Rock climbing is probably out for a while."

"You like to rock climb?" I asked.

"Yep. I'd tell you that I'm good at it, but it's Tuesday."

"It is?" I asked. "And what does that have to do with anything?"

"I never get away with lies on Tuesdays. Thursdays are the best for lying. I become a pyro on Fridays."

"Good to know." I smiled at him. "Are you always this funny, or is that the Percocet talking?"

He grinned at the bottle. "Did you hear that? She thinks I'm funny."

Definitely the drugs.

"Very funny, but I can't figure out why. Boom said you need surgery, but will have to wait until we get back to the base."

"Surgery, smurgery," Osberg replied.

Clearly wasted out of his mind, he gave me a big, toothy smile. "I like you," he declared.

Thrown off guard, I hesitated, and then replied, "Thank you. I lie you too."

"You should come around more. It gets boring. Magee is the only one who comes to see me, and he doesn't have a sense of humor."

"All right. I'll see what I can do. Do you need anything while I'm here? Some water? A cheeseburger?"

He chuckled. Then he started to say something but drifted off mid sentence.

Before I left, I bowed my head and quickly prayed for healing for his shoulder, and his heart. Careful not to disturb his sleep, I quietly ordered him to get lots of rest and let myself out of his tent.

* * *

The day looked bright and promising, and my spirit had been greatly lifted by the exchange and prayer with Osberg. Sure, bad things happened all around us, but so did good things. Determined to spend a little alone time focusing on the positive, I headed toward my tent.

Boom met me there. "You look happier," he observed with a smile.

I nodded. "Went to see Osberg."

"I take it he's doing well?"

"Really well. He's pretty funny for someone with a gigantic hole in his shoulder."

Boom chuckled. "He's always had a great sense of humor. Glad to hear that he's still in good spirits."

I nodded. "He still looks pretty rough. Will he be okay?"

"Only time will tell. For a veterinarian, Magee is one heck of a doctor. If he can keep the wound from getting infected, Osberg's chances are good."

"I'm relieved to hear that. Now, I have a feeling you weren't waiting for me just to talk about Osberg. What's up?"

A smile tugged at the sides of Boom's mouth. "Yes, well, what I need to know is what happened with Braden?"

"What do you mean?"

"How did you get him to break down like that?"

I shrugged. I didn't get him to do anything. I just saw a hurting kid, so I opened my arms to him."

"He keeps asking for you, you know?"

"He does? Why?"

"Maybe because you listened? I can't imagine that many people listen to him."

"Do you remember your childhood, Boom?"

He rubbed his chin. "Some of it. Moments, scenes. Special memories."

"In my memories of being Braden's age I was always too mature to enjoy with the young kids, and always too young to sit with the adults. It was a difficult time."

Boom nodded. "We tend to forget that sometimes."

"Remember. It will help you relate to them."

"Yes, speaking of remembering, have you recalled any more of what happened to the night Jeff brought you into camp?"

My mind drifted back to the escape from the Progression camp.

Everything hurt. I opened my eyes and people I didn't know stared down at me. Searching for a familiar face, I scanned the group. Connor. He was there and I was so angry at him. I sat up to give him a piece of my mind, but pain made me dizzy. Two men stood over me, diagnosing my state. Concussion, broken ribs, multiple cuts and bruises, black eye, split lip, possible internal bleeding.

I summoned the strength to stand, and Connor led me away from the camp where he professed his undying love, and then kissed me...

That stupid kiss had been invading my dreams ever since. But it was what happened after the kiss that had the whole camp scratching their heads.

I shook my head. "It's still a blur. I remember laughter and light that seemed to explode inside me. I couldn't handle it and fell to my knees. Then the next thing I knew, Connor was holding me, running toward the camp, and yelling names. Probably Osberg and Noke, now that I think about it."

The medics' eyes grew round when they saw me. They poked and prodded me, whispering and arguing amongst themselves. That lasted for who-knows-how-long, and then I woke up next to Ashley in our tent and I was fine. No, better than fine. Every bruise and cut that had previously marked up my body had been erased, as if someone had taken the ultimate magic marker to my skin. Even childhood scars and the initials I'd carved into my wrist were gone. All my aches and pains had disappeared. When I came out of the tent, all the soldiers were looking at me like I had antenna sticking out of my head.

"Magee and Osberg are both atheists," Boom said, bringing me back to the present. "You have no idea what you did to them that night."

"I didn't *do* anything. I don't know what happened."

"Exactly," Boom replied. "I'm glad we had this talk. I needed to remind you who you are."

I waited, but he didn't elaborate. I stopped walking and faced him. "And? Who am I, Boom?"

"Surely you know the answer to that."

Frustrated, I kicked a small rock. It rolled across the ground and came to a stop about a yard away from where it started.

"Yeah, I do," I replied. "I'm like that rock. It has no purpose whatsoever. It's in this huge forest full of rocks and it was doing absolutely nothing right here, and now it's doing absolutely nothing over there. Sometimes I feel like the Army is like that too. We keep moving and fighting and trying. Kids are dying, but are we really changing anything? Are we making any sort of a difference?"

Boom stared at the ground for a moment. Then he bent down and picked up a small stone, rubbing it between his thumb and forefinger. "A rock is a peculiar reference. Is there a reason you chose that particular object?"

I shrugged. "I don't know. I'm clumsy and I keep tripping on them?"

Boom chuckled. "Of course you do. It's scriptural. The stone that the builders rejected has now become the cornerstone. He is the stone that makes people stumble, the rock that makes them fall."

He handed me the rock. Grey and plain, there was nothing special about it, just like I knew there wouldn't be. "The cornerstone, huh? I've heard that passage before. Where is it from?"

"First Peter, second chapter."

I turned the rock over in my hand. "What is a cornerstone, anyway?"

"It's the stone that forms the base of a corner of a building. Where two walls connect," he replied. "All other stones are set based upon that stone."

"So, Jesus is the cornerstone. Okay, I get that." I still felt like I was missing some huge point that would cause everything to click and make sense. "So, Jesus causes some people to stumble and fall. That doesn't make sense. What does the rest of the scripture say?"

"It's a reference to their choice not to follow Him. Free will." Boom froze for a moment, closing his eyes as if accessing some gigantic Biblical database in his brain. Finally he looked at me and recited, "They stumble because they do not obey God's word, and so they meet the fate that was planned for them. But you are not like that, for you are a chosen people. You are royal priests, a holy nation, God's very own possession. As a result, you can show others the goodness of God, for He called you out of the darkness into His wonderful light."

"A royal priest, huh? I don't feel so royal right now."

"God's very own possession, built on the cornerstone. You are called to show His light."

"You do realize we're in the middle of a war, right?" I asked. "How the heck am I supposed to do that?"

Boom chuckled. "Oh, Libby, don't you see it? Your light has already affected two atheist medics, all of my soldiers, Connor and Ashley, and now Braden and Kylee."

He patted me on the shoulder, much like a father or a coach would do for a job well done. "It's in the darkest of night that the light shines the brightest."

Then he turned and walked back to camp, leaving me holding my fishing pole and pondering rocks, light and crazy Hispanic men who made my head hurt.

CHAPTER TWELVE

Connor

CONNOR FOLLOWED BOOM out of the main tent and into the glaring sunlight. He shielded his eyes for a moment to give them a chance to adjust to the change. He considered going to check on Liberty, but Boom motioned for him to follow.

"I need to check on the horses," Boom said. "Walk with me."

Connor nodded and accompanied his friend.

Once they were out of earshot from the tent, Boom turned to Connor and asked, "What are your thoughts on Braden and Kylee?"

Connor shrugged. "I'm not sure what to think. If they're with the Progression, we shouldn't have been able to bring them in alive."

Boom slowed as they reached the horses, and Connor followed suit.

"I do think they're hiding something," Connor added. "I just don't know what. Their whole story could be bogus, or it could be woven with the truth. I'm not sure. I don't pretend to be some big expert on kids, but when my parents died … well, I didn't act like them."

Connor rubbed the back of his neck and followed Boom toward a dapple grey stud. One by one, Boom checked over the horse's legs and hooves.

"What's your take on them?" Connor asked.

"Much the same. Although, Braden's reaction to Liberty surprised me. At first it looked fabricated, but toward the end ... there was too much pain for it to be all fake. There is some truth in it, but I'm not sure how much."

Boom stopped talking and waved at a soldier who was brushing down the horse Liberty had ridden when they picked up Noke. Dressed in full Army combat uniform, he looked like every other soldier in the platoon. At least until he stepped out from behind the horse and his dark brown cowboy boots made a stark contrast.

The soldier walked over and saluted. "Captain," he said by way of greeting.

"Connor, have you met Private Ryan Pearson yet?" Boom asked.

"Don't believe I've had the pleasure." Connor replied.

"Pearson, this is First Sergeant Dunstan, a brother of mine from Special Forces."

Pearson saluted. "Pleasure to meet you, First Sergeant,"

Connor returned the salute.

"Pearson was working as a ranch hand outside of Puyallup," Boom explained. "The ranch he worked for was supplying one of our units, so when we got word that the Progression was stealing their livestock, we went to help. We took out the threat, but not before the ranch had been drastically downsized."

Pearson chuckled. "I needed a job, and it turns out the captain needed someone who knew their way around a horse."

Boom patted Pearson on the back. "It's been a good arrangement. Since we will be mobilizing soon, I thought you might want Pearson to suggest a gentle horse for Ashley."

"The young girl, right?" Pearson asked.

Connor nodded.

"Does she have any riding experience?"

"No. Well, yes, but she was unconscious."

"Oh yeah, I remember hearing about that." He turned and studied the horses for a moment before pointing to the one Liberty had ridden. "That girl right there. She's no spring chicken, but she's gentle with an even temperament. I saw her walk right over a snake the other day and she didn't even flinch. Perfect for a new rider."

Connor thanked him for the recommendation, and then he and Boom returned to the camp, parting ways once they reached it.

Connor went in search of the girls. Although he couldn't find Liberty, Ashley was with Jeff. Connor stood back and watched the two of them train.

Ashley crouched down with her arms straight in front of her, while Jeff tugged her shoulders back.

"Your spine is supposed to be straight," Jeff told her.

Ashley sighed deeply. "This is so stupid. I told you, I want to learn how to do one of those really cool round house kicks."

"I can't teach you that until you perfect your stances," Jeff insisted.

Ashley relaxed her stance and fell on the ground, clearly too exhausted to stand. "You never let me do anything fun. You make me pose and flex in all these stupid, uncomfortable positions, and that's not what I signed up for. I want to kick and punch!"

Jeff threw back his head and stared at the sky, no doubt promising to never have kids of his own.

Despite his dark mood, Connor chuckled.

Ashley heard him and perked up. She pulled herself to a sitting position and asked, "Are you done questioning them?"

Connor nodded.

"Think Kylee will want to play cards again?"

He shrugged. "I don't know if that's such a good idea. We don't know much about them."

Ashley rolled her eyes. "They're kids, Connor, and it's not like we're leaving the camp or anything. We'll be right in the main tent. It's totally safe."

My daughter the negotiator. "Fine, you can go ask if she wants to, but you guys need to stay in the tent. I mean it."

"Thank you, thank you!" Ashley shouted and took two steps in the direction Connor had come from.

Then, as an afterthought, she turned around and said, "Sorry, Jeff, but this is boring." Before he could reply she sprinted toward the main tent.

Connor ran a hand through his hair, wishing he could push away all the worries nagging at his brain. He glanced around the camp, and then asked Jeff, "Have you seen Liberty?"

"No, First Sergeant." Jeff replied.

His weapons sat piled up on a box beside his tent. One by one, he picked them up and checked them over before equipping them.

After he finished, he addressed Connor again. "Will that be all, First Sergeant?"

Connor sighed. "When nobody is around, you can drop the title." He stepped forward and lowered his shoulders, trying to relax, hoping Jeff would do the same.

Jeff nodded, but still stood stiff and rigid, as if expecting Connor to pounce on him or something.

Connor made another attempt to offer the soldier an olive branch. "I know we haven't exactly seen eye to eye on ... well on anything, but I'm glad you've decided to join us."

It was an irrefutably true statement, since Connor would much rather have Jeff right where he could keep an eye on him than lurking around in the woods with a gun aimed at Connor's head. And if Jeff continued to stare at Liberty like some love-sick puppy, Connor wanted the boy where he could stab a knife in his eye.

As if reading Connor's mind, Jeff grinned. The upturn of his lips didn't look at all friendly.

"Where else would I go?" he asked. "I like it here."

Connor showed Jeff his teeth in what wasn't quite a smile.

"You're a good soldier, and I appreciate the fact that you would do anything to help Liberty and Ashley." He leveled a hard stare at Jeff. "But don't push me."

Jeff's gaze flickered to something behind Connor, and his smile widened.

"That sounds a little like a threat," Liberty said, sliding next to Connor, her fishing pole in her hand. "You wouldn't be threatening Jeff, would you?"

"No, ma'am," Connor replied, turning so he faced her. "Of course not."

Jeff snorted.

Liberty leveled a hard stare at Connor and he gave her his best innocent smile.

Jeff shouldered his rifle. "Hey, Lib. Good to see you, but I gotta go on patrol soon." He smiled and stepped forward to wrap her in a hug, squeezing her tightly and lifting her feet off the ground. She yelled at him and pounded her fists into his chest until he put her down.

"You're such a dork. Don't do that again," Liberty warned, but she smiled.

Connor did not.

Jeff seemed unfazed by Connor's glare or Liberty's chastising. He gave her a wide toothy grin and said, "Thanks for our talk yesterday. I feel better. About everything. You really helped me."

Liberty lit up. "Really? Good. I'm glad you're coming around about it all."

Connor felt like a fifth wheel, but he didn't care. Determined not to give Jeff the pleasure of making him uncomfortable, he crossed his arms and prepared to wait out their conversation.

"We should talk after your shift. Find me, okay, Jeff?" Liberty asked.

"Will do." Jeff turned his smirk back on Connor and saluted. "First Sergeant, Sir."

Connor dismissed Jeff, and then watched him stride away.

"He's come so far," Liberty said, watching Jeff's back disappear behind the trees. "I'm glad to see him growing and thriving. He's doing well."

Connor was just glad to see him leave. As he watched Jeff go, he wondered how the guy had gotten close to Liberty so quickly. Their friendship seemed easy and comfortable from the moment they meant, while Connor had to strive and sweat for every ounce of trust and affection he got from her.

"Connor?" Liberty asked, concern lined her forehead. "You okay?"

He shook himself out of his thoughts and focused on her. "Yeah, just a little worn out, but I don't have to meet with Boom until this evening. You want to go get something to eat and talk for a while?"

"Uh ... sure. I guess."

"Truth is, I'm worried about Ashley. We don't know much about these kids and I'm hesitant to leave her with them."

"I don't know, Con. They just seem a bit roughed-up to me."

"No, there's something we're missing. The kids don't look or act like Progression soldiers, but there's definitely something off about them."

Liberty's eyebrows scrunched up in disbelief. "They lost their mom and they have issues, but who doesn't nowadays?"

"It's more than that. The girl ... it's like she's always watching me."

A smile spread across Liberty's face. "Maybe she has a crush on you? You are pretty handsome, you know?" Her cheeks turned bright red and Connor got the feeling she hadn't meant to disclose that last little tidbit of information.

"You think so, huh?" he asked.

She rolled her eyes and turned away. "I just remembered that I have something else I need to be doing right now."

"Wait." Connor grabbed her arm. "Please come with me. I really am worried and don't want it to look like I'm spying on her, you know?"

One of Liberty's eyebrows rose in question. "So you think if you and I are just randomly hanging out and talking in the same place they happen to be, we won't look suspicious?"

"Less suspicious?" He smiled at her. "Please don't make me spy on her alone."

"Fine, but if we get in trouble, remember that this brilliant idea is all you, and I will totally sell you out."

Connor chuckled and followed Liberty. They entered the main tent just in time to watch Ashley jump out of her chair and point a finger at Braden.

"You can't do that!" she shouted. "It's not fair."

They paused at the door and watched the situation unfold.

"Yes I can," Braden replied. Jaw jutted and arms crossed, he asked, "Who's gonna stop me?"

"It's wrong. It's cheating. Don't you even care about that?"

"Why would I? I *can* do it, so I'm gonna."

"See," Kylee chimed in. "I told you he's a jerk."

"I'm not a jerk," Braden said. "I'm just not a loser."

Kylee giggled. "You've been losing the whole time."

"Shut up, Kye. These stupid rules are the only reason I'm losing. I'm sick of them."

"You can't just change the rules," Ashley insisted, dark hair flying as she spun her chair around and knelt on the seat. She then leaned over the table, practically stabbing Braden's chest with her finger. "It doesn't work like that."

Liberty elbowed Connor. "Her odd insistence on justice and rule following … she must get that from her mother."

Connor held up his hands to show his innocent and purity. "What's that supposed to mean? I follow the rules."

Liberty rolled her eyes. "Right. The question is, whose rules?"

Connor shrugged. She had him there.

"Oh, yeah?" Braden asked. Copying Ashley's pose, he turned around his chair and kneeled on the seat, sticking a finger in Ashley's face. "I can change any rules I want. Watch me."

"We should probably interrupt them before this leads to bloodshed," Connor said.

Liberty nodded and invited him to lead the way with a wave of her hand.

Connor marched into the tent and stood at the end of the table with his arms crossed, assessing the situation. Ashley and Braden looked like a couple of dragons posturing over their hordes of cards. Ashley's face reddened, and she gave up on her attempt to poke a hole in Braden's chest in favor of trying to filch his cards. She used her upper body and one of her hands to guard her own pile and had the other hand methodically snatching at his stack, around his blocks. Kylee sat in the chair beside Ashley, pretending to study the few cards in her hand, completely disinterested in the mighty battle before her. But, Connor could tell the girl was watching him out of the corner of her eye.

Yeah, I'm watching you too, sweetheart.

"A duel to the death?" Liberty asked.

Ashley glanced at Liberty, and then her accusatory pointer finger reappeared inches from Braden's nose. "He's not following the rules!"

"That's because they're stupid rules," Braden said.

"Only when you're losing. It's not my fault you're a poor loser."

"I'm not a loser!" Braden shouted. Then he launched himself across the table and scooped up as many of Ashley's cards as his hands would hold.

Ashley gasped in horror, her eyes wide, like she'd witnessed the most appalling act she'd ever seen. "Hey! You can't do that. Give them back," She launched for a counter attack, but Connor caught her in mid-attack.

"I think this card game might be a little too hardcore for you two."

She struggled against him for a moment, growling and snarling like some rabid animal. Then she seemed to realize he wouldn't release her until she calmed down.

"Fine." She relaxed against Connor. "I don't want to play with him anyway. Can I show Kylee around the camp?"

Kylee leaped from her chair and tossed her cards on the table.

"Please?" Ashley asked. "I'm so sick of this game."

"I remember telling you to stay in this tent." Connor frowned, releasing his daughter.

"It's so boring. There's nothing to do." Ashley tugged on his arm as her dark eyes pleaded with him. "Please? It's not like we can go far. There are soldiers everywhere."

There weren't nearly enough soldiers left for them to be everywhere, but Connor knew fresh air would be good for the kids.

"Okay, but don't go past the tree line, and be back in this tent before sundown."

Ashley agreed to his terms, and then tugged on Kylee's hand. The soldier that Boom had watching the kids glanced at Connor. Connor nodded, telling the man to follow the girls. When Connor turned his attention back to the table, Braden had scooped all the cards into his pile.

Connor chuckled at the peculiar behavior. "Feel better?" he asked.

Braden scowled at him.

Liberty sat in a chair next to the boy and rested her elbows on the table.

"They were stupid rules," Braden muttered.

"No doubt. I've never been a fan of rules myself." Liberty glanced at Connor. "When people tell me what to do it makes me want to do the opposite."

Connor's suspicion confirmed, he filed that tidbit away for later.

Problem with authority, check.

Braden's head tilted and his eyebrows rose. "You? Yeah right."

Connor chuckled. He could have named off numerous rules Liberty had problems with and he hadn't even known her for that long.

Liberty glared at Connor, then turned back to Braden. "No, I'm serious. I'm a rebel. Probably started when I was a kid. I hated things like shopping and dresses and the color pink. Mom could not fathom the depth of my hatred for these things, and she always dragged me shopping and stuffing me in pink, frilly dresses. So, to make our shopping trips interesting, I'd climb in the middle of the clothes racks and knock clothes off hangers until she made me go sit in the car. And every time she tried to dress me up, I'd play with the water snakes and frogs that swam in our irrigation ditches until my clothes got nice and muddy."

The visual of a young Liberty covered in mud and running some poor woman ragged drifted through Connor's mind. He coughed to hide the laughter that the image evoked.

"What's an irrigation ditch?" Braden asked.

"I grew up on a farm and irrigation ditches were just ditches we used to water crops. They were pretty gross, now that I think about it. Besides the frogs and water snakes, they also had snails and who knows what else in them."

"And you played in those ditches?" Braden asked, sounding shocked.

"Yeah, but only when Mom made me dress up." Liberty giggled. "Probably not one of my best decisions. I'm lucky I didn't pick up some sort of bacteria or fungus from that water."

Braden laughed. "I couldn't imagine Kylee swimming in a ditch, or playing with snakes. You're a pretty weird girl."

"You have no idea," Liberty replied. The briefest of smiles brushed her lips before she turned back to Braden. "I'm going to tell you something I wish someone would have told me at your age. Something that will make your life easier."

Braden shrugged. "Whatever."

Liberty watched the boy for a moment. He looked anywhere but at her, seemingly disinterested in anything she said.

She sighed and stood. "Alright. Never mind. Seems I misunderstood and you've got it all figured out and don't need my advice."

Braden reached for her arm "Wait."

She paused.

He looked at the table. "You've been okay to me. I'll hear you out."

The smile Liberty flashed Connor brightened her green eyes and smoothed away all hints of tiredness. It was a smile of hope, so rare and valuable that Connor wished he could engrave it into his mind to reflect on in the moments when all hope seemed lost. Her treasured smile faded, smoothing into a stoic mask as she sat down.

"Thank you," she told Braden. "Now look at me."

It took him a few moments to comply, but once he did, she continued.

"Don't be a rebel without a clue. It's okay to rebel, but make sure you have a cause and that your cause is worthy of the punishment you might face." Her chin rose a fraction as she continued to speak, "Rule breakers are responsible for all great things in the world: freeing the slaves, beautiful art, crazy dances, multiple music styles, innovative architecture, all sorts of awesomeness. Heck, even Jesus was a rebel. Rebels change the world."

Braden eyed her skeptically. Connor got the feeling the kid expected to hear the 'but' of the conversation, but Liberty kept speaking encouragement into him.

"You can be one of those crazy rebellious world changers, Braden; you just have to learn how to choose your battles. Don't fight stupid rules. Instead, fight bad ones. Fight for freedom and for people who are weaker than you are. Fight to keep life beautiful and extraordinary. Fight for life, love, peace and justice. Fight for truth and purity."

Her eyes glistened with passion as the air around them became charged with her hope for humanity. Liberty was usually animated when she talked, but while she spoke to Braden, she became something more. Something transformed. She embodied that which she spoke of, becoming beauty, life, love, peace and justice.

Connor leaned toward her, soaking up life from her. The hope in her words swept him up into her passion. Suddenly it no longer mattered that the Progression had them outnumbered, or that they didn't know whether or not they could make it back to Fort Lewis. But, despite all, they still had hope, and Connor chose to cling to it like life support.

"Rebels change the world, Brae," Liberty said, her smile of hope returning. "I'm glad you're a rebel."

Caught up in the moment, Connor realized he'd do anything to keep Liberty's hope alive.

CHAPTER THIRTEEN

Liberty

BRADEN REMINDED ME of myself at his age. He was broken. Feeling weak and worthless, he struggled to prove his strength and value. After the girls left, he meticulously arranged and counted his cards.

"Savoring your victory?" I asked.

He ignored me, but I could see something beyond his posturing and growling. Underneath the greasy hair and grubby fingers, Braden was gold, packaged in ripped jeans and holey sneakers. When I sat beside him, his worth—the worth he couldn't see or understand—seemed to take hold of my mouth and make me sing of his value. Like a diamond, he'd been created from pressure, and now he needed to be shined. So I encouraged him, words tumbling out of me, like some possessed motivational speaker hyped up on crack. Finally, after challenging this beaten down, kicked-in-the-teeth kid to change the world, my mouth finally closed.

Braden stared at me.

Whatever had come over me disappeared, and I became acutely aware of how lame my pep talk must have sounded.

Okay. What the heck was that about?

Braden didn't even blink. He just kept staring at me.

Awkward. What do I do now?

No brilliant ideas came to mind. I glanced at Connor, but he just stared back at me. No help there.

"Well, I should get going," I said to Braden. "I'll see you later?"

Still no response. If shock and awe were my goals, I'd accomplished them, but now I had no idea how to un-shock and un-awe him.

"All righty then." Desperate to escape the humiliating spotlight I seemed to have placed myself in, I stood and made a beeline for the door as quickly as my legs would carry me. Once out the door, I took off running. I sprinted toward the river, desperate for time alone so I could recount what I said and figure out why I'd said it.

The sound of footsteps behind me told me I didn't run alone.

Connor. Would you just go away and give me a moment?

I came to the bank of the river and turned south. His continued pursuit pressed me forward, and I ran harder, determined to keep going until he gave up. Time blurred as I followed the riverbank, sprinting until my lungs felt like they were going to burst. Even then, I didn't let up. I ran until my legs burned and the stitch in my side forced me to stop and catch my breath. After what seemed like forever, I halted and leaned over, gasping for air.

Connor came to a stop beside me. "You okay?" he asked.

Since I was physically unable to speak and suck down oxygen at the same time, I didn't bother answering him. Also, I wouldn't know how to respond. Instead, I turned and watched the river for a moment, focusing on my breathing. Staying vertical seemed like an unnecessary waste of energy, so I collapsed on the grass, staring up at the sky.

"We shouldn't be here," Connor said. "It's not safe to be out of the camp right now. We don't know how big their force is. They could be anywhere. Everywhere."

"You sound paranoid."

"I sound smart. But you make me wonder if I am."

I didn't reply, still not trusting myself to talk. In fact, if any evil sea witches lurked in that river, I planned to sell my voice to them so I never had to speak again.

Connor collapsed next to me, so close his arm brushed mine. I stared at the pale blue sky, trying not to let his proximity distract me from my self-loathing. We were far enough from the tree line that the grass had grown into a thick, lush bed that enveloped us. I tried to replay the stupid conversation I'd had with Braden in my mind, but exhaustion and comfort kept diverting my attention. The music of the river sang to me, lulling my body and mind into relaxation. I closed my eyes and let the sun warm my eyelids as my breathing steadied.

The warmth of Connor's arm reminded me that he lay beside me, sharing in this moment, and suddenly I needed to know why.

"Why did you follow me?" I asked.

"What?"

Rephrasing the question, I asked, "Why are you here?"

Connor shifted. I opened my eyes and he was lying on his side, facing me. Entirely too close, he propped his head up on one fist.

"It's not safe for you to be in the woods alone right now," he said.

I let out a deep breath. He'd followed me to babysit me. Figures.

"But that's not the only reason I'm here," he continued. "That kid—"

"Braden?" I asked.

"Yeah. What you said to him was ... wow. I don't think he expected you to support him. I bet no one has ever encouraged him before."

"I know." I sighed. "I sounded like an idiot. He must think I'm some sort of crackpot."

"No. He was posturing like he expected to be berated or disciplined. Instead, you spoke life and hope into him. He's a punk kid with a smart mouth, and you completely threw him off. He didn't know how to respond."

I eyed Connor, unsure of what think about this new development.

"You believe it, don't you?" he asked.

Looking back at the sky, I nodded. "Every word. I know it sounds crazy, but Braden is so much more than what he appears to be."

"Honestly, that's what I'm worried about."

"I'm not talking about him being with the Progression or something. I'm talking about who he is on the inside. He has the potential to be someone really special, but life has kicked him in the face so many times it's skewed his vision and he can't see a future for himself anymore. I just wanted to clear up his vision a little."

I could feel Connor's gaze burning a hole into the side of my face, but I didn't look at him. He watched me for a while.

"You really care about him—about all of them—don't you?" he asked.

"People won't care how much you know until they know how much you care," I replied.

"I've heard that before," Connor said.

"John C. Maxwell quote."

"Ah. Yep, that explains it, then. The firm had me read a few of his books when I was a new hire. They had a whole list of books selected to build competent leaders."

I chuckled. "Did they work?"

"The thing about self-help books is that they tell you what you want to hear and probably already know. They don't magically transform you into a different person. Take that quote you just used. I read the same quote, yet it affected me differently. It reinforced what I already knew: people need to believe I care about them before they will value my knowledge."

He shifted. "Don't get me wrong, I did care about my clients. I worked hard to get and keep them, and I appreciated the fact that they trusted me to win court cases. Leadership books gave me a different perspective, but they didn't change my views. That quote affected you, because it took what you already knew and put into a catchy phrase."

What Connor said made sense, so I nodded. "Okay, I can see that."

"There is a big difference between mutually beneficial relationships—like the ones I had with my clients—and your relationship with Braden, though. He can't do anything for you, yet you genuinely care about him, don't you?"

I thought of Braden, his small frame shaking with heart-wrenching sobs as he held me and accepted the fate of his mother.

"He's courageous," I replied. "He has a big, hurting heart and he's fiercely protective over those he loves. His life hasn't been easy, but he isn't giving up. He's a fighter."

Connor grabbed my hand.

I looked down, studying our interlaced fingers, but didn't pull away.

"You are the most beautiful person I've ever met," he said. With his other hand, he traced my face starting at my forehead and running his fingers down toward my chin.

"Perfect features, but you're so much more than this," he said. His fingertips ran down my throat and hovered above my heart. "Now this is what makes you truly beautiful."

Feeling like a deer in the headlights, I could see the truck coming straight for me, but I couldn't move. Part of me didn't even want to move. Something dangerously comforting drew me into Connor's sights. I wanted to close my eyes and drink his steady presence in like lemonade on a hot day.

He leaned toward me. My heart sped up as I waited for him. Closer and closer he came until only inches separated our lips.

I wanted to kiss him, but if I started, I didn't know if I could stop. If I'd even want to stop. Terrified of the erratic way my heart kept beating and desperate for reprieve from the desire that burned through me, I blurted out, "Why did you quit the Army?"

He pulled away from me. "What?"

"You were in the Army with Boom. Why did you quit it?"

Connor sat up and ran a hand through his hair. "Why would you ask that?"

My question seemed to touch a sore spot, and I considered it for a moment. "I'm not sure. I just want to know about you." I pulled myself up to sit beside him.

We sat in silence and watched the river. I could sense how upset and tense the subject had made him, and thought about withdrawing the question, but instead I waited. And my patience eventually paid off.

"I enlisted in the Army just out of high school," Connor said. He spoke so low I had to lean closer to hear him. "I scored in the ninetieth percentile on my ASVAB and the recruiters were tripping over each other to sign me up."

"ASVAB being ...?"

"Military placement test."

"Ah-ha. You scored well and the vultures swooped down on you."

I'd meant the comment to lighten his mood, but clearly failed because his frown only deepened.

"I volunteered for Special Forces and was selected. I made it through the Q-Course. I became a non-commissioned officer and went back to school, and then I ran the Q-Course again as an officer."

"What's the Q-Course?"

"Hell." Connor cracked a smile. "Also known as the Qualification Course. It's a six-phase assessment and training course designed to either make or break soldiers."

I tapped my shoulder against his arm. "Sounds pleasant. You went through it twice?"

Connor nodded and continued staring at the river. "Yep. I thought I was pretty impressive. After I graduated the second time, I was given my team. That's when I met Boom."

"He was your weapons guy."

Connor smirked. "That he was. You haven't seen an explosion until you've given Boom free rein. It's a glorious sight. I had an incredible team. Every one of them were like brothers to each other. And to me, and well ... I botched a mission and got a couple of them killed."

I watched Connor's jaw clench as he struggled with demons from his past. Desperate to offer some sort of comfort, I wrapped my arm around his and leaned against him. Since I didn't know what to say, I kept my mouth shut.

"I was an excellent intelligence sergeant, but I never should have become an officer. It changed everything when I became responsible for them all. I hated it." Connor leaned his head against mine, and I closed my eyes and breathed him in. At that moment, I realized I loved him. Not the arrogant attorney nor the clever and capable soldier, but the real Connor. The handsome, courageous and afraid-to-let-anyone-get-too-close Connor.

"Connor," I whispered.

"Yes?"

I wanted to tell him I loved him, but didn't want him to wonder if my declaration of love came from sympathy for his past. When I told Connor how I felt, I wanted it to be different, under better circumstances and without possible motives. So, I swallowed back what I wanted to say, and replied, "We should probably get back and check on Ashley."

I felt him nod against me. "Boom has someone watching her, but you're right. We should."

Neither of us moved.

Then suddenly Connor's entire body tensed and he whispered, "Somebody's coming."

CHAPTER FOURTEEN

Connor

CONNOR SAT UP and scanned the area, searching for a way out of the trap they'd set for themselves. The small meadow they rested in was too exposed. Looking back in the direction they'd come from, he saw that they'd never be able to hide their tracks. They needed to get out of there and far away before whoever approached stepped out of the trees.

"You have your gun?" he asked Liberty.

She nodded, her eyes wide.

"Hopefully you won't need it. Come."

He pulled her to her feet, gripped her hand and led her to the northeast, away from the river and toward the trees. Hand in hand, they sprinted through the forest without looking back. Shouts behind them told Connor that someone had found their tracks and would be following them. Confident that their best chance of survival meant splitting up so he could lose the soldiers, Connor tugged Liberty to a walk.

"I want you to run that direction." He pointed toward the northwest. "Stay in the trees, but follow the river back to the camp. Run as fast as you ran here, no matter what you hear behind you."

Liberty shook her head. "No. Not without you."

"I'm going to cover your tracks and lead them away. When it's safe, I'll follow."

She shook her head again. "No. We go together."

He cupped her face in his hands. "Dang it, listen to me. I know what I'm doing and I'll be fine. I won't be far behind you."

She didn't believe him. He could see it in the way her lips pursed and her eyes narrowed. They were wasting precious time, though, and he needed her to run.

"Libby, I was Special Forces ... a Green Beret. They trained us for tasks a lot harder than this." He brushed a quick kiss on her lips. "Now hurry and go so I can follow. If we wait, we'll both die here."

The sounds of pursuit grew louder. Liberty glanced back, and then leaned forward and returned his kiss. "Stay alive," she whispered.

"You can bet on it. Now go!"

Connor watched her sprint between the trees and disappear from his sight. With a sigh of relief he kicked leaves over her tracks, and then stomped to the east for a few yards, tearing up as much ground as he could.

Stopping to take cover behind a tree, Connor watched the direction he'd come from, awaiting his pursuers. After a few minutes, they made their appearance. First to show was a blond boy, packing a submachine gun and wearing fatigues but no armor. As five more unarmored soldiers joined the first, Connor realized that the crew must not have been expecting trouble, and hoped they'd recognize they weren't geared for a battle and turn back. The blond leader motioned for the boys behind him to look at the ground.

A brunette, who looked about fifteen, pointed toward Connor's direction and said, "They went that way."

"I know that, idiot," the blond replied. "But look how the tracks changed. There were two and now there's only one set, and it's heavier. Whoever it is wants us to go that way."

"Maybe one of them is carrying the other?" The brunette suggested.

"Or, they're trying to lead us that direction. Think, Ray. Pretend you're a well-trained soldier who knows what you're doing. I know that's a stretch for you, but try."

The brunette puffed out his chest and took a step toward the blonde. Another dark-headed boy on his left grabbed the brunette's arm and said something Connor couldn't hear.

"Aww, did I hurt your feelings?" The blond asked. Then he closed the distance between himself and the brunette, getting right in the kid's face. "We know you're an idiot. You don't need to prove it by trying to start crap in a forest potentially full of hostiles. You better stand down."

Connor watched the show, thankful for the time the Progression soldiers bought Liberty with their little pissing match. As the two boys stood unmoving in the clearing, he wondered if he'd have to do anything at all, or if they'd just kill each other. Finally the brunette lowered his head and took a step back.

"Right," the blond said. "As I was saying, we should split up and go in opposite directions."

So much for them turning back. Since Connor couldn't have them running off and finding Liberty, he aimed his Glock at the blonde and squeezed the trigger. The kid went down, and then Connor shot the brunette. Then, he ducked behind the cover of a tree and ran the opposite direction of the four remaining soldiers.

The group must have been filled with newer recruits, because it took them a moment to recover. By the time they returned fire, Connor was well away from them and weaving through the trees at a mad dash. Ducking behind a large oak, he waited and listened for the sounds of their approach. Once he heard them, he peeked around the tree and leveled his Glock, waiting for a clean shot. As soon as he got one, he took it. Another Progression soldier fell, and Connor ducked back behind the oak as the three remaining soldiers emptied their magazines in his general direction.

After a time, the gunfire stopped.

"Think we got him?" one of the soldiers asked, his voice high-pitched and young-sounding.

"Why don't you go check?" a second soldier asked.

"Parker?" the young-sounding soldier asked.

"Forget that," the third soldier replied. "We're not even geared for this. We should get back to the camp and report what happened."

"Parker, you're an idiot," the second soldier declared. "You saw what the major did to the guys who made it back from the last battle."

The silence that followed the second soldier's words spoke volumes. Connor cradled his Glock and wondered what to do. He could outrun the kids and get back to the camp, but because of their fear they'd follow and try to kill him. He couldn't take that chance. Quietly angling himself around the tree, he shot the boy who looked the oldest.

The remaining two boys scattered, and Connor slid back behind the tree.

"Parker, can we please go now?" the younger boy asked, sounding close to tears.

The boy didn't reply, but Connor heard them scurry away. He wondered where they planned to go and what their fate would be. Thankful that it was no longer in his hands, he slunk from the tree and continued his jog to the east. When the rest of the Progression showed up, he planned to lead them away from the camp and keep them guessing about the size of the Army forces.

About a half a mile into his jog, he came to a single lane dirt road that ran northwest to southeast. He followed the road to the north, shuffling his feet as he ran so his tracks wouldn't be as pronounced. When he came to an area with dense trees and short grass, he leaped from the road, and quickly covered his exit point with leaves and loose branches. Then he broke into a hard run that zigzagged through the forest a few times before heading for the camp.

By the time Connor reached the safety of the tents, twilight colored the sky as a mottled grey backdrop. Liberty and Ashley stood at the edge of the camp with their arms crossed, watching the trees around them.

After whistling his clearance, he stepped out from the trees and greeted his girls. He spent a few moments assuring them that he was unharmed, and then Boom showed up. Connor followed Boom into the main tent, past the tables and back to the section that had been sectioned off for Boom's private use. They entered through the thin flap and went straight to the table in the middle of the area.

A giant aerial map of Washington lay across the table, the corners weighted down with large rocks. Little red X's colored the map, marking off the areas where the Army had encountered Progression soldiers.

Connor wasted no time, and broke into a full recounting of his experience with the Progression soldiers. Boom studied the map as he listened, asking questions about the terrain and the boys. Then he took up his pen and hovered over an area by the river, preparing to draw another X.

"This is where you and Liberty were?" Boom asked.

Connor eyed the area and shook his head. "A little further to the south. She ran quite a ways. About here." He pointed at the map.

"Hmm." Boom drew the mark, and then scratched at his beard. "You weren't far from this bridge, where 530 crosses the Skagit River. I wonder if that's where they are."

Connor shifted to get a better view, and then studied the area, willing it to reveal its secrets.

"The bridge is too exposed, but this area right here—," he pointed to tree covered location right in front of the bridge, "this is the type of cover they'd want. They could ambush anyone who tries to cross the river. If I was running their camp, I'd plant snipers here, here, and here. They could take out anybody who even looked at that bridge without breaking a sweat."

"We could go north a few miles and take this smaller bridge." Boom observed. "But chances are they have that one covered as well."

Connor nodded. "I could take a team, and we could build our own bridge."

"That would take too long. Too much exposure. After today, Progression soldiers will probably start combing the riverbanks, searching for the two sets of footprints responsible for the deaths of their soldiers. I think the best chance we have is to send out scouts to find a shallow area to cross."

"You're right," Connor conceded.

"There hasn't been much rain lately." Boom crossed himself. "I'll send Stein and Soseki to begin the search first thing tomorrow."

They worked out the rest of the details, and then Boom left. Connor stayed behind to pour over the map and wonder how to safely get their people over the Skagit River.

CHAPTER FIFTEEN

Liberty

HEART POUNDING, I ran through the dark. Leaves and branches crunched under my feet, threatening to trip me, but fear kept me moving forward as fast as my legs could carry me. I lunged between two trees and right into a sticky spider web. It clung to my face and hair, and I slowed my steps to pull at it. As I did, a small hand reached up from the ground and brushed against my leg. The contact evoked images of the girl attached to the hand. She was hidden, young and afraid, calling out for help. She stood beside several others who reached out just as she did.

I reached down and touched her hand. It felt small and delicate in my own, and I gave it a brief squeeze to reassure her that I was there and trying to help. In the darkness, my fingers slid down her palm to her wrist and wrapped around it. I tugged on her arm, but she did not budge. Bracing myself, I tried again.

My tugging hurt her. Her cries of pain and desperation echoed in my head, forcing me to my knees. I dug at the hard, dry ground around her arm, trying to shovel her out with my hands.

"Don't give up, I'll get to you," I whispered, unsure of whether or not she could hear me.

Fear returned. It drifted over the ground like a fog, coming closer. I could see my own terror, but I couldn't leave the girl behind. Dark, sinister laughter accompanied the fear. It crept into my bones and made my blood freeze as it neared, growing louder and more ominous by the second. *My feet wanted to flee, but my heart knew I had to help the girl at my feet.* Choosing to follow my heart instead of my feet, I leaned over, wrapped both my hands around the small arm and pulled once more. Still, the ground resisted. I planted my feet and tugged harder. Dirt swelled around the arm. Small cracks spread outward, giving me the first sign of hope that I could pull her through.

"There she is!" someone shouted.

They'd caught me! Hundreds of Progression soldiers surrounded me, their guns aimed right at me.

"I'm not leaving you," I told the girl at my feet.

Shots rang out.

* * *

When I awoke, I was on my back. The roof above me started to close in.

Dirt! They shot me and buried me, but I'm not dead!

"No!" I reached up to claw my way out, expecting dirt, and felt the vinyl of the tent.

Right. I'm in the camp.

I took a deep breath and glanced at my watch. It was only two o'clock in the morning, so I closed my eyes, determined to get more sleep. But, tiny hands and shallow graves waited for me behind my eyelids, so I gave in and sat up.

Connor wasn't in our tent; he was probably on patrol or sleeping in his own tent. My outburst hadn't woken up Ashley. She snored lightly beside me. I envied her peaceful dreams and didn't want disrupt her sleep. Careful not to wake the girl, I slid out of my sleeping bag, exchanged my pajamas for fatigues, and slipped out of the tent. My thoughts became dark, terrifying monsters that I didn't want to be alone with, so I made my way to the main tent in hopes of finding a fellow insomniac.

To my surprise, Braden was awake and sitting in the same seat he'd occupied earlier. His head rested atop his arm, which stretched across the table. As if on autopilot, he flipped a single card over and over in his other hand. I watched him for a while, wondering if I should disturb him or leave him to whatever he was doing.

Before I'd decided what to do, Braden spoke. "Shouldn't you be in bed?"

"Funny, I was going to ask you the same thing. You been here all night?"

He gave me a lopsided shrug. "Nah. Just got here. Tried to sleep, but I couldn't."

I walked over and sat next to him. "Me neither. Your sister in bed?"

He nodded.

I picked up a card from the stack and flipped it over. Eight of hearts. Tilting it on its corner, I held the tip and flicked the card. It spun, becoming a red and blue blur.

Liberty Collins, master of mundane card tricks.

Braden sat up and copied my actions with his own card, making me feel like a very cool trend setter. Without speaking, we flicked cards until my fingers started to get sore. Then my curiosity got the best of me.

"So, tell me about yourself," I said.

Braden shrugged. "Not much to tell."

I leaned closer to him, wondering what I could say to get him to open up to me.

Maybe if I give a little, he will too.

"Okay, fine, I'll go first. I grew up with two sisters and my mom. Didn't have a dad around. What about you?"

"Just Mom, my sister, and me. Kylee and I got different dads. Hers used to come around every once in a while, but I never met mine." He flicked his card again. "Mom didn't say much about him. Just that he was worthless. Did you ever meet your dad?"

"Nope," I replied, wincing. The old wound still hurt. "I always wanted to, but it wasn't possible. All I had was a picture."

I could feel Braden studying me, but I didn't want to say more. To avoid further discussion, I gathered up the cards and started shuffling them. Then, I dealt us each two cards.

"Black Jack?" I asked.

"That's the game where we try to get twenty-one points, right?"

I nodded. "As close as you can without busting. If you go over, you lose."

"Okay, I'm in."

We each picked up our cards and studied them. I had a four of spades and an eight of clubs for a whopping twelve points. Definitely not a great start. I asked Braden if he wanted a hit, but the confused look on his face told me he wasn't down with Black Jack lingo.

"When you want another card, you say 'hit me,'" I explained.

"Ahh. Yeah, hit me."

I tossed him another card and took one for myself.

Queen of diamonds. Figures.

"I busted," I said, laying down my cards. "Twenty-two. What do you got?"

Braden set his cards down for me to see. He had an ace of spades, a jack of diamonds, and a four of hearts.

"Brae, you know an ace can either be one point or eleven points, right?"

He froze. His eyes widened for a second before he shrugged. "Yeah, duh. Everyone knows that."

"Cool. I figured you did, but just wanted to make sure."

He won the next two rounds, and then I won the fourth and fifth.

"I don't want to play anymore," Braden announced, tossing his busted hand on the table.

"Alright, do you want to play a different game?" I asked.

Braden tapped his cards a few times, and then turned his attention to me. "What happened to your dad?" he asked.

Frowning, I considered his question. I had no desire to air my family's laundry, but I wanted the kid to trust me, so I needed to be honest with him. I leaned back in my chair, making myself comfortable, and decided it couldn't hurt to tell him the story.

"My momma got married twice. Her first husband was a cheating jerk who left her for another woman. She was strong, though, and had a decent job. But still, she struggled to make ends meet, being a single parent raising my two sisters. Her boss was a nice guy who wanted to help. He offered her a promotion with a fat pay increase if she attended some sort of training seminar in Portland, Oregon. It just so happened that the training was held during the Rose Festival."

Knowing I couldn't do the story justice, my mind drifted back to the way Momma told it. Her eyes would always take on a dreamy cast, and she would pause and smile often, reminiscing about the good ole' days.

"The Navy ships were docked for the festival," I said, remembering the way Momma would lace her fingers and stare off into space. I glanced down and realized I'd unconsciously laced my fingers as well. Smiling to myself, I recalled the way she'd start. *'The grey sky dripped, and downtown Portland looked like an ocean of umbrellas and white hats.'*

She'd explain how a few of the sailors tried to catch her eye, but she didn't give any of them a second look. 'I wasn't lookin' for nuthin' but a pay raise so I could take care of your sisters. Last thing I needed was another man to come along and muck up my life even more. I was strong and determined to be alone. That is, until I met your daddy.'

Her eyes would light up and her cheeks would color. 'I was in line at a coffee wagon when he appeared. He tried to strike up a conversation with me, but I wasn't interested. I told him there were plenty of Portland women eager to hear his lies, but I wasn't one of them. He kept asking me questions, though. And he was a good listener. He insisted on buying my drink and we talked for far too long. I should have thanked him and walked away, but he was tenacious. That man!' she would exclaim. *'When your daddy looked at me ... he saw me. Nobody else in the world mattered.'*

"So he was in the Navy?" Braden asked, reminding me that I was supposed to be talking to him rather than replaying the conversation in my head.

"Yeah. He was in town on ... on free time. My dad was just a smooth-talking soldier who knew all the right things to say to make my mom lose her mind. That night he asked her to marry him, and she agreed."

"Wow," Braden said. "That's fast."

"Not just fast, it was insane. Might as well call it what it is."

I never understood how my level-headed, hardworking momma had been wild and crazy enough to marry a man she'd only known for a day. A man who would be shipping out a couple of days after they married. The first time I heard my parents' story I vowed to stay far away from soldiers, knowing they would marry me, knock me up, then abandon me and our child to run off and die in the service.

But now there's Connor, a little voice in the back of my head whispered. I shook it off and tried not to think about my own smooth-talking soldier. No, even worse than a soldier, he was some sort of Special Forces maniac.

Braden chuckled. "So it didn't work out?"

I wondered what the kid read in my expression. Feeling confused and flustered, I shook my head.

"The weird thing is that it worked out just fine. The next day they got a marriage license, and talked the deputy clerk into waiving the three-day waiting period. Then my dad's chaplain married them. They spent two days together, and then dad shipped out."

No matter how many times I told the story, it still made me feel hollow. I had been robbed of the father I'd so desperately wanted, and had spent my entire childhood recreating him based upon Momma's limited description. He stood tall and proud, with a handsome face and a muscular build. He laughed easily and had dreams of a big family. But the thing about him that I'd grown the most familiar with, was his absence. It left a gigantic hole in my heart that would never be filled.

Braden opened his mouth to say something, but I held up a finger to silence him before he could ask.

"He never came back. There was some sort of mechanical explosion when he was working on the ship. They said he died instantly."

Braden frowned. "I'm sorry."

I tried to smile, but I couldn't muster up the pretense.

"That really sucks," he said. "Sounds like he would have made a good dad."

I shrugged. "Who knows? I used to wonder what it would have been like, had my dad made it home. He could have taken me to father-daughter dances and threatened my dates with a rifle and all that great daddy stuff that my friend Michelle complained about."

Braden watched me, and I knew I needed to say more.

"I was angry for a long time. It's hard to move on with your life when all you can seem to focus on is what you don't have. You know?"

Braden nodded.

I let silence linger between us for a few moments, wondering if he'd open up and share a little of his story. He remained silent, so I continued. "I had to learn that I'm responsible for my own happiness. Out of pain and anger, I did a lot of stupid stuff, and I had to learn to forgive myself just like I forgave my dad. I realized I have a destiny—a purpose to fulfill—and I can't accomplish it while I'm dragging me feet through the past."

"What destiny?" he asked. "What's your purpose?"

"That's a very good question, but I'm not prepared to answer it at—," I glanced at my watch, "three thirty-six in the morning with no coffee in my system. Besides, I know *my* purpose. I'm curious as to what you think *your* purpose is."

He shrugged and looked away. After a time he frowned at me and asked, "Are you sure I have one?"

"Of course you do. Every one of us has a purpose. The soldiers, Boom, Ashley, Kylee, me and even you. You have a destiny, Braden."

"Liberty? Braden?" Boom stepped into the tent. "I thought I heard your voices. What are you two doing awake at this hour?"

I waved to Boom. "We couldn't sleep so we're having long, meaningful conversations about our pasts and our destinies."

Boom chuckled. "Well, amidst your nightly musings, you haven't run across Connor, have you? I left him in the back wing of this tent late last night, and no one has seen him since."

Braden and I both turned toward the back of the tent. My heart pounded in my chest as I watched the flap, imagining Connor leaning against it, eavesdropping on our conversation.

No. That's ridiculous. Why would he do that? Please don't be in there, Con.

The flap parted and Connor peeked out.

"Hey Boom, you looking for me?"

My jaw dropped. I felt it practically unhinge from the rest of my face, but I didn't care. I couldn't believe he'd been listening in on my private conversation with Braden. "You were in there? The whole time?"

"Not sure what you mean by the whole time." Connor stretched, trying to look nonchalant and relaxed, but I didn't buy his act. "I was asleep for a while. Passed out in the chair. Woke up to some chatter, and then heard Boom asking for me."

I stepped closer as my face warmed. "Some chatter? How much *chatter* did you hear?" I used my fingers to gesture quotation marks at the word "chatter."

"Uh ..." He shook his head like he was confused. "What do you mean, exactly?"

Hurt and disappointed, yet too exhausted to strangle him, I sighed. "Never mind. I have to go check on Ashley. I'll catch up with you later, Braden. Thanks for the talk." I patted Braden on the shoulder and turned to leave.

"Lib, wait," Connor called out.

I ignored him and fled from the tent.

CHAPTER SIXTEEN

Liberty

HUMILIATED BY CONNOR once again, I escaped from the main tent and sought the comfort found in Ashley's soft snore. It filled the tent with a sense of normalcy as I slid back into my sleeping bag and closed my eyes, trying to forget the whole experience in the main tent.

This is exactly why I don't do mornings. Nothing good comes of getting up while it's still dark.

Deep down, I knew my anger at Connor's presence in the main tent was a bit extreme. After all, it wasn't like I'd checked whether or not the tent was empty before I decided to spill my life story to Braden. And, if I'd paused long enough to give him the benefit of the doubt—which I'd promised to do—I had to believe he told the truth and had actually been asleep in there. So when he'd heard us, what did I expect him to do? Jump out and reveal himself and beg us not to say more? Would I have honestly been less pissed off?

But eavesdropping on me? Really, Connor?

I beat the back of my head on the ground a few times.

What if he's figured it out? Ugh. So embarrassing! I'm gonna have to kill him. Or at least maim him.

My eyelids drifted shut, and I realized that I was too tired to be enraged about the situation. Vowing to be more ticked off as soon as I had the energy, I relaxed against my pillow and let myself drift off to sleep.

* * *

The wooden door was back, looming before me. Beckoning to me. I drifted toward it while the broken stone path beneath my feet disappeared into mist. As I neared, the handle-less old door swung open.

As before, the stench of rot smacked into me. It assaulted my nose, making me want to turn away, but I couldn't. Past the door jamb, the floor glistened. Remembering that I'd slipped on it before, this time I proceeded with caution, holding the door as I slowly slid my feet across the floor. The instant I crossed over the threshold, the door slammed shut. I reached for it, but everything disappeared, and then suddenly, I stood in the middle of a grassy meadow. Taking a deep breath through my nose, I could smell grass and pine, but beneath it all, the stench of rot lingered. Wondering if the stink came from me, I sniffed my clothes. Nope, not me.

I sniffed the air again and smelled something I'd avoided for years. Dreading what I knew I'd find, I looked down. At my feet, a giant wine-colored rose bloomed. Beautiful and sorrowful, it released a perfume so fragrant it enveloped me and drew me to it. Squatting beside the flower, I reached out and touched its petals. The meadow shifted, and I found myself standing beside my mother on a beach. We stood barefoot, and the wet sand felt cool on my feet. The sky was overcast, and seagulls dove in and out of the small waves, hunting.

"Libby," Momma said.

Startled by the sudden sound, I looked up. "Yes, Momma?"

"It's time to say goodbye."

I could feel her sorrow, but couldn't understand it. She separated one red rose from the dozen in the crook of her arm. When the tide rushed in, devouring the sand and dampening our feet, she released the rose. The tide held the flower like a mother cradling a new baby. It swayed back and forth, and then carried the rose out to sea.

"Your father's out there somewhere. Tell him goodbye." She handed me a rose.

I stared at the flower, wondering how it could get a message to the man I'd never met. And why did goodbye have to be the message? There were so many other things I wanted to tell him.

Playing with the soft petals, my mind went blank. No. My dad was a stranger. I had nothing to say to him. In one swift motion, I plucked the petals from the stem and released them into the wind. They swirled around me, becoming a whirlpool of loss and sorrow.

The ocean and my mother faded away, and I found myself back in the meadow, now surrounded by hundreds of wine-colored roses. I hated the flowers. Not for what they were, but for what they signified: death. Their sweet fragrance overwhelmed me until I felt like I couldn't breathe through it. Gagging on the scent, I doubled over, heaving.

Juvenile laughter filled the meadow, accompanied by a thick blanket of fog that covered the wretched roses and neutralized their stench. Able to breathe once again, I stood and wondered why the fog had come so suddenly. Something tugged on my shirt, demanding my attention. I looked down, and a little blonde girl smiled up at me with dimples so deep she could store loose change in them.

I smiled back at her. "Hi there. What's your name?"

"I can't tell that to strangers." She put her hand on her hip and studied me, as if trying to decide if I qualified as strange or not.

"That is very wise." I crouched down to get eye level with her. "What can we talk about, then?"

"I'm going to be an astronaut when I grow up. What will you be?"

I scrunched up my brow and tried to remember my childhood career choice. "Um ... a firewoman."

She giggled. "I used to want to be a firewoman, but now that I'm older I want to walk on the moon." She held out her arms and started spinning in circles.

The landscape shifted, taking me to a forest setting. The sky grew dark and eerie, and the beautiful little girl I'd just seen lay at my feet. Her cheeks barely dented by ghosts of her dimples as her eyes stared vacantly at the sky.

"No!"

I bent down and shook her shoulders, but she didn't respond. I felt for a pulse, but her heart didn't beat.

"No, no, no."

I backed up. Another child lay to her right; a boy with messy red hair and chubby cheeks crowded with freckles. I checked his pulse. Dead. Beside him lay a caramel-skinned boy with curly, dark hair. Dead. Then a pale brunette. Also dead. I spun around and saw them everywhere. All dead. Despair burned my eyes as I counted the bodies. Eighty-three dead children. My heart broke for each sweet, innocent face.

Major Thompson's creepy laughter echoed throughout the valley.

* * *

The nightmare released me. I stared at the ceiling of the tent, shaking. So much death. They were all gone.

'Not yet.'

The "call" caught me off guard as it whispered into my heart and my spirit. I wanted more, so I listened, waiting for Him to speak again.

'Not yet,' He repeated. This time with His words came understanding. It swept away every web of doubt that netted my heart and filled me with anticipation for the future.

The kids aren't dead yet. There's still hope.

Peace and joy refreshed my weary spirit, and I leapt from my sleeping bag.

Somewhere out there is a little blonde girl with huge dimples, and there's still time to save her!

If I had any singing talent whatsoever, I would have sung at that moment. I wanted to share my joy with someone, but Ashley's sleeping bag lay empty. I unzipped the tent flap and peered out into the day. The sky was laden with heavy, ominous clouds, and soldiers took down the main tent. Curious, I slipped out of the tent to snoop.

Jeff was the first person I came across who I was reasonably certain wouldn't shoot me if I bothered him. I found him stuffing medical supplies into a box beside Osberg's tent. I waved and wished him a good morning.

"Hey there," Jeff replied with a nod and a brief smile.

"What's going on here?" I asked. "You really didn't want that promotion, huh? Now you're so desperate to get demoted that you're stealing medical equipment? I see how it is."

"Heh. I haven't gotten that desperate yet, but thanks for the idea. Haven't you heard? We're striking camp."

"Striking?" I asked. "I'll draw up the picket signs. What are you guys going for? Trying to get a raise, shorter hours or better medical benefits?"

"Wow, you're in rare form today," Jeff said. "What has you in such a good mood?"

Too excited to keep my news to myself, I leaned closer to Jeff and said, "There's still time!"

Jeff's forehead scrunched up. "Uh, for what?"

I laughed, feeling giddy and a little unbalanced. "We haven't lost yet. There is still time, and there is still hope."

As he lifted the box he'd just filled, I trapped his arms in a sideways hug and squeezed. Jeff almost dropped the box, and I laughed again. He tried to scowl at me, but I could tell he wasn't too upset by the way his frown kept waggling.

Pointing to the boxes at his feet, I asked, "Where are we going?"

"Scouts found a shallow place to cross the river, but Boom wants us on the other side of it before the rain hits." He looked up at the darkening sky.

I followed his gaze. "Yikes. Looks pretty ominous. Suppose we better hurry then."

"Once I'm done here, want me to help help you tear down your tent?" Jeff offered.

"No need," Connor said, appearing from the mists, or whatever the heck Special Forces soldiers traveled silently through so they could scare the crud out of people.

I jumped, and my heart went through my chest. Seemingly oblivious to my surprise, he sidled up to me and rested a hand on my arm. I pulled away since I needed some time to get over my bad attitude toward him.

Connor didn't react to my frosty reaction. Instead, he turned toward Jeff and explained, "I already took it down."

"Why?" I crossed my arms. "I can take down my own tent. Don't you have bigger duties to tend to? Someone to spy on, maybe?"

"Ashley asked me to show her how." He shrugged, looking all nonchalant and unbothered. "So I did."

I really wanted to argue with his logic, but couldn't. What sort of person would complain about a man teaching his kid how to strike a tent?

You may have won this time, bucko, but do not get used to it.

Since I couldn't say anything aloud, I settled for glaring at him, willing him to go away. When he didn't leave, I sighed and asked, "Is there something you need?"

"Yes, actually. We're going to have to transport Noke and Osberg. Magee is asking for your help."

Then I remembered that I was supposed to go to Magee for training. "Oops," I said.

"Everything okay?" Jeff asked.

"Yeah. Just remembering something I forgot to do."

"Anything I can help with?" Jeff asked.

"No, but thanks. I'll catch you later, Jeff."

He turned and went back to his packing while I took off toward Magee's tent.

"You're going the wrong way," Connor said from behind me. "He's by Noke's, preparing a gurney."

Without replying, I turned my steps. Connor lengthened his strides and caught up with me. Then he passed me and stopped directly in my path. I paused, and then tried to go around him, but he grabbed my arm.

"Would you please just listen to me?" he asked.

I stopped walking and crossed my arms.

"I'm sorry," he said.

"Really?" I asked. "Then why did you listen in on my private conversation?"

"I don't know." Connor shrugged. "I honestly didn't mean to, but I couldn't see a way out of it. And, I was curious."

"Curious? Connor, that information was secret. I didn't even want to tell the kid, but I felt like I had to for some reason. And you listened in because you were *curious*?" My cheeks warmed.

Connor's hands flung up in surrender. "Yes. Are you kidding me? Of course I'm curious enough to listen. You throw me the occasional bread crumb about yourself and expect me to be satisfied. I'm not. I'm trying to open up to you, and yet you give me nothing in return."

Knowing he had a point, I looked away. "Now that everything is crazy, my past seems like the only thing I have left to hold on to, sometimes. It keeps me who I am, and I'm scared that if I tell you about it, you'll have some sort of power over me. I know it's stupid, but I just … it's really difficult to open up about it."

He stepped closer and put his hands on my shoulders, pulling my attention back onto him. "I'm not going to hurt you. Ever. I just want to know everything about you." His dark eyes intensified and focused on me. He raked a hand through his hair and looked away.

The nearest soldiers stopped what they were doing and started watching us. Connor glared at them, and they went back to their tasks.

He frowned at me. "I get so frustrated that you won't tell me anything, and then there you are, opening up to this kid."

"Braden. His name is Braden. And I didn't want to tell him my embarrassing life story." My cheeks heated at the thought of what Connor now knew. "But he was upset and alone and I wanted him to know he has a friend. I don't tell you stuff about me, because … because … I'm just not ready yet, okay?"

"Libby, please." He reached for me, but I took a step back.

"I understand what happened and I'm not upset with you. I just … I need to be alone for a while. Thank you for the escort, but I can find Magee on my own."

Then I turned and fled like the chicken I was.

CHAPTER SEVENTEEN

Connor

CONNOR STARED AFTER Liberty, feeling frustrated and confused. His past had taught him that most women wanted to be pursued. Yet the one woman he wanted to chase just wanted to be left alone. It felt like some sick, demented joke that the universe insisted on playing with him.

He turned with a growl, and almost plowed into Jeff.

Jeff leaped back and held his hands up in defense. Jeff wore a smug smirk that made Connor wonder how much Jeff had overheard.

"Whoa, there. Don't kill the messenger." Jeff watched him for a moment too long before adding a belated, "First Sergeant."

Connor schooled his expression into neutrality. "And what message do you have for me, Corporal Thompson?"

"The captain is looking for you. He's with the horses."

Connor's hands itched to throttle Jeff, but he held them steady at his sides and managed to force out a thank you before leaving the man to fester in his smugness.

Once Connor found Boom, the two of them walked the camp, hurrying along the progress of the soldiers, securing loads and worrying about the ever-darkening clouds. Within the hour, Noke and Osberg were strapped into their gurneys and the camp was ready to move. Connor saddled the sorrel mare for Liberty and Ashley to share, but Liberty helped Ashley up and refused to climb up behind her. Instead, she hoisted Kylee onto the horse behind Ashley.

"What do you think you're doing?" Connor asked, pulling her aside.

"I can't ride the horse. I promised Magee I'd help carry Osberg."

"We have soldiers for that."

"Connor, I can't shoot. It's not fair for me to make one of the soldiers carry Osberg's gurney so I can sit on my butt and do nothing."

"You won't be sitting on your butt and doing nothing. You'll be keeping Ashley safe."

Liberty nodded. "Yep. I'll be keeping her safe by being on that gurney so we have one more gun ready to defend the platoon."

"Libby, we are heading back to Fort Lewis. Most of our soldiers are still untrained, and the Progression is probably watching our every move now. There's no telling what we'll come across. This situation has the potential to get very deadly, very fast."

"I'm waiting for the part where you explain how that's different from every other day of the past several months."

Connor could tell he wasn't getting anywhere, so he switched tactics. "I can't believe you put Kylee on the horse behind Ash."

"Why not? She's a young girl too. She'll keep Ash company."

He rubbed the back of his neck. "Dang it, Libby, we don't know anything about her and Braden. They could be dangerous. What if she takes off with Ash?"

"And leave her brother behind? Do you really think she'd do that?" Liberty raised an eyebrow in question.

"If they're with the Progression, it's hard telling what they will do."

Liberty looked past him to where the girls sat atop the horse. "Are you really gonna make me walk over there and rip Kylee off the horse?" she asked.

Connor turned and watched the girls. They talked and giggled about something. Braden tagged along behind Jeff, heading toward Noke's gurney. He sighed and shook his head. "We'll just have to keep an eye on them."

Liberty leaned against Connor's shoulder and said, "Thank you."

He nodded, uncertain of the wisdom of his choice. "I'm sorry. You're right and I shouldn't have listened in at the tent."

"I'm sorry too. I know you were in a tight spot. It's not a big deal. Just a little ... embarrassing."

Connor's brows arched. "Embarrassing?"

Color shot into Liberty's cheeks. "Yeah. We'll talk about it later."

"Right. I'd better go saddle my horse and catch up to Boom. Be careful. If anything happens, stay with Ash."

"I will. You be careful too."

Connor leaned forward and kissed her forehead, smiling against it. "I'm always careful," he whispered.

* * *

Once the platoon started moving, Connor looked back at the camp site. Nothing but graves remained, and he was more than happy to leave those behind. Turning to face forward, he clucked to his horse and drifted to the left side of the platoon—opposite of Boom. Once there, he patrolled up and down the line, keeping an eye on the equipment as well as the soldiers.

The platoon slowly traveled southwest, over the rough forest terrain, coming to an abrupt stop on the river bank. Boom dismounted and started walking toward the weathered John Deere barge wagon that carried the camp's gear, motioning for Connor to follow him. Connor hopped down from his horse and walked behind his friend. They halted toward the front of the wagon, where Pearson patted the neck of one of the two horses hitched to the wagon.

"What's the problem?" Boom asked.

The cowboy stepped around the horse and pointed at the bottom of the wagon. "The wheels. The river bed is too soft. They'll never make it across carrying all the gear."

"You sure?" Boom asked.

Pearson stared at the river. "Yep. Unless there's concrete under that water. The wagon's struggling with the dirt. These girls are having a heck of a time."

Pearson patted the horse's hindquarters, and Connor realized how badly the horses struggled to pull the wagon. He eyed the narrow wheels and nodded in agreement.

Turning toward Boom, Connor asked, "Unload and walk it across?"

Boom glanced at the sky, and then crossed himself. "That appears to be our only option."

Connor kneaded his temples. They could try to drag the loaded wagon across, but if it got stuck and flipped over they could lose all of their supplies. The risk was too great. He tried to come up with a better plan—one that wouldn't leave them exposed in the river for a half hour at best—but nothing came to him.

Resigned to unloading the wagon, Connor said, "On your order, Captain."

Boom started shouting orders. He sent six soldiers to secure the opposite bank and surrounding area. Then he positioned two more soldiers, to watch up and down the river. He ordered the rest to start unloading the wagon.

Connor sought out Ashley, and found her still on the horse, with Kylee. Kylee gave him a big, fake smile, and then tugged on Ashley's shirt until the girl waved at Connor. He nodded back and turned to search for Liberty, finding her with her team as they gently lowered Osberg's gurney to the ground. As the soldiers ran off toward the wagon, Liberty sat beside the gurney and drank deeply from her canteen, calling for Ashley and Kylee to come to her.

Thankful that Liberty kept an eye on the girls, Connor turned his attention back to the wagon and the troops. Once the supplies were safely on the opposite bank and behind the relative safety of the tree line, two soldiers—lead by Pearson—started walking the horses, hitched to the wagon, across. Pearson still wore his cowboy boots, and as he slipped across the slick river stones, Connor wondered if the man regretted that decision now. Although he wobbled a few times, Pearson still managed to stay on his feet. The wagon advanced at a slow and steady pace until about a third of the way through the river, when it suddenly stopped.

Pearson backed the wheels up, then tugged at the reins. The horses lurched forward, and then stopped again. He shook his head and backed the horses up. Several soldiers ran out into the water to help. They pushed on the back of the trailer. It gained momentum and then slammed into a stop once again, the trailer shaking. Connor feared the whole thing would fall apart if they did that again. Boom must have shared his fears, because he shouted out an order and Shortridge ducked under the water to figure out the problem. Seconds ticked by as he stayed under, and the entire platoon went deathly still, watching the river. Then suddenly, Shortridge resurfaced and announced that a giant rock—too large and heavy to move—was lodged in front of the two front wheels. Pearson backed the wagon up and took it at a different angle to miss the rock.

The whole ordeal took entirely too long. Connor couldn't shake the feeling of being watched. He searched for the girls, and found Ashley talking to Liberty. Kylee stared at him. He leveled a stare back at her and she looked away. Connor shook off his annoyance with the girl and headed toward. Before he reached his friend, gunfire erupted. Connor's horse reared. He rode to the commotion, and then slid from the back of the horse and scanned the riverbank while tying the reins around a tree branch.

Boom shouted orders, but knowing his job, Connor turned his attention to the trees. More shots rang out, and Connor followed the sound. About two hundred yards down on the east bank, he saw muzzle flashes, so he crouched behind a fallen tree and steadied his rifle. He saw movement through his scope, so he took a breath to steady his aim and squeezed the trigger. One soldier went down. Connor peered through the scope and fired again. Another figure crumpled. Stein joined Connor at the tree, and the two gunned down two more attackers. The rest of the enemy soldiers retreated back into the trees, disappearing from view.

Boom motioned for Connor to cross. Connor fell in line beside Ashley and Liberty, watching the tree line and hoping they made it.

The hooves of Connor's horse had just barely reached the opposite bank when the next series of shots rang out.

CHAPTER EIGHTEEN

Liberty

WE TRAIPSED THROUGH the forest carrying Osberg's gurney. It was a good thing they had him strapped down, because his body shifted restlessly despite the sedatives Magee had loaded him up with.

The silent tension of the platoon was as dark and ominous as the clouds that loomed above our heads. The forest lay still and quiet, surreal also in the fact that I couldn't smell its scents over the antiseptic aroma radiating from Osberg.

Osberg's body tensed and relaxed. Worried about the man, I started praying.

At first I prayed against infection, against pain and suffering, and for full healing of his wounded shoulder. I dismissed the limitations of the natural and prayed for the supernatural, asking for a miracle so big that Osberg wouldn't have to step foot in a doctor's office, let alone an operating room. The fact that Osberg was an atheist just made me pray harder. More than anything, I asked for God to show up in this soldier's life and make His presence and His power known. I prayed against all disbelief. As soon as I was done praying for Osberg, I started in on prayers for Noke.

With my mind occupied, the time started flying by. Before I knew it, we were at the river, setting Osberg's gurney down. The soldiers rushed off to help Boom with something, and I relaxed next to the patient and guzzled water, waving Ashley and Kylee over to me.

I patted the mare's nose and reassured her that she was a good girl. "How's she doing?" I asked Ashley.

"Good. But I wish I knew what to call her. 'Girl' is getting a little old."

I nodded. "She needs a name. You ladies should give her one."

Ashley and Kylee conversed about the matter for a moment. I watched them, thankful for the friendship that was developing between the two.

Glancing around, I asked, "Where's Braden?"

Kylee pointed to the soldiers unloading the wagon. Sure enough, Braden was right in the thick of them. He jumped up onto the wagon and started handing boxes down to the soldiers. I smiled, thankful that the boy seemed to be fitting in just fine.

"Cinnamon," Ashley declared.

"Hmm?"

"The horse. She's the color of cinnamon," Kylee added. "Don't ya think?"

Her coat resembled more sugar than cinnamon, but since the horse didn't object, I didn't either. "Yep. Cinnamon it is."

The girls each patted Cinnamon and muttered her name a few times, as if trying to commit it to memory.

Our impromptu naming ceremony was interrupted by a series of gunshots. I reached for Cinnamon's reins, expecting the mare to panic, but she just watched me while her tail swished back and forth.

I leaned against her neck and promised, "I don't even care where I get it, but I will give you an apple after this is over, Cinnamon."

Tugging on her reins, I jogged her to the cover of the trees, where I gave Ashley strict instructions to stay hidden and watch for Progression soldiers. With her as safe as I could keep her for the time being, I ran back to see how I could help our soldiers.

More shots echoed throughout the valley.

A black gelding, with stuffed saddle bags, reared and wrenched its lead rope from a soldier. Knowing how badly we needed those supplies, I lunged for the gelding's rope. The horse was too fast and too strong. Rough fibers bit into the flesh of my hands, and then the rope slid through my grasp. Empty handed, I fell forward and landed face down in the dirt.

The whole ordeal took maybe ten seconds. I didn't have time to dwell on it though, because another horse's hooves thundered straight at my head. They came down inches from my face as I rolled to the side and pushed myself up.

That was too close.

I let out a breath, immensely thankful for the opportunity to do so. Deciding to play it safe and get out of the way, I sat beside Osberg and assured him that everything would be alright. I don't know how reassured he felt, though, since he was still out cold. A quick glance at the trees showed me that Ashley and Kylee were still sitting atop Cinnamon, safe and sound. Next I scanned the area for Braden, finding him huddled beside Jeff. Jeff stood protectively in front of the kid while he tugged at the reins of a rearing brown horse.

When we get out of this, Jeff gets an apple, too.

Connor crouched behind a fallen tree, his rifle spewing out shells. Soldiers pushed the wagon and horses across the river toward the opposite bank. Feeling helpless, I continued to huddle close to Osberg, praying that it would end.

Then, suddenly, it did. The gunfire stopped, leaving my ears ringing. The few remaining horses calmed. Boom's voice shouted orders that I couldn't quite make out in a tone that screamed of urgency. Whatever we were doing, we needed to do it fast. After motioning for Ashley and Kylee to rejoin us, I stood and took my place at the foot of Osberg's gurney.

Ashley's eyes were round and her hands shook when she reined Cinnamon to a stop beside me.

"Wow," Ashley exclaimed. "That was … wow! Did you see those other horses? They freaked, but Cinnamon was so calm."

I looked down at my rope-burned hands. The skin was raw in a few places, and blood oozed from the wounds. I opened the small med-pack stored on the gurney and grabbed a couple alcohol swabs and bandages.

"Saw them and tried to stop one." I handed Kylee the bandages and held up my hands toward her. "Will you please clean and cover these?"

The rest of Osberg's team arrived and got in place to heft the gurney.

Ashley opened her mouth, no doubt to launch into a series of questions.

Silencing her by holding up a finger, I asked Kylee, "Quickly?"

Kylee ripped open the packages and adhered the bandages to my wounds. I thanked her, and then turned to lift up my quarter. As soon as Osberg was in the air, Boom shouted and gestured at our team to move forward. We broke into a run and rushed by him. Then Connor appeared on the other side of Ashley's horse.

"You two okay?" he asked.

"Yep, Cinnamon didn't even spook," Ashley said.

I followed my team down the bank and into the water, wincing at the icy water as it rushed up my calves. Cinnamon plunged into the water beside us without so much as a flinch.

Forget the apple, that horse deserves her own orchard.

Ashley beamed a smile at me. "Cinnamon's the greatest!" she shouted.

"Yep. She's doing fine. Now hurry and get to those trees," I replied, pointing at the opposite bank.

Ashley clucked and gave the horse her rein. Cinnamon broke into a trot and they scampered to the other side. When they climbed up the bank, I looked past them and saw Jeff almost to the trees ahead of them. He was at the head of Noke's gurney, and Braden walked behind him at the foot.

Now that I knew they were safe, I had a chance to realize how unbelievably wide the river was, and how exposed we were while crossing it. I looked to Connor, but he was watching the trees on the bank we'd come from.

My sneakers kept slipping on the slick river stones. More than once, I jostled Osberg and the crew before I caught myself. The group slowed, and I started testing each step before committing to it.

The deepest part of the river came just above my knees, and although the current was swift, we were in no danger of being swept down river. The day was chilly, but the exertion of carrying Osberg kept me warm. The frigid water was quite the contrast, biting into my skin, clearly determined to freeze my calves and feet. By the time we reached the opposite bank, my teeth had chattered loudly. Nobody complained about the cold, and I had no intention on being the first, so I closed my mouth and concentrated on putting one frozen foot in front of the other.

We climbed up the bank and stumbled toward the tree line. Shots rang out again. Our team of tired bodies, instantly renewed by the gunshots, kicked it into high gear. We rushed for the safety of the trees, and then gently laid our burden down on the grass. Ashley and Kylee rode Cinnamon to the other side of the wagon. The soldiers pulled their guns from their backs and ran back toward the river, like the slightly insane heroes they were. Jeff sprinted by me, with Braden hot on his heels.

I let Jeff pass, but put out my arm to snag the boy. "Whoa. Where do you think you're going?"

"With him." Braden writhed and wiggled, trying to get free.

"Why?"

"They might need my help," he said.

"*They* have guns. You don't."

Magee arrived and started looking over Osberg. "How's he doing?"

"He stayed asleep the whole time."

"Good. That's what we want." He motioned toward Braden. "The boy is leaving."

I thanked him for the heads up and grabbed Braden by the arm. "*I* need help." I pointed at the wagon. All its supplies lay scattered in the dirt.

Braden turned pleading eyes on me.

"Come on, Brae, we need to get the wagon loaded before they get back. This'll be a huge help to them."

Braden wanted to argue with me. I could tell by the way his teeth clenched when he looked past me to the trees where Jeff had disappeared. Magee cleared his throat, and then gave the boy a hard stare.

I laid a hand on Braden's shoulder and directed his gaze back at me. "Please, Bray? I can't lift those boxes by myself."

He huffed and he puffed, but he finally turned and followed me to the wagon. Ashley and Kylee dismounted and helped us as well. It was hard, heavy work, but together we got the wagon loaded in no time. Feeling accomplished and worn out, Braden and I sat down and leaned against the wagon wheel. Before I'd even had the chance to catch my breath, the soldiers began returning. A few of them headed to finish loading the wagon, and looked equally surprised and thankful to see it already done.

"See?" I asked, nudging Braden. "We done good."

He smiled back at me.

A stoic, dark-skinned man that Connor had once introduced as Master Sergeant Staten barked out an order, and the soldiers' surprise melded into determination as they shouldered discarded packs and prepared to move. Jeff ran through the trees and made a beeline straight for us.

"Time to mount up, ladies," he said to Ashley and Kylee. "Come on, I'll help you."

He led them toward Cinnamon, with Braden in tow.

Master Sergeant Staten blew past me like a thunderstorm, barking additional orders as he ran. "Pearson, get those horses moving! Soseki, you've got lead. Get us out of here!"

The soldiers sprung into action like a colony of ants preparing for a storm. I hightailed it to Osberg's gurney, arriving as the rest of team was going to lift him without me. They lifted and I reached for my handle just as the group lurched forward. Struggling to keep up, I spared one last glance over my shoulder, looking for Ashley. I was relieved to see her perched atop Cinnamon with Kylee behind her. Jeff and Braden had resumed their positions on Noke's gurney. Gunfire still resounded behind us, and I couldn't find Connor or Boom. The team broke into a jog and I was forced to keep up, or fall on my face.

After we'd ran for a while, and I noticed Connor and Boom were still missing, I asked, "Where are the rest of the men?"

"Holding them off," replied one soldier. "They're giving us a chance to get a head start, then they'll catch up."

What?

The world seemed to stop moving. I briefly wondered if I should run back and try to help them, but even if I got to them in time, I knew I couldn't really help. Besides, I didn't want to abandon Osberg. As we jogged through the forest, I kept looking behind us, hoping to catch a glimpse of the men, but I only saw trees. My feet kept pace with the team, but my heart lagged behind, wondering if I'd ever see Connor again.

We ran until the sounds of battle faded into the distance, and then we ran some more. Just when I thought my legs were going to fall off, Staten shouted an order and we slowed to a brisk walk. Following the lead of my group, I stumbled forward for what seemed like an eternity, over uneven terrain and through vegetation that grew tall enough to brush my thighs. My river-soaked jeans and sneakers felt heavy, making the trek that much more difficult. The stitch in my side evolved into ravenous hunger pains, making me regret my decision to sleep through breakfast.

As if the walk wasn't difficult enough, the heavy rain clouds no longer held back the inevitable. Rain came through breaks in the trees, giant drops falling from the leaves and pelting my head before sliding down the back of my neck. When I couldn't take it anymore, I used my free hand to yank my hair free of the braid that constrained it, providing a little more warmth and protection.

Osberg seemed to fare much better. He looked nice and cozy under a mound of blankets covered by ponchos. Every once in a while, we would break long enough for Magee to check on the two patients. During those times, I'd stretch and drink deeply from my canteen. The breaks never lasted long enough to do much else, though.

Exhausted and drenched, the platoon continued until darkness hid the landscape. By sheer force of will I kept up with my team, despite my constant desire to release my hold on Osberg's gurney and topple over. By the time Staten ordered us to stop, I was beyond spent. The team lowered Osberg, and I had to convince my cramping fingers to release their hold on the gurney so I could stumble to the wagon to retrieve my tent.

I slogged through the mud, searching for a relatively flat surface upon which to pitch my tent. Then I pulled a flashlight out of my bag and got to work.

"What do you think you're doing? Turn that off!" someone snapped.

I turned and found Master Sergeant Staten glaring at me. Confused and surprised, I fumbled with the light until it slipped out of my hands and fell to the ground, still switched on. I reached for it, but Staten moved faster. He snatched it up and switched it off.

"Are you trying to get us all killed?" he asked.

"N-no. Sorry, Sir." I replied.

"Well, the first sergeant isn't here, so you're going to have to start thinking for yourself. Let's start now. Any idea why a flashlight, in the dark, while we're running from people who are shooting at us, might be a bad idea?"

I didn't know what to say, so I stayed silent.

"Let's try again. Do you see anyone else using a flashlight?"

I glanced around. Not only were the soldiers not using flashlights, but I could see their silhouettes. They'd stopped what they were doing to watch the spectacle we created. Heat crept up my spine. "Again, I'm sorry, Sir. I didn't mean to put the platoon in danger. Can I please put up my tent now?"

"Well, nobody else is going to do it for you."

"I understand that, Sir, and I'm perfectly capable. Been doing it since I was ten."

He tapped my flashlight against his palm. "I'll just hold onto this for you. You can have it when your boyfriend gets back."

The cold exhaustion that had plagued me all day, instantly melted away. Heat filled my veins as I clenched my fists and resisted the urge to tell the self-inflated bully exactly what I thought of him.

Jeff stepped out of the shadows, sidled up next to me, and put a calming hand on my arm. "You need help?" he asked.

Staten snorted and walked away.

I shook my head. "Nope. I got this, thanks."

I yanked a side of the tent down and dropped the stake I was holding between my knees.

Jeff reached for it, but I stopped him. "I got it. Thanks, Jeff."

"All right, but if you need help, you know where to find me." He didn't wait for my reply before he turned and stepped back into the shadows.

Redirecting my anger toward the tent, I started pulling straps and stomping on stakes, and had the small, camouflaged dome up in no time.

"Hey," Ashley called out as she approached. "I got Cinnamon unsaddled and Pearson let me brush her down."

"That was nice of him." I unzipped the tent flap.

"You okay?" Ashley asked.

Since she didn't need to be burdened with the fact that our substitute platoon leader socially belonged back in high school, I nodded and lied. "Just tired."

"You're worried about my dad, aren't you?" she asked.

I nodded again and squeezed her shoulders. "Yes, but I know he'll be fine. He was trained for Special Forces, do you know what that means?"

Ashley shook her head.

"It means he has a PhD in butt-kicking. Special Forces are teams of the Army's best, who go into very bad situations and fix them. He has skills that I can't even comprehend. He's like our own personal Rambo."

Ashley stared up at me, her dark eyes round and somber. "Who's Rambo?"

"What?! Are you kidding me right now?" I held up my hands in disbelief. "How can you not know who Rambo is?"

She giggled.

I shook my head. "Kids these days! Well, come on and help me put up the tent, and I'll school you about the not-so-realistic Special Forces poster child."

"What made him not-so-realistic?" Ashley asked.

"Well, since he was an actor, he took stupid chances for movie bravado. Have you ever seen Connor take a stupid chance?"

Ashley seemed to consider the question for a moment before shaking her head.

"Exactly. Connor is very calculating. He's always paying attention and he has really great instincts."

Kylee stepped from the darkness and slid beside Ashley. "There you are. Did you find out anything?"

"No. Libby doesn't know when Connor will be back, either."

"Why don't you ever call him dad?" Kylee asked.

"It's complicated." Ashley turned back to me. "Right, Libby?"

Complicated didn't even begin to describe it, but I wondered why Kylee was so curious about the issue. I eyed the girl as Connor's warning about her ran through my mind. Kylee looked irritated, and I couldn't tell if her irritation was due to Connor's absence or Ashley's reluctance to expand on their family history.

"Hey, Kylee." I smiled at the girl, hoping it looked genuine and didn't betray any of the paranoia I'd caught from Connor. "Do you and Braden need help putting up your tent?"

She shook her head. "Nope. Jeff and Brae are already working on it."

I slid off my wet boots and slipped into the tent. "Cool. Come on, Ash, I'm starving and there's a tasty MRE in this bag with my name on it." I tossed my pack into the tent and bent down to untie my shoes.

Ashley groaned, voicing the level of enthusiasm she held toward the Army rations known as meals, ready-to-eat. I, on the other hand, was so ravenous that I didn't even care what the food tasted like. I just needed sustenance.

"Ash, do you want to come play cards with us for a while?" Kylee asked.

"No," I replied for the girl. "We need to get some sleep. Staten said we'll be heading out early tomorrow."

With the way Kylee stared me down, I got the distinct feeling that she was about to ask what business it was of mine. I held her gaze though, and she backed down without saying anything.

"I'm actually tired, Kye," Ashley said, looking back and forth between us. "Besides, when Connor gets back, I want him to be able to find me."

I was immensely grateful when Ashley followed me into the tent. After unrolling my sleeping bag, I yanked off my wet clothes, put on dry sweats and bedded down. I spent the next ten minutes rubbing feeling back into my numb toes between bites of the most disgusting meal I had ever put in my mouth. It tasted even worse than the expired creamed corn I'd eaten just south of Olympia. The MRE was labeled as chicken noodle stew with vegetables, but everything in the world tasted more like chicken than the meal that I gagged down. Still, since my body desperately needed the calories, I not only ate the whole thing, but I also licked the packet clean. Just goes to prove that people will eat just about anything if they're hungry enough.

Done with dinner, I collapsed into my sleeping bag and stared at the dark tent ceiling, wondering what the heck was taking Connor so long. I heard Ashley sniffling, and knew she had to be wondering the same thing.

"Come here, Ash," I said, opening my arms to her.

She scooted her sleeping bag next to mine and hid her face in my shoulder. "Where is he? Why isn't he here yet?"

I brushed the hair away from her face with my fingers. "I don't know, kiddo, but he'll be here. I promise."

When the sun came up the next morning, Connor was still missing.

CHAPTER NINETEEN

Connor

When the second round of gunfire started, Connor jumped from his horse and landed softly on the muddied river bank. He handed the reins of his horse off to the nearest soldier on foot, and directed him to take Paint and keep the horse with the platoon. The soldier scurried off, dragging Paint behind him, and Connor turned to assess the threat.

The last of the soldiers trudged through the middle of the river, followed by Boom atop his horse. Boom turned in his saddle and fired. His horse spooked and started bucking and rearing. Determined to give Boom the cover he needed, Connor leveled his weapon and fired into the tree line.

The enemy fire immediately let up, and Boom and the soldiers hurried across the river. Connor continued to fire at the enemy, while Boom popped into his peripheral and started doing the same just a few feet away. Connor drifted toward Boom. "Think they're going for the bridge?"

"Possibly. Or they're crossing just past the bend. Either way, they'll be upon us soon if we don't move."

"We need to give the platoon more time."

Boom nodded. "We can't leave, but we can't let them get around us either."

Connor heard some rustling in the trees behind him, and turned to find an olive-skinned soldier with dark hair step out of the trees. Boom had once introduced the soldier as Corporal Ron Gregoretti, saying he had joined the Army right before they dispatched Boom to deal with the Progression threat.

"We thought you guys might need some help," Gregoretti said. He moved to the side and revealed Stein standing behind him. Both soldiers had their packs on and their weapons in their hands.

"What do you need us to do?" Stein asked.

Boom grinned at Connor. "Ask and you shall receive."

Connor shook his head at his friend. "Coincidence."

"No such thing." Boom turned toward the newcomers. "Connor and I are about to check for stray Progression river crossers. We need you two to keep this crossing secure."

"Yes, Captain," the two said in unison.

Boom elbowed Connor. "You ready?"

"I got your back, old man, just don't expect me to pick you up when you keel over," Connor replied.

Boom chuckled and adjusted his gun. With Connor following him, he slipped back behind the tree line and angled south. They got about ten yards away from Gregoretti and Stein before the heavy clouds above them burst, resulting in a torrential downpour.

"Just perfect," Connor whispered.

"What, you can't handle a little rain now? You're getting soft, my friend."

"Soft? I'll show you soft." Connor lowered his head and pushed himself into a jog.

Boom caught up to him quickly, and the two raced downriver, with only a few rows of trees separating them from the Skagit. The heavy rain masked the sound of their boots pounding against the dampening ground.

Connor caught a glimpse of movement in the trees ahead and stopped short, hiding behind the nearest tree. Boom knelt and aimed his weapon. A pale flicker of light preceded hushed voices. Probably Progression soldiers, but they had to be sure. Connor signaled to Boom and Boom nodded, standing and pushing away from the tree that shielded him.

With guns aimed and ready, Connor and Boom crept forward. Connor watched through his scope, counting the intruders and searching for any clue that would distinguish their loyalty. When he lowered the scope, Boom held up four fingers. Connor nodded, confirming that he counted four as well. A branch cracked loudly under Connor's foot. He jumped back and ducked behind a tree. Gunfire from four assault rifles answered the noise.

Yep, they're hostile.

Connor looked to Boom, awaiting orders. He saw the glint of metal right before Boom stood and threw a small, oval object into the enemy soldiers. Knowing what to expect, Connor curled himself into a ball, covering his head. The earth shook. Then Connor and Boom followed up the blast with gunfire before they skulked forward.

There were no survivors, so they continued on their way. Connor and Boom dispatched two more enemy teams before heading back to Gregoretti and Stein. The rain slowed to a drizzle before they returned, but not before it made a soggy, slippery mess of the ground. The occasional discharge of a weapon could be heard along the river, telling Boom and Connor that Gregoretti and Stein were still engaged in battle. Boom whistled their approach right as lightning cracked the sky and thunder shook the mountains. He waited for it to die down and whistled again, waiting for Gregoretti's reply before stepping out of the trees.

"We've given the platoon all the time we can. Time to pack up and get out of here," he said.

Connor eyed the team's dwindling supply of ammunition and nodded. If they didn't get out of there soon, they wouldn't be able to leave at all. Connor opened the pack he'd previously dropped and pulled out his rain clothes. After slipping them on, he shouldered his pack and provided cover while the others prepared to run.

Boom gave the order, and the team took off at a fast jog. Rain dripped on them through the branches of ancient trees as they went. Stein led them along the tracks of their fellow soldiers until they came across a single lane gravel road. He pointed down the road.

"Wait," Boom whispered. He pointed up the road and raised his eyebrows at Connor in question. "What do you think?"

Connor followed Boom's gaze. The road they stood on stretched up the mountain behind them for about a hundred meters.

Then it veered off to the left when the mountain sloped steeply upward. A hundred meters up the slope and to the right, Connor saw a thick patch of brush. Connor glanced at the path they'd come from and read his friend's mind, realizing they'd have a clear view of the path from the brush. He nodded. "Perfect."

Catching on, Stein added, "I'll cover our tracks."

"Do we have enough ammo?" Connor asked.

Boom nodded. "We'll make do. Let's get set up and see what we're working with."

Connor followed Boom up the hill. They drifted away from the road and toward the thick brush. The dampened soil made digging easy, so they used their hands to dig out the ground into shallow fighting positions that provided cover. Boom directed Gregoretti and Stein to guard the area while he and Connor hid their heads under a shared poncho and pulled out a red lens flashlight. They stayed under there just long enough to distribute the ammunition and study a map. Once the plan had been established, Connor killed the light and they surfaced.

The four soldiers climbed into their prone fighting positions and waited.

Connor watched the path below, wondering what Ashley and Liberty were up to. Boom had described Staten as a hard man who would mercilessly push the platoon toward the base. Any Progression teams that were quick enough to catch them would be small and vulnerable.

After about an hour of waiting, Stein elbowed Connor and pointed to his ear. Connor hadn't heard anything, so he shook his head. But then, he heard a branch snap in the distance, followed by footfalls. The Progression approached. Connor strained his ears, trying to guess their number, and decided there had to be at least a dozen of them.

The team held their position, lying in the mud, as Progression soldiers filed into their line of sight. Connor counted heads as they popped into sight. Thirteen, fourteen, fifteen, sixteen. They stopped and looked at the road. Connor listened, but couldn't hear any more soldiers coming. The sixteen turned and started following the road down the hill.

Boom gave the signal.

Bullets rained down on the Progression soldiers from above. Some dove to the ground, and some turned and started firing wildly up the mountain. The Army had the high ground though, and the kids didn't have a chance. When the last body hit the ground, the guns went silent. The four soldiers froze and watched the kids for movement.

Boom lowered his head for a moment. Then he crossed himself and gave the order for the team to move. They descended on the corpses, checking for vitals as they went. No one survived, so they searched the bodies for ammunition and other supplies. Then Boom gave everyone their op order, and the team moved out.

* * *

The night darkened, and the team ran on. An old, familiar burn crept up Connor's legs and spread through his body. He relaxed his mind and opened himself up to the strain. M4 clutched in his grip, he trudged over hills and splashed through streams as Boom pressed them on.

Boom called the team to a stop by a small stream, somewhere around midnight. They took turns guarding and refilling their water supply. When Connor's turn came, he splashed water on his face and rinsed out his canteen. He refilled it, and then popped an iodine tablet into. Also refreshed and refilled, Gregoretti and Stein stood guard as Boom and Connor pulled out the map and the red lens flashlight and bent their heads together under a poncho.

"We cut across highway 530, and traveled down this national forest route 2010," Boom said, following the route with his fingertip.

Connor agreed. "They can't be too far ahead of us. Probably somewhere west of Boulder Creek. Are we going to continue on?"

Boom shook his head. "No. We're going to find a good spot to stop for the night, and then tomorrow we'll use the daylight to teach Gregoretti and Stein how to build traps."

"Smart. Keep them off our tail."

"Exactly. Tonight, we'll eat in shifts, then twenty-five percent security."

"I'll pull security first," Connor replied.

Boom and Connor climbed out from under the poncho and took up their guard positions, instructing Gregoretti and Stein to enjoy a tasty MRE, courtesy of the US Army. The two ate quickly, and then stood guard to give Boom and Connor the chance to fill their stomachs. After everyone had eaten, the team crossed the stream.

They continued on to the west until they found a patch of blackberry bushes.

"Lesson number one," Boom said, pointing toward the bushes. "You find the worst, most uncomfortable, most dangerous place you can find and sleep there."

Gregoretti and Stein paused, looking toward the bushes. Connor couldn't see their expressions in the dark, but he figured they had to be wondering whether or not Boom was messing with them.

"He's serious," Connor said. He walked past the two and stepped into the bushes, looking for the best place to post a lookout. "Come on, girls, it's cozy."

Boom stepped into the bushed and unrolled his sleeping bag between two bushes.

Gregoretti and Stein followed. They bedded down in the thick of the bushes, while Connor propped himself against a tree where he could see the majority of the surrounding area.

By now, the storm clouds were gone, leaving stars twinkling in the clear sky. Connor glanced up and wondered—not for the first time—if his brother Jacob could see him. He took a moment to wonder about Heaven and whether or its residents still kept watch over the living. Still uncertain of how the whole Heaven thing worked, he reassured himself that if Jacob was allowed to watch over people, he'd be keeping a close eye on Ashley and Liberty.

Are they safe? Connor wondered.

The stars didn't answer.

Connor's mind drifted in and out of memories of his brother, landing on a scene of them sitting in the Army recruiter's office.

"You don't have to do this, you know?" Jacob told Connor.

Connor nodded. Internally, though, he knew he had no choice, though. Jacob had been the anchor of Connor's teen years, but Connor was a man now. The time had come for him to venture out of his brother's shadow and start his own life. Desperate for more freedom than sleeping on Jacob's couch offered, he wanted to go forth and make his own mark on the world. Army recruiters with big promises said they needed him, and Connor enjoyed feeling needed for once.

"I want to," Connor reassured his brother.

Jacob watched him for a moment and then nodded. "I know. I'm gonna miss you, though."

"Which part are you going to miss? Cleaning up after me or cooking for me? I have to move out before you turn into a woman."

Jacob lunged at Connor, wrapped one arm around his neck and gave him a noogie. "This woman *can still take you down. Remember that, little boy!"*

The recruiter looked up from his desk and gave them a questioning look.

Jacob released his brother and leaned back in his chair. *"You're not gonna miss me? Not even a little?"*

"Maybe a little." Connor shrugged. A smirk tugged at his lips as he looked at his big brother. "You do make some bomb pancakes."

Jacob slugged Connor in the shoulder.

Boom sat up, returning Connor's thoughts to the present. The captain slid out of his sleeping bag and stood. Then he crept over to Connor and leaned against the tree beside him, looking at his watch.

"I'm a half hour over. Why didn't you wake me?" Boom asked.

Connor shrugged. "I can't sleep anyway. Might as well be useful."

Boom rested a hand on Connor's shoulder. "You'd be more useful if you got some rest."

"We've both gone without sleep for longer than this, and still managed to keep up," Connor replied.

"Yeah, but we were younger than. We're getting old now."

Connor chuckled. "Speak for yourself."

"All right, I'm old. Older, at least. To tell you the truth, I never thought I'd live to see thirty-five."

"I've seen some of your explosions, Boom. I never thought you'd live to see thirty."

Boom grinned. They stood in silence for a while before the captain asked, "So what has you unable to sleep, my friend?"

Connor rubbed the back of his neck. "I was just remembering the day Jacob took me to enlist. I still miss him. I keep thinking it'll get easier, but it's been months since he died, and it's not easier."

Boom scratched at his beard. "Your brother was a good man. I remember the first time I met him. It was at that meet and greet that Captain Lorouse threw."

Despite his dark mood, Connor couldn't help but smile. "I remember that night."

"I don't know how. You were ... what did you call it? Three sheets to the wind? And you left with that brunette server—the one with an extra button undone on her shirt—against the advice of your brother. I thought he was going to chase you down and drag you back to the Captain's party by your ear."

Connor chortled. "I'd forgotten all about that. Jacob didn't drag me by it, but he sure did bend my ear for days about it. I didn't think he'd ever let up about my 'unprofessional behavior.' I just kept asking him if he'd actually looked at her. The girl was built like Jessica Rabbit, and she invited me over for a nightcap. I would have had to be blind *and* stupid to refuse her, but Jacob didn't fully grasp the situation."

"Oh, I'm sure he understood just fine, but his wife was on his arm when you were describing that brunette's breasts." Boom laughed.

Connor joined in his friend's merriment, letting his worries wash away under the waves of laughter. Then he ran a hand down his face, wishing he could wipe away past mistakes as easily. "Man, I was stupid. When a woman that good looking is single, there's a reason. Took me close to six months to repair the damage she did to my credit."

"What do you mean?"

"She was a thief! Took pictures of my credit cards while I was sleeping, and then treated herself to one heck of an online shopping spree. Then, when I cut off the credit cards, she gave out my number to several of her suitors. I had to get my number changed."

Boom shook his head, still chuckling. "Jacob was a much better judge of character than you."

"If I remember right, it wasn't her character I was judging." Connor looked down at the ground and stuck his hands in his pockets. "Looking back, I probably deserved everything that sociopath did to me."

"Yes, you probably did."

"Thanks a lot, bro," Connor said.

"What? Back then you did deserve it, but thankfully, you've changed." Boom cleared his throat. "He lifted me out of the pit of despair, out of the mud and the mire. He set my feet on solid ground and steadied me as I walked along."

Connor looked at Boom. "Hmm?"

"You've been retrieved from the pit. Now He's strengthening you and steadying you. It's ... encouraging."

"Jacob?" Connor asked. "What pit?"

Boom shook his head, chuckling.

"Sometimes it's like we're not even speaking the same language," Connor replied.

Silence stretched between the two as they kept watch over the sleeping recruits. Connor's thoughts drifted back to his brother lying in bed with a broken leg, staring up at him.

'Please, Con, kill me. Save her.'

Connor looked away, wishing he could vanquish the memory for good, but knowing that he wouldn't, even if given the option. He needed to hold on to every last memory of the brother he had failed again and again.

Boom must have picked up on Connor's dark musings, because Boom patted his shoulder. "What is it?"

"Every time I'm away from Ashley, I feel like I'm letting Jacob down all over again. I should be with her, protecting her like I promised him I would. Yet, by staying behind, I did protect her. Seems like there's never a right answer." Connor's knees buckled and he slid down the tree. He sat and plucked a few blades of grass, and then ripped them in half and tossed them to the side. "I'm just afraid something's going to happen while I'm not there to help them."

"You can't be with them all the time. At some point you will have to trust them to survive without you." Boom paused and smiled. "Unless you're planning to lock them in a safe again."

"Oh, believe me, I would if I could get away with it! They'd escape though. Liberty would probably blow up the entire planet to get out of it."

Boom chuckled. "I do believe you're right. So, what do you plan to do with them?"

"What *can* I do? I love them, so I'll probably continue to do what idiots in love do. I'll follow them around like some crazed stalker, trying to keep them safe and protected while I slowly lose my mind."

"Quite the definition of love."

Connor nodded. "I'm thinking of making it into a ballad."

Silence stretched between the two as Connor considered Boom's question. *'What do you plan to do with them?'* There hadn't been much time to plan for anything beyond keeping Ashley and Liberty safe. No one could possibly expect more from him. Yet, with Boom's question lingering in the night air, Connor realized how much more he wanted.

"I plan to marry her, Boom," he announced.

Stein rolled over in his sleeping bag. An owl hooted somewhere to the north of them. Connor watched his friend, waiting for a reaction.

"Then what?" Boom finally asked.

"I don't know." Connor shrugged. "Go off the grid, raise a family …"

"There's no safe place to do that anymore, Conman."

Connor chuckled. "Figures. Now that I want one."

Boom patted Connor's shoulder. "I hear that safety is overrated anyway. Never tried it myself, and I wonder if Ashley and Liberty would even enjoy it."

Connor nodded, smiling. "Yeah, well, there is that too." And with that, he pushed himself off the ground, stood and stretched. Then he bid Boom a goodnight and drifted off toward his sleeping bag.

CHAPTER TWENTY

Liberty

I SAT ON a wooden bench, hunched over the plain white face of a porcelain doll. In my hand, I held a fine-tipped paintbrush, the thin bristles dark with black acrylic paint. In contrast, the bright summer sun beat down on the top of my head, providing what my grandmother referred to as 'ideal painting light.' I could feel my freckles multiplying under the warm rays, and knew my nose would be a lovely shade of pink by the time we finished. A wiser kid would have applied generous amounts of sun block, but I had neither time nor concern for such things.

Grandma stood beside me, holding a plate. She leaned closer to me and the smell of wheat toast and warm apple-butter tickled my senses, teasing my taste buds. When she smiled, little lines spread out from the corners of her eyes and around her lips. She sat the plate of toast on the bench next to me, and slid spectacles the color of her short silver curls up the bridge of her nose. Some grandmothers made cookies. Mine suffered from diabetes, so she fed me wheat toast smothered in sugar-free homemade apple-butter whenever I came to visit.

"Yum, thank you, Grandma," I said, eying the treat.

"That's for afterward," Grandma said, waving her hand toward the brush. "We gotta paint first. This light won't last forever, and those eyelashes are impossible to get right without good light."

Right. The eyelashes. *My attention turned back to the doll head in my hands and I wondered what had possibly given my grandmother faith that I could do the task she'd set before me.* "But what if I mess up?" *I asked her.*

"Oh, you will, honey," Grandma adjusted my grip on the paintbrush, making it feel awkward and unbalanced in my hand.

"Sheesh, Grandma, aren't you supposed to build my confidence or something?"

She smiled at me, her eyes sparkling with humor. "Everyone messes up. Why should you be any different?"

Suddenly she sat beside me on the bench, and the paintbrush and the doll head disappeared. She cupped my cheeks in her hands and studied my face. "You've got young eyes. You see things in the young that others don't. You can do this."

She kissed my forehead, and then disappeared.

* * *

I awoke still reaching for the dream, as if I could step back through time and once more find safety and security under the watchful gaze of my grandmother. My eyes burned at the memory of painting eyelashes while she looked on and corrected every mistake I made. Although I made a lot of mistakes, she never got angry or even frustrated with me. Instead, she kept reassuring me that, between my young eyes, steady hand, and her expertise, our dolls would have the most beautiful eyelashes ever. The task required lots of time and energy, but she was right. Our dolls did have incredible lashes.

Grandma's back porch felt so far and long ago that I couldn't help but wonder if it had actually happened.

Maybe it was a dream. Maybe it's all been a dream.

Closing my eyes, I searched for more memories of my grandmother. They came in flashes: Christmas, dinner at a restaurant, a drive, a birthday party. I held each memory close to my heart like the precious life-restoring gem it was.

Where are you, Grandma? Are you okay?

My imagination took a dark turn, showing me images of death and destruction. Since that path ended in a bottomless pool I wasn't prepared to dive into, I focused on the dream and tried to analyze its meaning.

'*You see things in the young that others don't. You can do this.*'

I don't remember her saying that. What the heck does it mean?

The words bounced around in my mind for a while, but no obvious meanings stuck, so I sat up and stretched. Every square inch of my body protested, insisting that I lie back down and sleep. Unfortunately, with the soldiers packing up around our tent, I knew I couldn't get that. Ignoring the complaints of my muscles, I reached for the clothes I'd taken off to dry the night before. They were still wet, so I wadded them into a ball and went through the pack Connor had given me.

In the front pockets of the pack, I found a waterproof parka and pants that would have helped me immensely the previous night, had I only known about them. Connor had also stuffed an extra pair of fatigues in the bag for me. After smacking my forehead for not checking the pack earlier, I closed my eyes and sent up a quick thank you for the dry pants and for Connor's forethought. Then I woke Ashley up.

She fought me for a few moments, and then popped up. "Is Connor here?" she asked.

"I haven't seen him yet, but we should go check."

Her body collapsed, and she pulled her sleeping bag back over her head. "If he was in the camp, he would have come and told us."

"Dang. Nothing gets past you."

I spent the next ten minutes alternately tickling, bribing, and threatening her until she crawled out of her sleeping bag and agreed to come with me for breakfast.

Our search for breakfast ended in front of one of those weird in ground fire pits with an extra air hole. A large pot of oatmeal sat on top of it, so I grabbed two bowls and served us some. Bruised, battered, and disheartened by Connor's continued absence, Ashley and I sat in silence, shoveling food into our mouths.

Jeff and Braden joined us as we were finishing our meal.

"Mornin'" Jeff said.

I nodded to him.

Kylee stumbled out of her tent a few minutes later. Her hair stood up from her head in a dark, knotted halo, making her look anything but angelic. She patted it down a couple of times, then gave up and staggered toward us.

I gave her my best attempt at a smile. "Hey, sunshine."

She frowned.

"You're having one of those days too, huh?" I replied.

She sat down and Braden handed her a bowl of oatmeal. After a few bites, she seemed to come back to life. She turned to Ashley and asked, "Has your dad shown up yet?"

Ashley shook her head.

"Sorry," Kylee replied. Her face drooped.

Weird. Why is she so interested in Connor?

"I'm sure he'll be here soon," I told the girls, eying Kylee. "Connor is fast and stubborn. Nothing will be able to keep that man from finding us. Trust me, I've tried to lose him numerous times."

Ashley gave me a fake smile that looked more like a grimace.

I squeezed her shoulders. "Hey, why don't you go see if someone has saddled Cinnamon for you yet?"

She seemed like she wanted to object, but then scampered off to check on the horse. I poured myself a cup of coffee, and then sat back down, staring into the fire. Jeff finished eating, and then said something about packing before he stood and left, followed by Braden and Kylee.

I tuned out the buzzing of the camp around me and focused on the flames, silently praying for Connor to be safe.

What if he doesn't come back?

The thought blindsided me, inundating my heart and mind with fear. Tears stung my eyes as I replayed all the times he had shown affection toward me, only to have me run away or brush him off. Now that I faced uncertainty about his return, regret felt like a rope around my ankles, threatening to pull me under a wave of despair.

I should have told him how I feel.

Truthfully, though, I was a coward. Revealing my emotions to Connor meant opening myself up to a vulnerability that I wasn't ready for yet. But, if he stood in front of me right now, I would have come clean and confessed my feelings for him. He wasn't, though, and since I had no idea if and when he'd come back, I brushed away the last of the stupid moisture from my eyes, hitched up my backpack and went to pack up my tent. That killed a whole five minutes, so I meandered over to check on Ashley.

When I found her, the girl was having an in-depth conversation with Cinnamon about the necessity of holding still while she mounted the horse. Cinnamon chewed a mouthful of grass, eying Ashley like she was crazy.

"Yes, like that," Ashley said. "Just stand there. Don't move."

She stepped to the horse's side and stuck her foot in the stirrup. The minute Ashley put weight on the stirrup, Cinnamon drifted away from her. Ashley hopped a couple of times, following the horse, before pulling her foot away and stomping on the ground.

"You said you'd hold still."

With the skeptical way Cinnamon eyed Ashley, I doubted she'd made any promises. I watched the two of them, deciding that the scene would have been hilarious if only Connor would have been there to share it with me.

"Is there something I can do to help?" I asked.

"I don't know what her problem is." Ashley looked to be on the verge of tears as she gestured toward the horse. "She usually lets me right up. Why does she keep moving away?"

"It's okay. We'll figure it out," I replied, squeezing her shoulders.

Ashley and I studied Cinnamon. The horse chewed on a mouthful of grass around her bit, watching us as we approached.

"She seems fine, Ash."

Ashley rolled her eyes. "I know, but watch." She gripped the reins and saddle horn, and then slipped her foot into the stirrup.

Cinnamon shuffled to the side. I scratched my head. Ashley had mounted Cinnamon several times without incident.

"All right girl, what's going on?" I asked, patting Cinnamon's flank.

She didn't answer, so I picked up a stick and used it to clean out her hooves, checking for rocks or anything else that would make her uncomfortable. Finding nothing obvious, I grabbed the saddle and stuck my foot in the stirrup. When I shifted my weight to pull the other leg up, the saddle slid off Cinnamon's back, falling toward me. It happened so quickly that I lost my footing and had to hop several times to regain it.

"Well, that's your problem," I said. "This horse is a genius and she knew the saddle was loose. She didn't want you to fall off. Who saddled her?"

Ashley looked down at the ground.

"You did?"

"I told them I could do it myself. I've watched them do it a bunch of times and it didn't look that hard."

"It's not difficult at all, but you have to cinch it tight. If the saddle moves, it's too loose." I righted the saddle, and then lifted the fender and hooked the stirrup on the saddle horn. After undoing Ashley's knot, I looped the cinch straps through the ring a couple of times and showed her how to tie it correctly. I demonstrated how to pull the cinch strap tight, and then looped it through the keeper. Then I led Cinnamon around in a couple of circles and tightened the cinch once again.

"Oh," Ashley said. "That's different than how they do it."

"Yeah, well, that's the cowgirl way," I replied.

"Okay, but will Cinnamon let me on now?" Ashley asked.

I shrugged. "Only one way to find out."

She inched up to the horse, and then gripped the horn. Then she slowly slid her foot into the stirrup. Cinnamon craned her neck to watch the girl, but other than that did not move. Ashley swung her other leg over the horse and settled herself into the saddle. In response, Cinnamon let out a huff, as if exasperated by how long it took us to figure out the issue.

"You were right." Ashley beamed me a proud smile and patted Cinnamon on the neck. "She is a genius."

Cinnamon whinnied in agreement.

* * *

That day we marched on, through the scorching sunshine, around mountains, and across shallow lakes. In an effort to distract my mind from worries about Connor and the pain, exhaustion, and possible heat stroke of my body, I prayed for Osberg and Noke. I prayed against infection and for muscle and flesh to knit back together, leaving no evidence of their wounds. I prayed for a complete healing that would blow everyone's mind and help them see that God was still in the healing business. Then I started praying for their hearts and minds as well as their bodies. Mostly I prayed beneath my breath, but judging by the way the soldiers would occasionally cast suspicious glances my way, a few of my prayers must have escaped through my lips.

By the time Drill Sergeant Staten—as the soldiers had not-so-lovingly taken to calling him—finally called us to a stop that evening, I was half dead. After we lowered Osberg to the ground, I collapsed beside him and closed my eyes. The knowledge that I should be putting up my tent did not fill me with the energy to do so. My arms felt like useless lead-filled lumps, and I didn't know if I'd ever be able to move them again.

A dark shadow loomed over me. "You dead?" Connor asked.

My heart sped up at the sound of his voice. I didn't open my eyes, just in case I was dreaming. "I can hear you, so would that make you dead too?" I asked.

He chuckled.

I shifted and winced at the charley horse that zapped my leg. Since I didn't have the energy to stand, I kicked my leg a couple of times and tried to knead the muscle. "Nope. I'm definitely alive. My body wouldn't hurt this much if I was dead."

He knelt beside me and pushed my hands away so he could massage my thigh. His thumbs dug into the muscle. It hurt so bad I wanted to scream and writhe, but I didn't have the energy move, let alone adding drama to it. He must have sensed as much, because the next thing I knew his arms slid under me, and then he lifted me into the air.

Energized by the fact that Connor carried me, I opened my eyes and attempted to flail wildly. "What the heck? Put me down!"

He ignored my protests and pulled me to his chest, holding me closer. Too weak and tired to win the fight, I gave up and collapsed against him.

"You know I'm going to have to kill you for this, right?" I asked.

His chest rumbled against me, so I scowled at him to let him know I was serious.

"You can kill me later, after you've rested."

I yawned. "How very accommodating of you."

"I try."

For one brief, insane second, I considered professing my undying love for Connor, just in case …

"You're not planning on abandoning us again, are you?" I asked.

"Aww." He smiled. "Did you miss me?"

"Maybe for a second, but thankfully, it passed."

He chuckled.

Connor made me stay awake long enough for him to stuff another disgusting MRE down my throat. Everything after that was a blur.

CHAPTER TWENTY-ONE

Liberty

I PEACEFULLY SOARED among the clouds, enjoying the cool breeze in my face as my wings stretched effortlessly across the sky. The world felt peaceful and free, smelling of nature and life. Then, suddenly, the breeze changed. It darkened, becoming heavier and tainted with smoke. Dipping below the clouds, I turned and searched until I saw found dark plumes billowing from the trees to the north. Fire. Curious, I flew toward the source to investigate.

Eighty-three flames danced across the forest floor in some sort of wild revelry. They burned unchecked and unrestrained by county lines, rivers or lakes. Animals fled ahead of the flames, but I knew they couldn't run fast enough to escape the fire. Through pops and crackles, the flames sang of their goal to destroy it all, leaving nothing but ash and ruin in their wake.

Terror squeezed my heart, and I screamed for the flames stop. Life couldn't end like this. Not at the hands of such mindless destruction.

'Stop them,' the "call" whispered into my heart.

I stared at the flames, wondering how I could stop them. Not even the rivers could dampen the destruction, so what could I possibly do?

The "call" answered my unvoiced question, emboldening me with courage and strength, and promising protection and direction. Although I had no idea what I would do when I got there, I *closed my eyes and flew straight into the heart of the flames. The heat beat against me. It licked the pocket of air that surrounded me, but it could not touch me. As I hovered above the ground, waiting for inspiration, a song filled my heart. I opened my beak and sang of the beauty being destroyed. I mourned for the lost, and crooned about the future that could be if only they'd stop burning.*

"It doesn't have to be this way," I told the flames. "Come and see a different future."

When I opened my eyes, all eighty-three flames surrounded me. They swayed back and forth, dancing to my solo. They were listening! I was so close to making a difference, but I had run out of words. Silence enveloped us, and fear crept up my spine. The bubble surrounding me thinned as the fire crept closer. Anticipating the worst, I closed my eyes and waited for the flames to consume me.

* * *

When I awoke, ghosts of clouds and fire lingered in the back of my mind, hinting at a dream I needed to remember. Desperate to recall the dream, I squeezed my eyes shut and focused. Suddenly, it came back to me. I was a sparrow, singing to eighty-three tongues of fire.

Oh yeah, that's helpful and important.

Dismissing the dream, I sat up. Ashley was still asleep in her bag, but Connor was nowhere to be seen. I remembered his hands under me, lifting me into the air, probably provoking my crazy dream.

Was Connor a dream too?

As I struggled to sort reality from dream, the tent flap unzipped and Connor ducked in. "Hey," he said.

"Hey." I tried to pat down my unruly curls. They felt frizzy, like someone had attacked my head with Velcro while I slept. Wondering how ridiculous I looked, I glanced at my bag and longed for five minutes alone with the brush and toothbrush inside it.

Connor clearly wasn't going to give me that time, though. He slid into the tent beside me and handed me a steaming cup of coffee. Then he turned and zipped the tent flap behind him. "Still want to kill me?" he asked.

Too tired to commit to any decision, I replied, "Maybe after my coffee." Closing my eyes, I sipped from my cup. It was bitter and almost strong enough to chew, and it tasted like heaven.

When I opened my eyes, Connor smiled at me. "Just shout out a warning first. Otherwise people might say you're un-sportsman like."

"We wouldn't want to make people talk."

Connor moved closer. The corner of his lips turned up, creating a dangerously sexy smirk. "Not even a little? You should probably know that soldiers gossip like little old ladies. They're already talking."

"What? Why?"

Connor shrugged. "I sleep here a lot. They can probably sense the chemistry between us."

"Chemistry?"

"Yeah. Enough to build a nuke with. Don't you feel it?"

With no way to backpedal the conversation, I considered kicking Ashley to wake her up. As Connor closed the already small gap between us, I couldn't decide if I wanted to scream for help, run away or lean into him. All three options terrified me. Closer and closer he came, gobbling up my personal space as if it were a meal served to him.

"Regardless of whether or not you missed me, I missed you," he whispered.

His voice had deepened and gone husky. It wreaked all sorts of havoc on my stomach. I loved him. Like some co-dependent maniac, I wanted to wrap my arms around him and smother him with kisses so he could never leave me again. I longed to be forever by his side and on his arm.

No. That's not me. I'm independent ... and alone.

My affection for Connor threatened everything I'd ever wanted for myself. He was like morphine for my aching, lonely heart and I wanted to open my veins and let him in. But, I knew that if I took a hit, I'd only need more of him. The tent and the sounds of the camp faded into the distance and all that mattered was Connor. He leaned closer and I wanted to grab his shirt and pull him to me. In anticipation, my hands shifted. Heat ran down my chest, scalding me.

The coffee!

Literally scalding me. I tried to jump to my feet, but smacked my head on the roof of the tent. "Ouch! Ouch! Ouch!"

Connor grabbed the hem of my shirt and pulled the fabric away from my stomach, providing a little relief. I thanked him and leaned back, tugging my shirt from his fingertips. With a smirk still affixed to his face he watched me expectantly, as if any moment now I would throw myself into his arms like some stupid damsel in distress.

Nope. Not today, mister.

"I make you hot. Literally," he said.

I rolled my eyes, while my stomach attempted to unknot itself.

"Ash, wake up, honey." My voice sounded desperate even to my own ears. "We need to get packed and ready to move."

She stirred.

Connor watched me, obviously amused.

"Ash." My shirt had cooled, so I dropped it to fall back against my skin and used both hands to shake the girl. "Time to get up."

Please. Don't leave me alone with this maniac. He's looking at me like I'm a steak and it's freaking me out!

Finally, she stretched and sat up, rescuing me from my alone time with Connor.

CHAPTER TWENTY-TWO

Connor

STILL SMILING ABOUT the desire he'd seen in Liberty's eyes, Connor slipped from her tent and went to refill his coffee cup from the pot by the in-ground fire pit. Taking a moment to sit and reflect on her obvious affection, he ladled himself a bowl of oatmeal and watched the trees. Within moments, a soldier hopped out from between two tents, laid two roughly-made crutches beside Connor, and then plopped down. He breathed heavily as he adjusted his splinted right leg to stretch out in front of him.

"Noke?" Connor asked, amazed.

The soldier nodded, chuckling at whatever he saw in Connor's expression.

"Last time I saw you … it didn't look good. That was only a few days ago. What are you doing out of bed?"

"The doc cleared me." Noke grinned. "So I reckon it's about time to stop letting people carry me around."

"Well, good to see that you're healing so quickly. I'm shocked actually. You're not planning on walking the next stretch, are you?" Connor continued to gape at Noke.

"No, Sir. I can hobble around camp just fine, but I'm betting these wooden armpit supports would chafe like nobody's business. I can ride, though. Doc says he don't see why I can't sit atop a horse for a bit. The ride can't be much rougher than the gurney." He gave Connor a wide, toothy grin. "You're lookin' at me like

I'm some sort of anomaly. Don't soldiers survive bullet wounds all the time?"

"Your wound was pretty extensive," Connor replied. "When Liberty and I picked you up, your leg was soaked with blood and you were leaving a trail behind. We didn't know if you'd make it through the night, and now you're walking? Don't you think this is odd?"

"It's not odd. What it is, is a miracle. The good Lord must not be done with me yet."

Connor forced himself to stop staring. He returned his attention the trees and stretched out his hands above the fire pit. As he warmed himself, he thought about other bullet wound victims he'd known, recalling their recovery times and comparing them to Noke's. Although the soldier's speedy recovery seemed impressive, Connor decided to talk to Magee before using any crazy words like "miracle" to describe it.

"Well, I best go pick out a horse," Noke said. Pushing himself up with the help of his crutches, he stood and hopped away.

Connor stared after the man, still unsure of what to make of their exchange.

"Excuse me, Sir," someone said from behind Connor,

He turned to find Soseki watching him. "Yes?"

"The Captain is looking for you. He says it's urgent, and he's waiting in his tent." Soseki's words were clipped, emphasizing the urgency he spoke of. He stood tall and tense, and his eyes darted across the camp, clearly on alert for something.

Wondering what had set the soldier on edge, Connor nodded. "I'll go right now."

Soseki nodded and hurried away.

What now? Connor wondered. The camp buzzed with its normal activity, and the soldiers looked relaxed and at ease as they packed. Whatever news had rattled Soseki obviously hadn't reached the rest of the camp yet.

Boom's tent was one of the few structures still erect. It was the same size as the tent Ashley and Liberty shared, but it stood closer to the center of the camp. Connor came to a stop in front of the open flap and peeked inside.

"Enter," Boom said.

He sat atop his sleeping bag in the small space, his head just inches from the ceiling. Mouth drawn in a tight line, he clutched a single sheet of paper that his eyes seemed glued to.

Dread crept up Connor's spine as he wondered what could have Boom so absorbed and somber. Ducking into the tent, he asked, "You were looking for me?"

Boom nodded, still not taking his eyes off the page. "Have a seat. We have much to discuss."

Connor sat, and then watched as Boom continued to scan the paper. After a few moments, Connor cleared his throat, finally earning Boom's attention.

"Oh, right. Close the flap," Boom said.

After Connor zipped the flap closed, he pointed at the paper in Boom's hand. "What's that?"

Boom put it face-down on his lap. "We will discuss this in a moment, but first, I have something for you." He grinned and opened his hand in front of Connor's face, revealing a ring.

"I thought you'd never ask," Connor said.

Boom chuckled. "Sorry, but I've already chosen my bride. She's a harsh one that'll no doubt be the death of me, but she's much more exciting than you are."

Connor laughed. "Indeed. The Army will most likely drive you to your grave. So what's this for then?"

"This ... this is for your bride."

"Boom, where did you get this?"

"It was my mother's. Take it."

Connor studied the ring, hesitant to pick it up. The large, round diamond in the center sat surrounded by a circle of sapphires. The band was thin white gold and although Connor knew little about jewelry, it looked expensive and old. "I can't take this. It's too much." But, he wanted to. He could envision the ring on Liberty's finger, and it looked perfect.

"It's been stuffed in my weapons crate, collecting dust for a long time. *Madre* would want it to go to good use. Take it, Conman."

Suddenly excited and a little anxious, Connor scooped up the ring and studied it closer. "It's amazing. She's going to love it."

Boom grinned. "Yes. I'd imagine she'd even take you along with it. Just don't wait too long to ask her."

Connor nodded and stuffed the ring into his pocket. "Thank you."

"Of course, *hermano*. Now, let's talk about these marching orders. A message came across the radio this morning."

Connor cocked his head to the side. Boom had been complaining about issues with the radio. Fort Lewis promised to communicate with the platoon at oh-five-hundred every Sunday morning, but so far, the radio had just relayed static, with an occasional beep. Boom had voiced his suspicions that the Progression was jamming the signal. Radio waves had become a battlefield to be won by the team with the best technology. The Army seemed to be losing that war.

"You finally picked up something?" Connor asked.

"Yes. They're calling us back to the fort. Immediately. Intel says that Lieutenant Justice is on the move." Boom picked up the page he'd put down and offered it to Connor. A jumble of letters had been scribbled across the top of the paper, decoded into a message at the bottom. "The signal was interrupted before they finished."

Connor scanned the document. Although he'd never met Lieutenant Donovan Justice, he'd heard plenty about him during his stint in the service. As both creator and head of the Progression, Justice had started the child soldier division of the military out of the Mountain Training Center in central California. The program had spread quickly, though, branching out first to other bases and eventually into public schools. The idea that Justice would venture from the safety of his California home both intrigued and terrified Connor.

"Why would he leave Cali?"

Boom shrugged. "Good question. He's coming, though. If he's planning to invade the fort ... I don't know if we can stop him."

"What?! How big are his forces?"

"Big enough that the Army is worried enough to call us all back in." Boom folded the paper and stuffed it into his pocket.

Connor's mind raced, trying to make sense of what Boom had said. "Fort Lewis could easily defend against an attack. I've been there. I remember the security and the—"

"No, Conman. You were there before the collapse. You haven't seen it since. The Progression knew. They were prepared. When chaos hit, we recalled everyone we could. We secured the base, and then started sending out teams to regain control. I was out, leading one of those teams, when our own jets started dropping missiles on the base."

Connor felt like he'd been punched in the gut. "What? How?"

"The Progression was part of us. They had access."

"But they had voted to shut it down."

Boom shook his head. "After you left, the powers that be reached a negotiation to keep the Progression alive, but limited."

Connor rubbed a hand over his head. "The other bases?"

"Varying degrees of the same fate."

"When you said our forces were limited, I had no idea." Connor swallowed, feeling like the proverbial rug had been ripped out from under his feet. He had a ring. He even planned to ask the woman he loved to marry him. They might be able to squeeze in a few moments of happiness before the Progression wiped everyone out. "Now Justice is bringing his Army to finish what they started."

Boom nodded. "Have you ever met him?"

"Can't say I've had the pleasure."

"I met him once, and it definitely wasn't a pleasure. We were at a dinner for some official, and Justice set up a series of demonstrations to entertain the dinner guests. During one of the demonstrations he had his kids attack the host's guards. They fought dirty, encouraging shock and awe from the party goers."

"Showing off his bloodthirsty children to impress the crowd." Connor frowned. "Sounds like a swell guy."

Boom nodded. "A few of the other guests voiced concerns like yours. Justice shut them down quickly. Reminded me of the Scripture: 'For a time is coming when people will no longer listen to sound and wholesome teaching. They will follow their own desires and will look for teachers who will tell them whatever their itching ears want to hear.' Justice helped the rich get richer and the powerful grow even greater. But in the end, he crushed them all to satisfy his selfish desires. I can't begin to imagine what has him marching north, but it cannot be good."

"So what's the plan?" Connor asked.

"We move. Quickly. I'm thinking about sending you and Soseki ahead to scout. Whatever the Progression is planning, it must be big. You can bet they'll want to keep us from reaching the base and interfering. We will have to prepare for whatever traps they're setting."

Connor nodded. He didn't want to be away from Ashley and Liberty, but he understood the necessity. "Say the word and we'll make it happen. We must assume they know our approximate location, and therefore know our route. We will have to change it up a bit to surprise them."

Boom rubbed the stubble on his chin, considering the map once again. "Yes, you are correct. My original plan was to continue south to Highway 203. Then we'd take 203 to 18, and then follow 18 to the fort. It's a good route that will keep us off the freeway and away from the more populated areas, but we'd still have the convenience of the road for the wagon. Travel would be quicker."

Connor nodded. "Smart, but predictable. It's exactly what they'd expect you to do. What's the one route they'd never expect you to take?"

Boom stared at the map. His brow furrowed and he shook his head. "You're talking about I5. The Progression has held control of the freeway for months. There's no way … " Boom shook his head again, but Connor could almost see the wheels spinning in his friend's brain.

"Of course it's crazy. That's why they'll never suspect it. Major Thompson is an arrogant, self-inflated leader who would never suspect that we'd be brazen enough to hit that road. I'd personally guarantee that he only has a few patrols running supplies on it right now. With any luck, we might even be able to intercept one of those supply wagons. Refill our ammo and maybe steal some meals from the Progression. If we send out scouts and keep our pace up, it could work."

Boom scratched the whiskers on his chin and looked up at the roof of the tent. Then he turned back to Connor and laughed. "You're right. You're crazy, but you're right. We could do it."

They had just bent their heads together and started making plans when Connor heard Liberty panicked voice shouting for Ashley.

CHAPTER TWENTY-THREE

Liberty

CONNOR LEFT TO go refill his coffee, and I collapsed on my sleeping bag and breathed deeply.

"You okay?" Ashley asked. Although she wasn't quite laughing at me, she couldn't mask the amusement in her voice.

"My shirt is soaked."

"What happened?"

I sighed again. "Connor. Connor happened. He made me crazy until I dumped coffee on myself."

She giggled.

"If I had a pillow, I'd throw it at you."

That only made her laugh harder. I started thinking up creative threats, but Kylee called Ashley's name from outside the tent. Ashley turned and unzipped the flap, revealing both Braden and Kylee.

"Hey Libby," Kylee waved at me. "Ash, you wanna go get some breakfast with us?"

The girls both looked to me with big, pleading eyes.

"We're supposed to be packing up," I reminded them.

They upped the pathetic on their pleading and continued to stare at me.

"Please," Ashley asked. "We'll go get breakfast really quick, and then I'll be back to help."

We both knew that by the time Ashley got done with breakfast, I'd have our tent torn down and ready to go. But, I didn't want to stand in the way of the girls' budding friendship.

"Fine, go," I told her. "But hurry back. I want you to saddle Cinnamon this time so I can make sure you know how."

"You're the best, Libby!" Ashley squealed before disappearing into the sunlight.

"Yeah, yeah, I love you too. Just don't forget to hurry back," I yelled. Unsure of whether or not she heard me, I decided it didn't matter. There were only so many places the kids could go in the camp, and I'd find them as soon as I was ready to help her with the horse.

"Thank you," Braden said, startling me.

I looked up at the flap, and there he stood with a forced smile, thanking me for some strange reason. Startled, I asked, "For what?"

"Brae, come on!" I heard Kylee shout from behind him.

"For teaching me how to play Blackjack, of course." Then he disappeared from my view.

The whole exchange felt odd, but I had so much to do that I couldn't give it much thought. Dismissing Braden's words, I got straight to work rolling up our sleeping bags and attaching them to our packs the way that Connor had taught me. Then I stuck them outside the tent and climbed out beside them. Another beautiful July morning greeted me. The blue sky was clear, birds sang from the trees, and the camp busily packed up around me. I started tearing down our tent to the tune of soldiers shouting orders and loading boxes.

Jeff showed up, looking fresh-shaven and dapper in clean fatigues. "Need help?" he asked.

"Not really." I pulled one of the stakes from the ground. "If tent striking were an Olympic sport, I'd qualify for at least a bronze."

He chuckled. "I don't know, you'd have some pretty steep competition, but let me rephrase that. Do you want help?"

"Sure, since Ashley abandoned me to hang out with Kylee. Speaking of which, your shadow was here this morning, acting kinda odd. What's up with Braden?"

Jeff shrugged. "Don't know. Haven't seen him yet today." He plucked another stake from the ground.

We finished striking the tent in record time, then Jeff took it to the wagon to be loaded. With nothing else to do, I went to go check on the kids.

I made it only a few yards before Magee stepped in front of me and asked if I could spare a minute. Minutes were one of the few thing I had in abundance, and I still hadn't spoken to him about being his assistant, so I let him lead me toward Osberg's tent. We ducked into the two-man tent and he closed the flap behind us. Osberg was wide awake and greeted me with a giant smile.

"Hey there," I smiled back and scooted to the left side of his bed, opposite of Magee. "You look way better than you did the last time I saw you."

His skin no longer had an ashy grey hue to it, and his eyes appeared clear and focused.

"I clean up well," Osberg replied.

"Thank you for coming," Magee said, tossing me a bottle of sanitizer. "First step, clean your hands."

I did so, and then handed the bottle back to him. "What can I help with?" I asked.

"We need to prep him for transport. To start, we'll remove his bandages and check for infection. Then we'll redress the wound. You will mostly just be watching as I explain the process."

"Got it."

"Because the wound is open, I'm going to need you to put on this." He handed me a mask.

While I put on my mask, he slipped on a second one and a pair of gloves. Magee pulled the top of Osberg's sleeping bag down to his stomach, revealing the wounded soldier's bare chest. Then he started tugging at the medical tape adhering the gauze to Osberg's shoulder.

"This is the worst part," Osberg said with a wince. "I'm surprised I even have any chest hair left for him to rip out."

Since I'd seen the extent of the damage to Osberg's shoulder, I seriously doubted that undressing the wound was the worst part, but I nodded like I believed him. "I bet."

Magee removed the last of the bandages and put them aside. He pointed at the wound and said, "What we're looking for is discoloration or odor. Do you see any odd coloring?"

I looked at Osberg's shoulder and almost lost my breakfast. About a three-inch diameter area of skin was missing, exposing two dark holes in the bright red meat of Osberg's shoulder. The skin around the wound had a yellowish tinge to it. I leaned back and took a couple of deep breaths, trying to swallow back the bile rising up in my throat.

"You okay?" Magee asked.

"Yeah. Just need a minute. I wasn't expecting ... that. Is that yellow color on the skin normal?"

He nodded. "It's from the ointment we put on it. He's also been taking an antibiotic to ward off infection."

"Along with pain pills," I added. "He likes those a lot."

Magee chuckled. "I bet he does."

"Were you able to get the bullet out?"

"Bullets, and yes. Do you think you can come smell his wound now?"

"Never thought the day would come when I was sniffing wounds," I replied.

Osburg chuckled, but I think Magee rolled his eyes.

I lowered my mask to rest under my nose, leaned over Osberg, and took a whiff. "I smell the medicine and antiseptic, but that's it."

"Good. That's all I smell as well." Magee plucked a small white tube from the tray beside Osberg's head and unscrewed the top. "Now we apply more ointment and redress it."

I watched as he squeezed a liberal glob of goo onto the wound, and then covered it with a large square of gauze. He added a protective backing with adhesive sides, and then turned toward me, removing his mask and gloves.

"And we're done. Do you have any questions?" he asked.

"No. You explained it well, thanks." I still didn't know my role in helping Magee, but he seemed like the type of guy who'd let me know when he was good and ready, and not a minute before. After almost getting sick all over Osberg, I didn't mind waiting to find out more.

"Good. There should be a couple of men outside. Will you please tell them I'm ready before you go?"

I opened the flap, stepped into the sunlight, and relayed Magee's message to the two men outside. Then, I turned to begin my search for Ashley. Jeff called out my name. I searched for him, but several soldiers stood around, blocking my view.

Suddenly Jeff appeared beside me, his brows knit together and his shoulders so tight I could see the tendons standing out in his neck.

"What is it?" I asked.

He breathed heavily, and beads of perspiration ran down his hairline. "Have you seen the kids?" he asked.

"No. Why? What's going on?"

His hands trembled as he lifted a sheet of paper and offered it to me. "I think they're on the way to Granite Falls."

"What? No they're not. I just saw them a little while ago." I looked down at the page he'd given me. The loopy, handwritten note had only two words on it: Granite Falls. "What is this, Jeff?"

"When I went back to grab my pack, that note was on top of it."

"Looks like the writing of a teen girl. It's not Ashley's, though. Kylee's?"

"That's what I thought too. I went to ask her what it meant, but I can't find her. I can't find any of them."

His words suggested a possibility that I couldn't accept. "What do you mean you can't find them? They went to go eat. They're here somewhere."

"Libby, you're not listening. They're not here. The security Boom assigned to them is missing as well." He ran a hand over his head and closed his eyes. "I'm so stupid. I should have seen it earlier. We suspected they were Progression and were watching them, but they took so long to make their move. I thought we were wrong."

A chill ran up my back as his words sunk in. I scanned the area, expecting Ashley to pop up and tell us she was fine. "Ashley wouldn't have left."

"Not voluntarily, no."

I shook my head. He was wrong. He had to be wrong. "No. They're probably by the horses, goofing off."

"I checked. They're not there. They're not anywhere in this camp." Jeff grabbed my wrists and I realized I was trembling. "All three of them are gone. I think they've taken Ashley to Granite Falls, and we have to find Connor."

No. I was in a nightmare. Desperate for it to end, I pulled away from Jeff and started yelling. "Has anyone seen Ashley? She's missing!"

The soldiers all turned and looked at me.

"Ashley's missing!" I shouted again. "I need Connor!"

"Ma'am, please calm down. We'll find her," said a dark-haired soldier. "When was the last time you saw her?"

I turned away from him, desperate to find Connor. If I could just reach him, he would fix it. He'd find her and bring her back safely, because that's what he did. Then suddenly he was there, standing in front of me with worry etched into his features. Tears stung my eyes as I held out the paper toward him.

"Ashley is gone!" I cried. "They took her and we have to do something!"

"Are you certain?" Connor read the note, and then swore.

"I've searched the camp," Jeff said. "Ashley, Braden, and Kylee are all gone."

Boom climbed out of the tent behind Connor. Connor turned and offered him the note. Then he moved closer to me and interlaced his fingers in mine as we waited for Boom's reaction.

"I've heard rumors of a base in Granite Falls," Boom announced. "It would make sense."

Then the captain sprung into action.

"Mathers, find Stein," he barked to the soldier standing closest to him. "Tell him the kids are missing, and take him to where their tent was. We need to find out which way they went and make sure they're heading toward Granite Falls."

The soldier saluted and ran off.

Boom shouted for Marr.

Marr stepped forward with a salute. "Yes, Captain?"

"We need you to run a supply check. If they took so much as a bullet, I want to know about it," Boom ordered.

"Right away, Sir!" Marr hurried away.

The soldiers crowded in around us, awaiting orders. It felt so surreal, like I stood in the middle of some wartime movie, where the troops were amassing to go after the girl in distress. Only this time the girl in distress was Ashley. We'd been betrayed.

"They tricked us," I whispered.

Connor squeezed my shoulders. "We'll get her back."

"How could they do that?" I asked.

Nobody answered.

"Where the heck is Shortridge?" Boom asked. "He was pulling security on the kids. Someone find him. Now!"

Boom seemed to scan the group around us until he found who he was looking for. "Pearson, get a head count on those horses. Staten, take over security detail. Bump us up to forty percent. Connor, Liberty come with me. Everyone not pulling security or currently assigned, get this camp ready to move!"

Boom turned and rummaged through a case outside his tent. He pocketed something before marching toward the trees. Connor tugged on my hand, and we followed Boom away from the group. Once we could no longer see nor hear the camp, Boom turned and faced us.

"I have little or no intel on the Progression's Granite Falls base," he explained. "We came across a miner a while back who came from the town. He said that he'd packed up and left the minute the Progression made their appearance. He couldn't tell us much, other than the town had been overrun quickly. I wish there was more to give you."

"Give *us*? You mean you're not coming?" I pointed back at the camp as tears stung my eyes. "But they're packing up. I thought ... how can we save Ashley without the help of the soldiers?"

Connor squeezed my hand. "He can't come. They have marching orders."

"What does that even mean?"

Boom's eyes looked haunted and torn. He shook his head. "I'm sorry, Libby, but we cannot accompany you. A large Progression force is marching toward Fort Lewis, and they need us back to defend."

Boom and the Army weren't coming with us. I felt numb and hollow. I looked up and Connor and shrugged. "Well, we should get going then. Maybe we can catch her before they get to Granite Falls?"

Connor put his hands on the sides of my face, and then looked me in the eyes. I saw sorrow and defeat in his gaze, and it terrified me.

"I need you to go with Boom," Connor said.

"No." I tried to pull away from him, but he held on to my face.

"Libby, please."

"No! And how dare you even suggest such a thing. This is Ashley we're talking about. There is no reality in which you to talk me out of going after her, so you can put that out of your mind right now." I yanked my face out of his hands and stepped away from him.

"This is a trap, Libby. This whole thing has been a setup. Major Thompson planted his soldiers, and I scooped them up like an idiot and brought them into our camp. Now they have Ashley."

"Right." I nodded. "Because she's your daughter and the major has his shorts in a wad because you got away and humiliated him. I get it. Just like I get that you need help. You're not walking into this trap alone."

"I'm a professional, and they set this trap for me. Not for you. You can go on with the Army and be safe … safer … at Fort Lewis."

A breeze picked up, blowing against my face. With it came images: clouds, wings, fire. A series of chirps sounded from above me. I looked up to see a small sparrow perched on a branch and watching me, its head tilted to the side as it sang.

"A sparrow," I whispered as the dream came flooding back. "I sang and they listened."

"What?" Connor asked.

"The sparrow." I pointed at the bird. That's the answer. "I have to go with you."

"You're not making any sense. What does a sparrow have to do with anything?"

Knowing he wouldn't understand me, I turned to Boom. "Last night I had a dream. It seemed stupid at the time, but now, I think I understand the meaning. I was a bird … a sparrow. This fire was raging out of control, destroying everything. God called me to be the sparrow. I'm supposed to talk to them. I have to tell the kids that there's another way. Only, I don't know what that other way is."

"Another way?" Boom asked. He shook his head and crossed himself. Then he looked up at the sparrow and nodded. "Of course."

Connor took a step back and glanced from Boom to me. His eyes went round and wild, like a doctor in an asylum, trying to decide which whacko to sedate first. "What are you two talking about? There is no other way."

Boom reached into his pocket. "Actually—"

Footsteps interrupted him, and then Jeff appeared, looking grim and worn. "Excuse me, Captain," he said.

"You have a report for me?" Boom asked. He had retrieved a folded paper from his pocket and he held it in his hand.

"Yes, Sir. Two horses are missing, but nothing else. Stein has confirmed that they're heading northwest, toward Granite Falls. The camp is ready to move on your order, Sir."

"Was anyone able to locate Shortridge?" Boom asked.

"Yes. He's dead, Sir." Jeff frowned. "We found his body just north of the camp. He was stabbed in the chest."

"How the heck did they get their hands on a knife?" Boom asked. Shaking his head, he crossed himself again and muttered a quick prayer. Then, almost as an afterthought, he said, "Thank you, Corporal Thompson."

Jeff had been dismissed, but he did not leave. Instead, he walked over and stood on the side of me opposite of Connor. Boom's eyebrows rose in question.

"I'd like to request permission to accompany the first sergeant on his mission, Sir."

"No," Connor replied.

Jeff tensed. "With all due respect, First Sergeant, you're going up against my father. Nobody knows him better than I do, and you will need my help if you have any chance at getting her out of there alive."

"No. Since we are going up against your father, you have a conflict of interests. Who's to say where your true loyalty stands? Speaking of which, where were you when the kids took off?"

I rested my hand on Connor's arm. "Jeff isn't the enemy here. He wants to help us, and we should let him."

"There is no 'us'!" Connor snapped. "You and Jeff are going with Boom and I'm going for Ashley alone."

I crossed my arms. "So, that's it? You're just going to storm the town and kill as many soldiers as you can before they put a bullet between your eyes? Because, you know, that'll get her back, right?"

"Libby—"

"Don't." I held up a hand. "I know you're good at what you do, but not even you can take down an entire town of soldiers. You think you're the only one who has a role to play in this? It all rests on the shoulders of the great and mighty Connor Dunstan, right? Well, you know what? I will follow you anyway. Boom will not hold me against my will, and I swear I will crawl to Granite Falls if that's what it takes. This is about more than Ashley, Connor. I know this sounds crazy, but I can't shake the feeling that I'm needed in that town. I keep having these dreams and … and these kids need a chance. They need a choice, and I think I'm supposed to give them that choice."

"What could you possibly say to them to convince them to leave the Progression?" he asked. "These are not sweet kids who just need a hug. These are trained killers and we are their enemies."

I could tell he didn't believe me, and I didn't know how to explain it. Turning toward Boom, I saw the paper in his hand, and asked, "You had something about another way?"

"Oh, right!" Boom handed the paper to Connor.

Connor unfolded it and scanned the page, his eyes growing round as he read. "The Army is really willing to do this?" he asked.

Boom nodded. "These are desperate times, and the US military recognizes the fact that many of the Progression soldiers were coerced into service by extreme measures. Most were never even given a choice. Unfortunately, I have not had the opportunity to use this resource, but perhaps you will." He spoke to Connor, but looked at me.

Although Connor didn't show me the document, I knew the Army had to be offering something good. Something worthwhile. I made a mental note to get the details from him later.

Straightening my back so I stood taller, I said, "I'm going, Connor."

Jeff smiled and leaned closer to me. "Me too."

The veins pulsing at Connor's temples made him look dangerously close to an aneurism.

Boom slid next to Connor and lowered his voice to barely above a whisper. "Both Liberty and Corporal Thompson would make valuable assets on this mission."

Connor shook his head. "*Et tu, Brute*?" he asked.

Boom nodded. "It doesn't count as betrayal if it's in your best interests."

"Keeping Liberty alive would be in my best interest."

Boom ignored him and turned toward me. "He doesn't deserve you, but I'm glad you've decided to stick by him. Thank you."

Boom held his hands out to me and I stepped in to hug him. He kissed my cheek, then held my face steady as he whispered, "His eye is on the sparrow."

I froze. Despite the warmth that rushed through my veins, goose bumps sprouted up across my flesh. *Of course.* My mind spun, recalling verses and a song talking about how even the life of a sparrow was precious to God.

"Thank you," I whispered and gave Boom's shoulders a squeeze before letting go and backing away to wipe my eyes.

Next, he turned toward Jeff. "You're a good soldier and a great friend, Thompson. I cannot officially grant you permission to go after Ashley any more than I can grant permission to Connor. But, if you were to leave with him, I also cannot spare the men to stop you."

"Thank you, Captain," Jeff replied, shaking Boom's hand.

Boom faced Connor. "Also, if you were to take a couple of horses, while I wasn't looking of course, I couldn't be expected to prevent that. I bet there will be two all saddled and ready, since we are packing up to go south."

The gratitude in Connor's eyes made my heart melt. I didn't quite understand what went on between the two of them, but I could tell it meant the world to Connor. Finally Connor lunged forward and embraced Boom. When they pulled apart, the two studied each other for a moment.

"*Hermano,*" Boom said, holding out his hand.

They did some sort of complicated handshake, and Connor's smirk returned, dissolving the somberness of the moment. He cocked his head to the side and said, "Don't tear up, old lady, you aren't free of me yet. We'll catch up to you on the road to Fort Lewis."

"Looking forward to it." Boom smiled back. "Give 'em hell, Conman."

CHAPTER TWENTY-FOUR

Liberty

AFTER BOOM FINISHED saying his goodbyes, he turned and headed back toward camp. Connor grabbed my hand and we stood there for several minutes, looking in the direction Boom had gone. Jeff stood beside us, but nobody said anything. Valuable time ticked away, and I started to get antsy.

"Don't we need to go get our supplies and the horses?" I asked "What are we waiting for?"

"Boom needs time," Connor explained.

Time for what he didn't say, and I didn't ask. After what seemed like an eternity, Connor tugged on my hand and said it was time to go. When we returned to the camp, we found our bags just outside the tree line. Boom had the soldiers lined up, facing away from us, while he paced in front of them, talking. I heard the words 'marching orders' again before Connor pulled me back into the trees. As Boom had blatantly hinted, two horses waited, saddled and ready for us, grazing away from the rest of the herd.

"That Boom guy was cut from some pretty great cloth," I declared, following Connor, who crept toward Paint.

Connor nodded. "The best."

Jeff slunk in beside us, and then split off to mount the second horse, a chestnut colored Arabian that gave Jeff a dubious stare down as he approached. I looked past our horses into the herd, searching for Cinnamon. Since I didn't see the horse, I assumed she was one of the two the kids had taken.

Connor tossed Jeff his pack, which Jeff tied to his horse's saddle. Then Connor mounted Paint, offered me the stirrup, and pulled me up to sit behind him. After I settled myself on the horse's back, I wrapped my arms around Connor's waist. He clicked his tongue and Paint lunged forward.

As we walked away, I leaned against Connor's back, finding comfort in the contact. "That was too easy. I'm sure the soldiers heard us and knew what we were doing. Why didn't anyone try to stop us?" I asked him.

"Every soldier in that camp feels responsible for Ashley's disappearance. Each of us let our guard down, and now, she's gone. They can't come with us, but they won't keep us from getting her back."

With my cheek pressed against his back, I nodded.

I shouldn't have let her go.

My throat constricted. Squeezing my eyes closed against the guilt I felt, I reminded myself that Ashley didn't need me to turn into some sniveling, regret-encrusted weakling. She needed me to be a strong and courageous warrior who would walk through the enemy's camp and retrieve her.

"We'll rescue her," Connor said over his shoulder. He tapped Paint's sides with his heels, springing the horse into a gallop.

I fully understood the meaning behind his message. Either we'd save Ashley, or we'd die trying. Considering the implications of death made me squeeze Connor even tighter. There were so many things I wanted to do before I died, and I couldn't—in good conscience—neglect the words I'd put off for so long. Leaning against his back, I vowed to summon my courage and tell him how I felt before we ran off and got ourselves killed.

Jeff followed as we raced up the Pilchuck River until it crossed the Granite Falls-Pilchuck Road. The map showed that the road that would take us right through the town, so we left the riverbank and climbed onto the pavement.

As we distanced ourselves from the river, an eerie silence engulfed the land. Connor's back tensed against me, and I pulled away from him enough to scan the area for threats, but I didn't see anything. He reined Paint to a fast walk as trees and foliage fell away to large fenced-in yards and razed buildings. The clop-clop of the horses' hooves shattered the quiet, announcing our presence to the world. Connor led Paint to the side of the road, where the grass would muffle the sounds of our arrival.

Throughout our ride, my mind kept drifting back to Braden. I replayed our conversations in my head, making mental notes of the way he'd reacted to everything we'd talked about. Although I knew the kid had issues, I could have sworn I'd been getting through to him.

If I'd been getting through, though, would he really have taken Ash? And, who killed Shortridge? How could I be so wrong about Braden?

Then I thought about the last time I saw Braden. He had thanked me, and then paused, as if he wanted to say more, but couldn't.

Was he trying to warn me? Did he want to say goodbye? Maybe I did get through to him ...

Connor turned Paint down a gravel driveway. It wound between a few rows of trees before ending in a circular driveway. A cobblestone path led away from the driveway, through a set of marble pillars. The path pressed on, inviting guests to walk between a second set of pillars that stood on either side of an arched, double-door entry way. To the left of the pillars was an attached three-car garage. To the right, giant windows wrapped around the two story home, exposing it to the trees. Every inch of the home that wasn't covered in windows was wrapped in Tyvek.

"Where are we?" I asked.

"A client was building this house," Connor replied, reining Paint to a stop on the path between the pillars. He dismounted and peeked in the nearest window. Since I didn't know what he sought, I stayed on the horse and shrugged at Jeff.

"What's the plan?" Jeff asked, leading his horse to where Connor stood.

"We're almost to town," Connor replied, turning away from the house and facing Jeff. "Any idea where that sick psycho would take her?"

Jeff rubbed his chin for a moment. "The major likes to make a show of it. He usually goes for irony or drama. Or both. Libby, does your map show buildings?"

"No, just roads," I replied.

"My client was using settlement money to build this house," Connor said. "Before we took his case to court, I spent some time in and around town, checking out the safety issues he reported at the quarries. I'm relatively familiar with the area, and if I knew what the major was looking for, I could probably tell you where it is."

Jeff tapped his forehead. "Think coliseum or theatre. The bigger and brighter, the better. If we were in Seattle, he'd be at the Seahawks stadium. If we were in Portland, it would probably be the Rose Garden."

"Granite Falls doesn't have anything like that," Connor replied. He started pacing in front of the garage. Then he stopped and turned toward Jeff. "Granite Falls is better known for what's outside of town: the quarries, some waterfalls and the ice caves."

Jeff shook his head. "No, he'd want something in town. He's pulling you into this trap, so he's not going to hide it from you. What's the biggest building here?"

"They've got some nice houses in the area. The City Hall is downtown, but it's not very big."

"What about a school?" I asked. Both men turned to face me and I got the distinct feeling they had forgotten I was even there. I tried not to let that bug me as I plunged ahead. "I grew up in a small town and the biggest building we had was the high school. All the town's major functions were held there."

Jeff looked to Connor. "He'd love the irony in taking his kids back to school."

"Libby, you're a genius." Connor laughed. "The Granite Falls High School is a beautiful building, built only a few years ago. I would bet money that's where he is."

I slid down from Paint's back and plucked the map out of my pocket. "All right. Can you show us where it is?"

CHAPTER TWENTY-FIVE

Connor

CONNOR STOOD BEHIND Liberty, eying the map in her hand.

"This is where we are," he said, pointing just south of the town. "The school is on Burn Road, between Quarry and Jordan. We should tie the horses up here, and leave them and our supplies behind so we can sneak in. Maybe if we take a couple of these side streets, we'll be able to avoid their notice for a while."

As he visualized the route they would have to travel, he couldn't deny the impossibility of their rescue mission. They had no intel and limited weapons and ammo. He leaned closer to Liberty, drawing strength from her presence, and accepted the fact that the best case scenario of any plan he could concoct would end in his death so she and Ashley could survive. He held her hand and wished he had time to put the ring in his pocket on her finger.

Determined to save Ashley first, Connor's mind kept running scenarios. They'd somehow get past the unknown number of guards, and do reconnaissance on the school. As soon as they found out where Ashley was being kept, they'd go in with guns blazing and … and probably die horribly. The major knew who Connor was, and this time he'd be ready for him. There'd be no creeping past security and no Boom to come in and blow the place up to rescue them. The major wouldn't have lured Connor to Granite Falls if he wasn't prepared to take him down.

Feeling defeated, Connor sighed. "You guys don't have to do this."

"I'm pretty sure we've already had this discussion," Liberty replied.

"Yes, but let's be real about this situation. I have no idea what we're up against. There could be a thousand Progression soldiers waiting for us just inside this town."

"I know."

"We're going in blind with almost no resources."

"I know," she said again.

"Look," Connor growled. "Nothing but death is waiting for me in that town. I would like you to live. Please? For me?"

She looked up at Connor, her green eyes bright and full of fire. "If you have faith as small as a mustard seed, you can say to this mountain, 'Move from here to there,' and it will move. Nothing will be impossible for you."

"Faith? Libby, we're talking about armed soldiers here. What if your God wants you to die in His name? Will that help Ashley? No, these guys are going to mow down your faith with their assault rifles. Do you have any idea what thirty rounds per magazine will do to your faith?"

She took a deep breath and stepped back. For a moment, Connor thought she would keep stepping. He wished she would mount Paint and ride south until she caught up with the Army. Boom would see her safely to the fort, where she could live out the rest of her days in peace.

At least until the Progression comes and levels the fort.

Even if Liberty walked away now, nothing would guarantee she'd even make it to Boom's platoon, much less survive the next Progression attack. Safety was just an illusion that had been shattered the moment the economy fell. There was no "safety" anymore.

Liberty turned and handed Jeff the map. "Can I please have a moment alone with Connor?" she asked him.

"Yeah, of course." Jeff replied. "Just yell if you need me."

He turned and walked around the house.

Liberty watched him go. When he disappeared sight, she slid in front of Connor. She put her hands on his chest and looked up at him, her bright green eyes brimming with unshed tears. Connor felt the weight of his rebuke and wished he could apologize for the reality check he'd given her. Truthfully, though, she needed to know what she was getting into.

He pushed a stray curl behind her ear and let his hand linger there.

"It's my fault they took Ashley," Liberty whispered.

Connor tried to object, but she shushed him.

"No, it is. I never should have let her go to breakfast with Kylee and Braden. Speaking of which, I'm seriously stumped about Braden. Connor, I swear I was getting through to that kid."

Connor frowned. "I thought you were, too."

"He thanked me before he left."

"He did?" Connor asked.

Liberty nodded. "Said it was for teaching him how to play Blackjack, but it wasn't. He tried to warn me, and I totally missed it."

Connor considered this new information for a moment before asking, "Do you think Braden wants out of the Progression?"

"Yes. I don't know. Maybe I just want him to want out? It feels like ... I feel like we're missing something. My heart keeps telling me that we're not too late to help the Progression kids. We just need to figure out the way." She looked away and blinked back tears.

Overwhelmed by her passion, Connor leaned forward, wanting more of this crazy woman who refused to give up hope. "I love you." he whispered.

She turned back to face him, and his lips landed on hers. His intention had been to just give her a quick peck, but she grabbed the sides of his vest and pulled him into her, deepening the kiss. Heat blossomed in Connor's chest, spreading through his veins as the kiss continued. He wrapped his arms around her and held her close.

Liberty broke contact. Then she leaned her head against his chest.

"I know," she replied. "I love you, too."

Connor breathed deeply, and allowed himself to enjoy the moment. She loved him, and her admission of that love had finally opened the door he'd been trying to unlock. If they had a chance of living through this, things would change between them. He'd be able to pursue her fully, without fear of scaring her off. He'd marry her.

If only we could get through this alive.

Liberty looked at him like she wanted to say more. He stared into her eyes and waited, knowing from past experience that if he waited long enough she'd say more than she intended.

"I love you," she said again, this time with a smile. "And I need you to trust me."

Wondering what she was up to, he answered, "I do trust you."

"Have you ever seen the movie 'The Princess Bride'?" she asked.

"Long ago. Why?"

"There was a scene in the Fire Swamp, where Wesley was attacked by giant rats and Buttercup just gasped and sat there, helpless. Do you remember the scene?"

Feeling a little lost and confused, Connor answered, "Vaguely."

"The last guy I dated … we watched that movie together, and I asked him why Buttercup didn't pick up the sword and kill the rat. He told me that Wesley had to be the ultimate hero and save her. He couldn't do that if Buttercup could take care of herself. I broke up with him the next day. You need to understand something. I will never be your Princess Buttercup. I will pick up that damn sword and kill whatever rat threatens you. But those kids … they're not rats."

"Okay. Where are you going with this?"

Liberty's smile widened. "This thing is hopeless, right? No way we can survive it?"

Connor frowned, wondering why she seemed so happy about their assured demise. "I have been trained to survive, but the major knows what I'm capable of. He's no fool, so I'm sure he'll be prepared."

She pulled away from Connor and started to pace. "So … I have this idea."

"Yes?"

"It's completely insane. Seriously, it makes no sense at all, but I know we have to try it."

She'd whipped up some cockamamie plan that would, no doubt, put her directly in danger. Connor could feel a headache coming on in anticipation of the details. He rubbed at his temples and asked, "This has to do with the dream doesn't it? And the sparrow? What's the plan?"

"Yes, but there were multiple dreams. And, you can't say no until you hear me out. Oh, and just a friendly reminder that we're all going to die horribly anyway. This is a 'why the heck not try it?' type plan."

"Sounds terrifying."

"Most definitely the craziest thing I've ever considered." Holding her hand out expectantly, she added, "I'm gonna need that paper Boom gave you."

* * *

Once Jeff returned, Liberty laid out her plan, and she was right, Connor didn't like it at all.

"So, you're just going to march up to the door and ask for a conference with the Progression soldiers so you can explain the error of their ways and encourage them all to defect to the Army?" he asked.

"I'm not going to ask for a conference, you're going to buy me one."

"The major will never let you get a word in. They'll break your beautiful neck the minute you start talking."

"She doesn't have to speak," Jeff said. "At least, not at first. When they search her, they'll find the letter from Fort Lewis. The major always has one of his cronies read things he finds aloud to him. Everyone within earshot will hear it."

Connor frowned at Jeff, wishing he wouldn't encourage Liberty's insanity. "Okay. Then they'll know about the Army's offer. What then?"

Liberty put a hand on his arm. "I'll need you to buy me some alone time with the soldiers. You'll have to keep the major busy."

"He's not dumb enough to leave the safety of the school, so how do you propose I do that?"

Jeff chuckled. "That's why you treat him like he's the most intelligent man on the planet, and assure him that we're all mere mortals, cowering in his high and mighty shadow. Use his vast ego to bait your trap."

Liberty lit up, smiling at Jeff. "Right. Pride comes before the fall. You can utilize his arrogance to get him out of the school."

Connor thought for a moment. "He'll have guards posted. If I take down enough of them ..."

Jeff nodded. "Exactly. Now you see."

"What about you?" Connor asked Jeff.

"Me? I'm going with Libby."

Connor blinked. "Come again?"

"I'm walking in there with Libby."

The idea swished around in Connor's head while he tried to figure out if he liked it. On one hand, he didn't trust Jeff. But on the other hand, he knew Jeff would keep Ashley and Liberty safe. Best case scenario, Jeff could be trusted, would try to help, and would most likely die alongside them. Worst case scenario, the major's son would roll over on Connor to save Ashley and Liberty. Since Connor could live with either option, he nodded. "All right."

"What?" Liberty asked. She turned toward Jeff. "Are you sure? Your dad—"

"Won't kill me," Jeff interrupted her, "—He'll be mad as hell, but he won't. I'm coming so you won't have to go in alone."

"Jeff, you don't have to do this."

"I know. But I'm going to."

"All righty, then. Might as well remove the gear now." Liberty's expression melted into an odd mixture of relief and sadness. She undid her holster and held it toward Connor. "Remember when you gave me this? You were such a cocky jerk."

Connor accepted it and slid it through his belt loops. "Why? Because I pointed out the lack of wisdom in storing your gun in your waistband? Yeah, I was such a jerk that I gave you a present that saved your butt. Probably literally."

She rolled her eyes and tried to hide a smile. "You're still a cocky jerk, but I know you're gonna save my butt again." Next, she handed him her Sigma.

Connor's chest tightened, touched by her faith in him. "I still think it's a bad idea. You're talking about negotiating with the Progression. They don't negotiate."

Liberty cupped his cheek in her hand. "I know, but I have to try. And there's one more little detail I forgot to mention."

"Why do I get the feeling this is about to get a lot more complicated?"

"I need you to promise me something."

He sighed. "Do I get to find out what it is first?"

The side of her mouth turned up into a smirk. "Yes. Please promise me you'll try not to kill any of the kids."

"I don't think you realize what you're asking. The odds are already stacked against us. These kids are going to be armed and shooting at me, and now you're telling me I can't shoot back? This is suicide."

"No, that's not what I'm saying. Shoot back all you want. Just try not to kill them."

"Sometimes they leave me no choice."

"I know," she admitted. "But, if at all possible ... please?"

"They're dangerous."

She nodded. "You're more dangerous."

She had a point. Connor looked from Liberty to Jeff. Jeff's mouth hung open as he stared at Liberty's back, but when he noticed Connor watching, he closed his mouth and shrugged. Connor wondered if Jeff was having second thoughts after the revelation of Liberty's "no kill" policy.

"Please, Connor," Liberty said, drawing his attention back to her. "This is important."

He shrugged. "I'll do what I can."

"Life, Connor, and time. I need them in abundance. Pretend they're currency, and get me enough of each to purchase the fattest diamond on the planet."

He holstered her Sigma and said, "You've never struck me as the type to be interested in diamonds."

Liberty grinned. "I'm not, but Ash is." She slid her pack from her shoulders and walked toward the house to stash it.

Jeff removed all of his weapons. He stepped forward and offered them to Connor. Connor declined each except a small dagger that he sheathed around his ankle.

"I need to travel light," he explained. "You should put the rest in the house. We'll come back for them on the way out."

"Right." Jeff nodded. He watched the house and lowered his voice. "You can cut the crap with me. We both know we're going to die in there."

Connor cocked his head to the side. "If you really believe that, why are you coming?"

Still watching the house, Jeff replied, "Because she's the only person alive who would do the same for me. Besides, who knows? My dad might spare them if I slip back on his chain." With that, Jeff marched toward the house with his weapons in hand.

Moments later Liberty reappeared and scurried toward Connor.

"I should get going," Connor said when she drew near.

Chewing on her lip, she nodded.

He grabbed her hand and pulled her into a hug. "When this is over, you'll break down and give me a fair shot, right?" he asked.

Liberty raised an eyebrow. "Like in the arm?"

He squeezed her tighter. "You know what I mean. A shot at making *us* work. No more running away or dumping coffee on yourself to avoid alone-time with me. A real chance to see what this is between us."

She nodded slowly. "Yes. Jeff and I will find Ashley, and then you will march through the doors playing the part of my knight in shining camo. How could I not throw myself at you?"

"Oh, throw yourself, eh? I didn't go that far, but if you insist…"

She shoved him, but her smile told him she wasn't angry. "You're being a cocky jerk again."

He shrugged. "Sorry. Habit."

She took a step back, but he grabbed her arm and pulled her to him. "One last kiss?" he asked.

"No." Liberty silenced his lips with her finger. "Don't talk like that. There will be many more kisses."

She slowly lowered her finger, but her gaze didn't leave his. He looked into her eyes and saw persistent endurance steeped in courage and faith. He stroked the side of her face, marveling at her. She didn't pull away, so he leaned down until his lips were almost touching hers.

"One of many, then," he whispered.

Liberty threw her arms around his neck and kissed him. She tasted of fear and desperation, and he wished he could pick her up and whisk her off to safety, as if such a thing existed anymore.

All too soon, Liberty pulled away and gave him a sad smile. Her eyes were moist, but she didn't look away.

"I love you," he said.

"I know. I love you too, and I'll see you on the other side."

CHAPTER TWENTY-SIX

Liberty

JEFF AND I stood on the corner of West Galina Street and Portage Avenue. I pointed up Portage Avenue and Jeff nodded. Yep. We were going the right way.

"You okay?" Jeff asked.

"Yeah. I just need a minute." I bent over to tie my shoe. Since it was already tied I pulled the string loose, and then tied it again. *Just breathe. You can do this. You have to do this.*

"All better," I lied. Nothing was better. We were about to do something really stupid and it had all been my idea.

Jeff waited for me to summon my courage and stand up. "You okay?" he asked.

I nodded. "Never better."

Because he was a good friend, he didn't call me out for being a liar. Instead, he waited for me to join him, and then we walked side by side up the center of Portage Avenue. Strolling down the center of the street, we made a lot of noise, trying to make sure all eyes were on us while Connor did his thing. It worked in our favor, really, since the more nervous I got, the more I talked and the goofier I got. I felt like an adrenaline junkie about to jump off a cliff.

We walked past a thrashed house with a "For Sale" sign sticking out of the roof. I pointed at the home and asked Jeff what he thought of it.

"Too small. I'm looking for something that will hold the twenty or so kids I want to have."

"Twenty or so? Your poor wife."

He laughed, and I loved that about him. Terrified out of our minds, on the way to see his sick and demented father, and still we laughed about real estate and kids.

"There are great schools in this district, though. Are you sure you won't reconsider?"

He tapped his chin thoughtfully. "Perhaps, but let's see what else we can find."

Taking our own sweet time, we continued on. At the end of the street, we found a ransacked fast food restaurant on one side and a partially burnt down teriyaki joint on the other.

"So … about lunch. What do you say? Teriyaki or burgers?" I asked.

"Both," he replied. "I'm famished."

"Ohh, good answer!" I rubbed my stomach. "I want fries. Steak fries, waffle fries, sweet potato fries, pretty much all the fries ever made. I want them all."

We turned left on 96th Street and passed a coffee hut.

"With a salted caramel latte," Jeff added.

"And that's why we're friends. You'd get me one too, right?"

He nodded, way too vigorously.

We passed a few more stores, one of which had a table and benches in front of it.

"Shall we sit for a moment?" I asked, gesturing toward the table.

"We shall."

The glass front doors were shattered, and the remains were strewn throughout the entrance. Jeff and I made a big show of walking over and plopping down in front of the large, unbroken window. Then we stared into the shop and discussed the menu, arguing about what we'd order. I opted for roast beef, while Jeff crooned on about pastrami.

While we chatted it up like old friends who'd happened across each other, I caught movement out of the corner of my eye. Jeff waggled his eyebrows at me, and I knew he'd seen it too. We had an escort, which was great, because that was the plan.

That's the plan, stomach, stop twisting in knots!

My discomfort must have shown on my face, because Jeff leaned forward and whispered, "It's not too late to back out of this."

We were so far past backing out that we could no longer see the entrance sign, but I smiled at him anyway. "Think I'm afraid of a couple of kids? Please."

"Shall we be on our way then?" he asked.

"We shall!"

I stood on wobbly legs. The stupidity of what we were about to do was finally catching up to me, assaulting my nerves. Mumbling under my breath about eyes and sparrows, I pushed on. We turned right on Jordan Road, and I heard feet scampering behind us.

"Are you sure this is the right way?" I asked Jeff.

The scenery changed. It felt like we'd stepped out of the town and into the forest. The surprisingly wooded area held only a few houses, with no hint of a school anywhere close.

Jeff nodded. "This is what the map said."

"Hmm." I scratched my head. "It must be the school where Sleeping Beauty attends. Any moment now the twelve dwarfs will jump out and take us captive."

Jeff chuckled.

We turned left on Burn Road. The right side led to a middle-class housing community, with small homes and tiny fenced yards. The homes sported broken windows, and were covered in graffiti that had taken them from cheerful and quaint to creepy and defiled. The forest lined the left side of the road, complete with lush bushes and tall trees. Elephants could have been hiding behind those trees and we wouldn't have known.

While my mind counted the number of possible Progression guns that could be aimed at us, my feet stumbled on a pocket of air. Jeff grabbed my hand and narrowly kept me from falling on my face. After that, I focused on putting one foot in front of the other.

We passed a red brick elementary school on the right side of the road. A long parking lot stretched through the rest of the block, making me feel exposed and vulnerable. To the left, the forest was broken up by a small parking lot that led to a brick church with a tall white steeple. I stopped and stared at the building for a moment, thankful for all that it symbolized.

"Uh, Libby," Jeff said, tugging on my sleeve and pulling me back to reality. "Look at the road."

Lewd and suggestive graffiti covered the blacktop. I read a few creative ideas about what people could do with themselves before I saw what Jeff was talking about.

My name was scrawled across the street in giant red letters, with an arrow pointing toward the main entrance of the high school.

Goosebumps rose across my flesh as we crept closer to the paint. The paint smelled fresh. Curious, I reached down and swiped my finger across the surface.

"Still wet," I said, holding up my paint-stained finger for Jeff to see.

He paled, reflecting my thoughts on the matter.

His fear made me even more nervous, so naturally, I opened my mouth. "I always wanted to be the popular girl in high school. Be careful what you ask for, I guess."

I turned toward the school, wishing I could run the opposite direction. But, somewhere in that building, Ashley waited for us.

Jeff rested a hand on my shoulder. "You ready?"

I sighed. "Nope. Where do you suppose the welcoming committee is?"

"They don't need to come to us. They know we're coming to them."

"Good point. Well, I'd hate to keep them waiting."

We stepped over my name and turned into the high school driveway. As Connor had said, the school had a unique, modern design, different from any other public school I'd seen.

Pillars sprung up in the front, leaning outward and supporting the roof, which also appeared to be leaning forward. Large windows covered the front of the second story as well as the front entrance, and wrapped around to the sides.

The glass panels of the front door were broken. Little shards still clung to the sides, looking jagged and dangerous. Strangely, the door handle was locked, so Jeff reached in through one of the panels and opened the door.

Out of habit, I reached for my Sigma, pausing as I remembered that Connor had it. "Leaving the weapons behind might not have been the wisest idea," I told Jeff.

He shrugged. "They never would have let us get this far if they thought we were armed."

Although I'd only actually used my gun once, being without it sure made me feel naked. Shaking off the feeling, I crept forward.

Glass crunched beneath our feet, making stealth impossible even if that had been our plan. We eased past the entryway and into the wide entrance hallway to get a look around. A large glass window on the right side of the hall had web-like cracks running through it. Beyond the window, chairs surrounded an office counter. A decomposing body occupied the high-backed chair behind the counter. I glanced at the corpse long enough to verify that it wasn't someone I knew before continuing on.

The first classroom we came to was on the left, and we paused to peek in. A few chairs had been turned over on their sides, and the teacher's desk was flipped upside down with the drawers gone.

"Looks like the kids had a party, but where did they go afterward?" I asked.

Jeff shrugged. "Guess we better keep looking."

The building was quiet, but not silent. We could hear faint sounds of conversation, but couldn't tell which direction they came from. The whole place smelled musty, with a hint of decay and paint. Sniffing, I followed the paint smells to the right, until I ran into another note for me. This one, just like the last, was tagged in red spray paint. 'This way,' it read, with an arrow pointing to the right.

"Aww, sweet. They left us directions."

Jeff grunted and wiped his eyes. He was sweating. A lot, judging by the glistening sheen across his forehead. Even terrified of what his father would do to him, the lovable idiot had followed me into the school. I was pretty certain that Jeff and Boom were cut from the same cloth.

The front of the building was bright with natural light from the large windows. As we ventured inward, however, the rooms grew progressively darker. I didn't want to walk into the dark places like some stupid girl in a bad horror flick, but the note they'd left me pointed us further in. I looked to Jeff, and he nodded. Yes, he thought we should do what the message said and venture into the dim, sinister hallway.

Awesome.

We took two steps in, and then heard footsteps. Jeff and I froze, leaning against the wall more out of habit than any sort of delusional belief that they didn't know exactly where we were.

Jeff held up one finger, signifying that only one solder approached. Wondering why they were only sending one, I peeled my petrified self off the wall and waited in the middle of the hallway. Kylee marched forward, coming to a stop directly in front of me.

CHAPTER TWENTY-SEVEN

Connor

WITH A HEAVY heart, Connor left the house. The thick trees surrounding Granite Falls provided him cover as he drifted to the west and skirted the town. Traveling at a steady jog, he crossed Ray Gray Road and stayed west of Gardner Lake. Then he sprinted across Crooked Mile Road and paused when he reached the trees, catching his breath while waiting to see if he'd been spotted. No alarms sounded and no enemies confronted him, so he turned north.

Crossing Highway 92 proved a bit more problematic. He peeked out of the trees. The wide highway would leave him open and exposed the moment he stepped onto it. Searching for an alternative place to cross, he looked both directions. The town lay to the east, and west led to a four-way intersection with an island in the middle. Deciding the intersection was his best option, he slipped back into the trees and went to investigate.

Three empty flagpoles jutted up from the island, stretching into the sky. The poles were surrounded by bushes and a spattering of six-foot-tall evergreens. Prime location with plenty of coverage for a lookout. Watching the island, Connor picked up a small rock and tossed it into the street. The rock hit the pavement, and then bounced a few times before coming to a stop on the solid yellow line.

On the island, bushes shook and a young man wearing fatigues crouched and aimed an assault rifle at the highway. Connor ducked behind a tree as the soldier scanned the area with his weapon.

"Come on, check it out," Connor whispered.

He heard no movement, though, and when he peeked out from behind the tree, the soldier was nowhere in sight.

Well, that's pretty lazy.

Connor picked up a second rock and tossed it into the street. It rolled and came to a stop beside the first one.

This time the soldier on the island grumbled as he stood. With his gun drawn, he crept out from behind the brush and headed toward the road, scanning the trees as he went.

Still trying for stealth, Connor unsheathed Jeff's dagger and waited as the soldier walked to the center of the road and glanced down at the rocks. Then he shook his head and leveled his gun in Connor's general direction.

"Anybody there?" he asked. "If you're there, come out with your hands up, and I won't shoot you."

Yeah right.

Sweat glistened across the boy's forehead. He wiped it away with a shaky hand, and then swung the weapon from side to side, searching.

Connor lowered his M4 to the ground, sheathed Jeff's knife, and put his hands in the air. "Okay, I'm unarmed and coming out." He stepped out from behind the tree in time to see the soldier jump.

"I'm just passing through town. Don't mean anybody any harm." At Liberty's insistence, Connor had shed his fatigues in favor of jeans and a t-shirt. He was beginning to see the wisdom in her suggestion.

"That's close enough," the soldier said. "Where are you coming from?"

"Sultan."

"Where you headin'?"

"Arlington. I have some family up there that I want to check on. See if they're still alive."

The soldier eyed him for a moment before saying, "You're gonna have to come with me first."

"Why?" Connor stepped forward. "Is there a problem?"

"Everyone has to meet the major. Now, keep your hands in the air and don't make any sudden movements. I'm going to come over and make sure you don't have any weapons on you."

Connor stood still as the soldier approached him. Before the soldier made it to the side of the road, Connor lunged forward and grasped the barrel of the gun from underneath, knocking it upward. With the gun now aimed at the sky, he kicked the soldier's left kneecap. Bone cracked as the soldier cried out in pain and fell over. Connor yanked the gun free and spun it around, aiming it at the soldier writhing in pain at his feet.

"You're no civilian," the soldier said. He glared up at Connor.

"Never said I was."

"You're the guy the camp is talking about, aren't you?"

"Maybe. What are they saying?"

"You're with the Army," he spat.

Connor saw the cap of a small container in the soldier's shaky hand. He swooped down and plucked it out of the kid's grasp.

"You say 'Army' like it's a bad word," Connor said, studying the vial.

"Traitors. Liars. Murderers. You guys created us, but when we stopped being your puppets, you came in like friends, only to kill our brothers and sisters."

Connor chuckled. "That's a pretty speech, but guess what? You're still a puppet." He held up the vial and let the sunlight shine through the glass.

The soldier's brows pinched together, but he did not respond.

"I could have killed you a dozen times by now, starting with when you first peeked your head over that bush. The Progression values you so much they gave you crap training and sent you out here to face threats alone."

"I'm not a—" he clamped his mouth shut.

"I'd imagine there are several one to two man patrols walking around—also a careless waste of soldiers. The major's not trying to stop me. He's throwing away your lives to lead me to him. And, just in case I don't kill you, he gives you a little something to do it yourselves." Connor frowned. "What does he tell you to make you do it?"

The soldier stared at the ground.

"That we're the ones torturing you all?"

"I think you broke my kneecap."

"Yeah, I did." Connor leaned over and searched the soldier, finding a handgun strapped to his ankle. He disarmed him and stood. "And I did it so I could leave you alive."

He dropped the vial on the ground in front of the soldier. Then he scooped up the soldier's weapons and took them back to the tree where he'd stashed his own. He reequipped himself and returned to the soldier lying on the road.

"Your guns are behind the second tree on the right. In case you haven't figured it out, everything the Progression told you is a lie."

He left the soldier stewing in the middle of the road with only his thoughts and the vial of potassium chloride to keep him company.

As Connor continued on his way, he thought about the young soldier's reaction as Liberty's words replayed in his mind.

'This is about more than Ashley, Connor. I know this sounds crazy, but I can't shake the feeling that I'm needed in that town. I keep having these dreams and ... and these kids need a chance. They need a choice, and I think I'm supposed to give them that choice.'

He contemplated the brainwashed soldier he'd left behind, wondering if any of the Progression kids could truly be reclaimed, whether or not they should be reclaimed. They had signed their own death warrants the instant they signed on with the enemy. No one could deny that they deserved death for what they'd done to the country, but they were just children. Liberty was right; there had to be a better way. Connor wondered how many more kneecaps he'd have to break in order to get the Progression kids to think for themselves. Their world consisted of lies and murder. How could anyone reform that? Fueled by anger for the man responsible for all of this, Connor glanced at the sky and made a vow. Even if he and everyone he loved died today, he would kill Major Jack Thompson.

CHAPTER TWENTY-EIGHT

Liberty

I HAD SO many questions for Kylee. I needed to know why she had sold us out, taken Ashley, and killed Shortridge. Desperate for answers, I opened my mouth to unleash a full-on investigation, but the only question that came out was, "Is your mom still alive?"

Jeff squeezed my arm. "That was a scam," he said, making me feel like the biggest fool on the planet.

Kylee chuckled and shook her head. "Of course it was a scam. You really are naïve, aren't you? Forget that though, and let's get to what's important. Where's Connor?"

I didn't have a chance to answer before a deep baritone voice shouted, "Tinstel!"

I had been expecting the Major. Even knowing he would be here, hadn't prepared me for the way his voice unhinged me. The terror of my nightmares came to life and breathed fear down the hallway and up my spine. Just that one word paralyzed me.

Suddenly I realized just how stupid my idea was, and I wanted out of it. I turned and tried to tug Jeff along with me, but he was frozen like an ice sculpture by my side. Wide eyed and tight lipped, he stared in the direction the voice had come from. Jeff had said his father wouldn't kill him, but he didn't look so certain anymore.

Kylee straightened to attention and turned back the way she'd come. "Yes, Sir!"

"Are you going to keep our guests to yourself, or are you going to bring them back here?" the major asked.

No. Don't take us to him.

The sound of heavy footfalls filled the hallway. She didn't have to take us to the major, because he was coming for us.

A whisper of conversation came from the major's direction. He laughed, sounding every bit as nightmarish as I remembered. The echo of his merriment bounced off the hallways and smacked into me, freeing my feet. I took a step back and another. Kylee reached out and grabbed my arm, pulling me toward the laughter. Amusement lit up her eyes.

I swallowed past the lump in my throat to ask, "How could you? Haven't you seen the things he's done?"

Her nails dug in to my flesh until I cried out in pain. It didn't matter, though. All I could focus on was the sound of Major Thompson limping toward us. Closer and closer he came as Kylee held me in place, keeping me from escaping. Jeff moved. I didn't see what he did, but the pressure and pain from Kylee's grip disappeared.

She snatched her hand away and snarled at him. He glared back at her. She ignored him and addressed me. "You haven't seen the things *I've* done. I stabbed that soldier right in his weak and pathetic heart."

"What? Why?"

"Because we're enemies. That's what enemies do, genius. Either they kill us, or we kill them. That's how it works, Liberty."

Kylee's eyes hardened, and I finally understood the depth of her deception. She'd fooled me. They'd all fooled me. They didn't want to be redeemed, they wanted to kill us.

What was I thinking? It was just a dream. I can't help them! I can't even help myself!

I wanted to run, but we were out of time. Major Thompson was upon us.

He clucked his tongue at Kylee. "Now, Sergeant Tinstel, I sent you to welcome our guest, not frighten her."

Kylee snapped to attention. "She tried to run away, Sir."

The major gave her a stern look. "That's because you broke character early, Sergeant. I told you, you have to hold the ruse until the end. Adds to the affect. Besides, Liberty wouldn't get far, would she now?" he asked with a wink.

"No, Sir."

He looked at each of us, and then frowned. "I see the reports are accurate. Dunstan has decided to play games with us."

"He didn't enter the town with these two and we haven't been able to get a visual on him yet," said a male voice behind me.

Since I hadn't heard anyone come in after us, I turned to see who it was. Camouflage and guns crowded the hallway as young soldiers stood at attention.

"Move your men into position. It's time we changed the rules of Dunstan's game. Secure the building, and when Connor appears, tell him we have his ladies and demand his surrender. Bring him in unharmed," the major commanded.

Just like that, the hallway behind us emptied.

"Don't worry, Liberty," the major crooned. "We won't let this minor setback ruin the day we have planned."

He reached for me and I winced, expecting an attack. Instead, he gently took my hands in his, and gazed at me with his lips turned up in an eerie smile.

"Look at you!" he said, acting like we were old friends. "It's good to see you again. Although, it took you quite a bit longer than we anticipated."

He leaned closer and whispered in my ear, "To be honest, I was beginning to wonder whether or not Sergeant Tinstel actually left the note to lead you and Connor here. It's a comfort to know she remains loyal to me. Loyalty is such a fragile thing, you see." The major scowled at Jeff. "Isn't that right, my son?"

Jeff didn't answer.

The major released my hands moved in front of Jeff. "And yet, you came back. I cannot help but wonder why?"

Again, Jeff didn't answer.

The major slid something out of his pocket. There was a flash of silver, and then Jeff cried out in pain. The major leaned back, pulling a short, thin knife from Jeff's forearm.

"No!" I shouted. "Leave him alone!"

"Shh, I'm fine," Jeff insisted, covering the wound with his hand.

I gently grabbed his arm and studied it. A collection of small, thin scars ran up and down the arm. Most were faded with age, but a few looked recent.

Shocked and appalled, I asked, "Are these all from him?" Jeff looked away.

I shook my head. "You shouldn't have come, Jeff."

The major laughed and wiped his blade on Jeff's t-shirt. "Yet, he did. It seems that you somehow managed to instill in Jeff the main character trait that I could not: Loyalty."

I spun on my heel and faced him. "And why would he be loyal to you? You're a monster who attacks his own child and terrorizes his own country."

Jeff grabbed my arm and pulled me back away from his father.

The major clicked his tongue at me. "There's no need for name calling. Jeff causes his own discomfort, and as for the country ... I believe Mark Twain said it best. 'Loyalty to the country always. Loyalty to the government when it deserves it.' Our government hasn't deserved loyalty in a long time. So, we started a new one."

Four soldiers filed into the hallway behind the major and stood at attention.

"Everything's ready?" the major asked his men.

"Yes, Major."

A grin spread across the major's face, practically splitting it in two. "Great! We should get going then. The show is ready to begin!"

Dread soured my stomach. "What show?"

He ignored me. "Search them quickly, so we can go."

Soldiers vigorously patted me and Jeff down. One them stuck his hand in my front jeans pocket and pulled out Boom's paper. He offered it to the major.

"What have we here?" the major asked. "Could it be a note of surrender maybe? Or perhaps some silly order from Dunstan demanding that we release the girl?"

When neither Jeff nor I answered he let out a dramatic sigh and waved us off with a hand. "Well go on, read the thing," he said to the soldier who'd found it.

The soldier's brow furrowed as he scanned the page. "It's from a General Douglass from Fort Lewis and is addressed to the Progression soldiers under the command of ... of you, Major."

The major chuckled. "Oh yes, I'm sure it is. Knowing those windbags, they're ordering us to lay down our arms, shove our tails firmly between our legs and crawl back to them on bloodied knees. Then they'll promptly position us in front of a firing squad and put us out of their misery for good."

Frowning, the soldier shook his head. "No, Sir. It says here that if we defect to the Army we will receive immunity for the crimes we have committed and a full pardon—"

Before he could finish, the major snatched the paper from his hands and read it. "Lies!" he announced, ripping the paper to shreds. Then he ripped those shreds into shreds and threw them on the floor.

"Immunity! Pardon!" he shouted. "These are lies that they will promise you, but we all know the truth. They attacked first. They tried to shut us down. They didn't want us, so we took over and proved to them how valuable we are."

He chuckled. "Now they see the error of their ways, just like General Justice said they would. It's too late for us to come back. Even if we wanted to return to their counterproductive micromanagement, they wouldn't take us back. No, any who defect to the Army will wish for a firing squad after the torture they will subject you to."

"Yes, Major," the soldier replied, but I could see the lines of doubt fracturing his composure. Boom's document had affected him. "It's why you give us the pills. To keep us from all that they would do to us."

The major nodded. "Remember that. The Army will offer you nothing but pain and suffering. Whereas I offer freedom to get what you want."

"Freedom?! You call this freedom?" I asked. "You treat them like killer puppets and send them out to do your dirty work. This isn't freedom, this is—"

A blur came at my face with a loud smack. My neck twisted and my cheek stung. Stars danced before my eyes and I tasted blood. The major had backhanded me. He stood, glaring at me, inches from my face, and I knew he wanted to do much more.

"You will not speak to my soldiers again, or I will kill you," he spat.

I cradled my cheek in my hands.

"Understood?" he asked.

I nodded.

"You have no regard for their lives. You do not know them. You would them to their deaths for some lies on a piece of paper? You will *not* speak to them!"

I stepped back, cowed by the intensity of his tone.

The major calmed and adjusted his shirt, and then held a hand out toward me. "Ah well, your stupidity cannot be helped. Come now. This has put me in a foul mood and I wish to get back to the festivities to lighten my disposition, so I don't kill you before it's time."

I gulped. Jeff filed in beside me, and then we followed the major and his cronies around the corner and through another hall. Each hallway grew a little darker than the last. Finally, we stepped through double doors and entered a pitch-black room. The major paused at the doorway and I squinted into the darkness, trying to make out anything at all.

I heard rustling, followed by a click. The beam of flashlight illuminated the immediate area. We stood atop terrazzo floor, only a few feet from a row of black upholstered seats. I could barely make out an additional row in front of that one, but couldn't see much else.

The major leaned close to me—his fermented breath making my eyes water—and asked, "Did you ever do any acting, Liberty?"

"A little, in school," I replied.

"Did you enjoy it?"

Wondering where his line of questions would lead, I answered, "Yes, but I wasn't very good at it. I could never seem to make myself pretend to be someone other than who I am."

"I could give you a few pointers," Kylee offered.

The major frowned at her. "Sergeant Tinstel, there's no need to be disrespectful. Although it's unfortunate that Liberty doesn't share your acting prowess, you shouldn't belittle her shortcomings."

He grabbed my arm and turned me toward the stage. "But truly, I must disagree about the fundamentals of acting. It's an art form to be able to take on a different identity. Sergeant Tinstel is one of my most accomplished artists."

I shrugged. "I'm sorry, but deception seems like such a waste of talent to me. Kylee could have been so much more. She still could be."

Kylee glared at me.

Loud, raucous laughter surged from the major. I waited, wondering why he found that so funny.

"You're such a delight," he said once he finally regained his composure. "So authentic and transparent. Even in the enemy camp you're trying to save the world. Completely unlike these bootlickers that only ever tell me what they know I want to hear. We could use someone like you in the Progression."

Eying him suspiciously, I replied, "I'm quite certain you'd kill someone like me."

He considered me for a moment before replying. "Yes, perhaps you're right. Well then, enough dilly-dallying. On with the show."

He put his arm through mine and led me past the chairs. We followed the beam of his flashlight to a center aisle, and then turned again and walked deeper into the darkness.

"Lights!" Major Thompson shouted, startling me.

A generator hummed, and then one lone spotlight sputtered and clicked on. It sat above us on a stage and lit up a large circle in the middle of dark velvet curtains. Beside me, Major Thompson giggled like a psychotic child on a sugar high.

"I do so love the theatre, don't you?" he asked.

Certain I wouldn't love anything he was this excited to show me, I chewed on my lip.

"Come now," he dragged me along. "We have to get good seats!"

CHAPTER TWENTY-NINE

Connor

CONNOR STARED ACROSS the four lane road in front of Granite Falls High School. Even if he could magically teleport himself across the street, he'd be dead before he came within ten yards of the school. The major's choice for a base had been a brilliant one, since open parking lots with sparse landscaping bordered the school. A few vehicles sat abandoned in the parking lots, but getting to them safely would prove tricky.

Although, if Jeff was right about his father, Connor wouldn't have to walk across that parking lot until the Major stood waiting for him on the other side. That was—of course—assuming Connor could trust Jeff. Connor was still pondering the wisdom of the plan when the front doors of the school swung open. He ducked down and watched through the scope of his assault rifle as soldiers filed out of the building and pressed against the walls. They split up, and he counted them as they fanned out into their positions around the building.

One crouched in the shadows to the left of the door. He lost sight of two, three and four behind bushes and trees. Five knelt behind a bench. Six disappeared for a moment, and then reappeared right before ducking behind an abandoned truck in the lot. Glass crunched and something on the roof caught Connor's eye. Number seven broke the window and started crawling out.

Without killing them? Right, Libby.

Connor sighed and aimed his M4. He squeezed the trigger and planted three shots into the wooden paneling that encircled the window, forcing the roof climber to rethink his position. Connor kept an eye on the window, but the soldier didn't try again. If he had any chance of surviving this, he needed to keep them on the ground.

"Connor Dunstan!" one of the soldiers shouted, his pubescent voice cracking on the last syllable.

Connor peered into the scope on his M4 and watched the young soldier stand and project his voice.

"We have your daughter and your—," he paused and whispered to the soldier beside him. They shared a brief conversation, and then he projected his voice again. "And a woman named Liberty. Lay down your weapons and come in, and neither of them will get hurt."

"Bring out my daughter!" Connor shouted back. "I want to make sure she's unharmed before I surrender."

"I'm afraid we can't do that, Sir. Our orders are to bring you in, but I assure you, she has not been hurt."

The soldier was arrogant enough to stand in the open, giving Connor a clear shot. He scanned the boy's body, trying to decide where to shoot him. He settled on the outside left thigh and squeezed the trigger. Return gunfire erupted and Connor hid behind a tree and waited for the shots to die down. When there was a lull, he peeked out again. From his angle, he could still see the foot of another soldier—the one behind the truck—so he aimed and fired.

More gunshots replied.

Zero dead, two wounded and five left. Connor stood and projected his voice. "I've taken a leg and a foot. I could have killed both of them, but I don't want to. I don't even want to hurt you guys, but I will. So help me God, I will wound every single one of you until my daughter is brought out."

"But if you'd just surrender, we can take you to her." A different soldier spoke now.

"That's not going to happen, so I suggest you get in there and tell the major I want to see my daughter."

Arguing came from the front of the school as the soldiers discussed their options. Then finally, one replied, "Okay. We'll go talk to the Major. Just don't shoot."

Connor peeked around the tree and saw them file into the school. Two of the five had a soldier riding piggy back.

Connor leaned against the tree and waited.

CHAPTER THIRTY

Liberty

As JEFF AND I followed Major Thompson down the center aisle to the front row of seats, we heard a few shots from outside the front of the building. I paused and looked back, wondering if Connor was okay. The major motioned us along, and then sat once he was a few seats in. He directed me to sit beside him, and I did, with Jeff sitting on the other side of me. Soldiers filed in around us. I heard them behind me and resisted the urge to turn around and look at them. I deliberately laced my fingers and put my hands in my lap so I wouldn't fidget as we stared at the spotlight on the curtain. I couldn't stand the waiting, though.

"Where is Ashley?" I asked.

The general shook his head. "Now is not the time for questions. For now, we will sit and wait for the actors."

More gunshots erupted outside. I winced, and the major frowned.

"Ahh," he said. "I see our 'star' has decided not to come quietly. That's a pity. I do hope they don't accidentally kill him. That would be most inconvenient."

Why? What the heck are you planning?

"At any rate, I suppose we should get started." The major sat back in his chair and cleared his throat. Projecting his voice, he ordered, "Open the curtain."

The curtains slowly parted to reveal Ashley sitting, mid-stage, on a high-backed chair. A Progression soldier stood beside her, with a hand gun pressed against her temple. She squinted into the sudden light, and she tried to raise her arms, but her wrists were tied to the chair.

A strangled sound escaped from my lips as I stood, intent on rushing down there and freeing Ashley, but Jeff grabbed my wrist. Surprised, I turned toward him and he shook his head at me.

"He wants you to react," he whispered, nodding toward the major.

Right.

Mentally kicking myself for being so stupid, I sat and put my hands back in my lap.

She's okay. She's alive and they're holding her. She's okay. Just breathe and be smart.

I recapped the plan in my head, vowing to stick to it. After I collected myself, I nodded to Jeff to let him know I was back under control. When my gaze returned to the stage, I felt the major watching me.

Enjoying the show?

Since I couldn't trust myself to speak, I kept my mouth closed and watched Ashley. Moments ticked away as I wondered where Braden was. I also silently questioned the absence of the major's evil daughter, Gina. Surely she'd want to be here, savoring this moment of hell for us. If we survived, I'd have to ask Jeff where she was stashed if we survived.

When we survive. Think positive. When, not if.

Footfalls hurried through the hallway, growing louder as they approached. Jeff and I turned and watched the door, awaiting news about Connor. Three anxious young soldiers burst into the room and paused to scan the area. Then one of them marched over to us, bent down and whispered something to the major. Two more soldiers filed in, each carrying a wounded boy on his back.

Wounded, but not dead. Thank you, Connor.

"Why did you leave your post?" the major asked. "Were your directions unclear?"

"No, Major, our orders were perfectly clear." the soldier standing closest to the major replied. "But he shot Briggs and Stuart and asked us to bring you a message."

The major glanced over his shoulder at the two wounded soldiers, who were being lowered to the ground.

"They need a medic," the soldier insisted.

"They're still breathing, so they should not have turned from their directive. You are all facing insubordination for this!" the major shouted. He stood and took a couple of deep breaths. "You all know the cost. We do what we must to keep our brothers and sisters safe. To stay free. Are you failing me, Corporal Noyes?"

The soldier stiffened. "No, Major."

"Well, you might as well tell me his message."

"He says he'll surrender as soon as he sees the girl. He wants to make sure she's unharmed."

"Just the girl?"

Noyes nodded.

"Interesting." The major looked at me and asked, "Why just the girl?"

I was a horrible liar, so I swallowed back the lie I'd planned to tell and stuck as close to the truth as possible. Shrugging, I replied, "I didn't like Connor's plan, so I decided to try my own. His feelings might be a little hurt about that."

"I see." The major nodded. "And what, exactly, is your plan?"

"Walk in the front door and ask to see Ashley, no killing, no dying."

The major chuckled. "And what was Connor's plan?"

"Use lots of big guns and storm the castle."

"Can you think of any other reason why Connor wouldn't want me to take you outside?"

I chewed on my lip for a moment. "Yeah. I talk a lot. He might be kind of tired of that."

The major laughed. "She talks a lot," he said to the soldiers.

A few of them chuckled, but most remained quiet.

"I can go talk to him, Major," Jeff volunteered. "I'll convince him that the girls are in danger, and that he needs to lay down his weapons."

"What sort of fool do you take me for?" The major sneered at Jeff. "I don't know what you two have planned, but I do remember telling you what your fate would be if you chose to ignore my commands again. I trust that you haven't forgotten that?"

"No, Major." Jeff lowered his head.

As the major stood, he gestured for the soldier on the stage to bring Ashley to him. The soldier nodded and started untying her.

"My apologies for the delay in our show, but I must see to a momentary inconvenience outside. It turns out that the old adage is correct; if you want something done right, you truly do have to do it yourself."

The soldier from the stage tugged Ashley from the platform and stood her beside the major. She watched me as he grabbed her arm and tugged her toward the aisle. He paused long enough to direct Kylee to sit in his vacated seat beside me.

"She likes to talk, Tinstel. So, if she so much as opens her mouth, kill them both."

"Yes, Major," Kylee replied.

Then he was gone. With his final declaration, he'd demolished our plans. I sat, dumbfounded, wondering how to win over these kids without speaking. The task was impossible. I had to explain—to make them understand—that there was a better way. I looked to Jeff for support, but he wouldn't meet my eyes. He had to feel as disheartened as I did. I closed my eyes and prayed, waiting for the right answer to come to me. Time ticked away and I had no answers.

I opened my eyes and searched until I finally spotted Braden standing directly behind me. Head bowed and shoulders lowered, he seemed sorrowful and upset. I closed my eyes and prayed again. This time a sparrow greeted me behind my eyelids. She was brave, fierce, and completely untouchable by the fire. For the first time in a long time, I felt protected.

'His eye is on the sparrow,' Boom's voice whispered in my ear.

Encouraged, I opened my eyes and said, "Brae! Thank God you're okay."

Confusion creased his forehead.

"Shut up," Kylee said. "Talk again and I'll kill you."

She should have killed me when I first said his name, but she didn't. Braden looked at me. The remorse in his eyes encouraged me far more than Kylee's promise of death scared me.

"I was worried about you! I had a letter with me, but the major ripped it up. The army has offered immunity and pardon to anyone who defects."

"I said shut up!" Kylee screamed.

I could see her out the corner of my eye. With both hands, she aimed a handgun straight at me. Anger distorted her features as her body stilled.

"I know you were afraid before, but you don't have to be afraid anymore. You can join us." I looked around. "You can all join us."

Braden lunged for me, jumping over the seat. There was a loud bang, and then he crashed into me. I toppled over. My left shoulder hit the hard floor first, and excruciating pain blossomed from the point of contact. My left hip hit next, causing a lesser wave of pain down my side. Braden landed on top of me, his upper body smashing my head into the floor. I smelled copper, my ears rang, and stars danced through my vision.

Was I shot?

My entire body was full of pain and pressure, making it difficult to breathe. I tried to ask Braden if he was okay, but couldn't form the words, much less speak them.

"No!" someone shouted. "Oh, God, no!"

Kylee. She continued screaming as the weight of Braden's body lifted off me. Jeff appeared inches from my face, his eyes wide and his face white as he looked me over.

He said something, but I couldn't hear him over the ringing and the screaming.

"What?" I asked.

"Were you shot?" he asked.

The ringing started to fade, but Kylee's cries grew louder. Jeff's gaze drifted down to my shirt. Blood drenched the front of me.

"I don't know," I replied.

Kylee screamed again. She knelt in front of Braden. "Why?! You're so stupid, Brae. Why would you do that?"

"Because Liberty's right," I heard Braden say, his voice barely audible over the fading ringing of my ears. "I'm sick of killing and I'm sick of taking. There has to be a better way."

"What about dying?" Kylee argued. "You sick of that, yet? Because that's what they'll do to all of us."

"No. We saw what the Army's really like. The major's been lying to us all along, Kye. We can trust the Army. We have to help them."

"What's wrong with Braden?" I asked.

Jeff looked at the kid and shook his head, his eyes sorrowful.

"He was shot!" Kylee shouted. "He was shot because you couldn't keep your big mouth shut!"

"What?! No!" It no longer mattered how much my body hurt, I had to get to him. I pushed myself to a sitting position, leaned over, and slithered along the floor to where he lay. Jeff objected at first, but when he saw he couldn't stop me, he put his arms under mine and helped me until I stopped front of Braden.

The boy was sprawled out on his back with his arms and legs stretched out as if he was making a snow angel on the auditorium floor. Kylee leaned over him with her hands pressed against his chest. Blood oozed around her fingers and covered the front of Braden's shirt. Still shocked, I watched as she tried to staunch the bleeding, and started screaming for a medic. The rest of the soldiers just stood there watching, their jaws hanging open.

He's dying!

The realization hit me like a knife to the heart. My eyes flooded with tears. "Why? This should be me, Brae. I'm sorry. I'm so sorry."

"You're damn right it should be you," Kylee snapped. Keeping one hand pressed against her brother's chest, she put her gun to my head. "You just couldn't shut up, could you? You did this!"

"No," Braden replied. "We did this. And now we must fix it. Libby, I figured out what my purpose is."

My heart wanted to shatter at the bravery of the kid. Tears fell from my eyes as I watched him affect the soldiers around him and witnessed what a great leader he would have made. He had given up his life not only for me, but for all of them.

I swallowed back the emotions that threatened to consume me and asked, "What is that, Brae?"

His legs and arms started shaking. Sweat beaded on his pale forehead.

"My purpose was always to die." He gave me a weak smile, and then turned his gaze on his sister, who still had her gun pointed at my head. "I get to die saving a life, Kye. Please promise me that my sacrifice wasn't for nothing."

The gun resting against the side of my head started trembling violently.

"I can't do that."

"Yes, you can," Braden whispered. "I love you, sis."

Before she could reply, his eyes rolled up into his head and his body relaxed.

The pressure from Kylee's gun disappeared, and then metal clanged on the floor. Any ounce of composure she had left shattered. She grabbed hold of his shoulders and him, begging him to wake up. Sobs ripped through her, jerking her body with the force of guilt and sorrow. I didn't know what to say or do, so I leaned against Jeff. He draped an arm over my shoulders as I cried beside Kylee.

The doors darkened, reminding me that we were still very much in danger. I looked up to see Connor between two soldiers, walking alongside the major who was still using Ashley as a shield in front of him.

"What's going on here?" the major demanded.

CHAPTER THIRTY-ONE

Connor

CONNOR DROPPED HIS weapons behind the tree, knowing they'd be taken from him if he didn't. He watched the school entrance, wondering—once again—if Jeff was right about the major. After what seemed like an eternity, the doors swung open and two soldiers stepped through. They were followed by Ashley, Major Thompson, and two more soldiers. The major held Ashley directly in front of him, with a pistol pressed against her head, while the soldiers surrounded him, scanning the parking lot with their guns drawn.

Connor considered the scene. He could shoot the major without hurting Ashley. But, how would the soldiers respond? Would they shoot back at Connor or just kill Ashley right away? He wasn't willing to gamble with his daughter's life, so he dropped his last gun—his Glock—and waited for the major to tell him what to do.

"Dunstan, I'm appalled at your manners," the major announced. "Here I have your daughter completely unharmed, and you waltz up and start shooting my men."

"I could have killed those boys. You wanted me to, didn't you? You practically served them to me on a platter, Major Thompson. Your disregard for the lives of your soldiers is disgusting. You should give them to me. We both know I'll treat them better."

The major twisted Ashley's arm until she cried out in pain. "Do you think it's wise to antagonize me?" he asked.

Game over. Connor stepped out from behind the tree with his hands up. "No. I'm sorry. Please don't hurt her."

The soldiers all aimed their weapons at Connor as the major released Ashley's arm. She rubbed it while Connor inched toward her, trying to buy Liberty as much time as possible without putting his daughter in further danger.

"Good to see that you've come to your senses," the major said.

Connor crossed the street and stepped into the parking lot.

"Just keep coming, nice and slow. Keep your hands where we can see them."

Since the major had ordered it, Connor slowed his pace to a crawl. When he finally reached the major, soldiers swarmed him, patted him down and announced that he was clean.

A gun went off inside the school. Someone screamed.

"Well, I did instruct her not to talk," the major said with a shrug.

Fear swept up Connor's spine, and Ashley brushed tears away with her shoulder as the soldiers herded them into the school.

Another scream followed indecipherable orders. It didn't sound like Liberty's voice, but still, Connor worried. The soldiers at his sides prevented him from sprinting ahead to find out what had happened. The major limped along as they slowly led him down two never-ending halls and into a dark auditorium. A single spotlight lit up the stage, illuminating a vacant chair center stage. Soldiers clustered around the floor in front of the stage.

"What's going on here?" the major asked, his deep baritone echoing off the walls.

Kylee stood. Blood covered the front of her shirt and her face glistened with tears in the dim light. "Braden's been shot!" she replied.

"What?" the major asked. "By whom?"

Since Jeff and Liberty both entered unarmed, Connor wondered the same thing. The major and the soldiers looked puzzled and distracted as they watched Kylee. Connor had an opportunity. He eyed the long knife holstered around the waist of the soldier next to him. Two armed soldiers stood within striking range, but both neither was paying attention to him. One snap of a strap, and Connor slid the knife free. He spun and lunged, simultaneously knocking the major's hand upward and sliding the blade across his neck. Adrenaline and pride flooded Connor's veins at the sight of the major's blood, making him feel invincible. The gun fired, and plaster sprayed down on Connor from above.

Everyone in the room turned to stare at Connor and the major. Guns aimed, jaws dropped, and Connor spun the major so his dying body shielded Connor and Ashley. While the major grabbed at his throat, trying to staunch the flow of blood, Connor disarmed him, and then pushed Ashley away, shoving her into the hallway behind him.

"Stay low and out here," he said before slamming the door closed.

He turned back around, expecting to be riddled with bullets the instant the major stopped breathing. Instead, the soldiers seemed frozen as they watched the major frantically cling to life.

Gurgling sounds came from the major. Then, finally, his head bent forward. A crimson necklace stretched across the front of his throat, dripping down into his shirt.

The two soldiers who had brought Connor in turned their weapons on each other. Around the auditorium, fights broke out. Some weapons were still aimed at Connor, but several turned on other soldiers. A caramel-skinned boy dropped his gun and lunged at another soldier's throat with his bare hands. A brunette girl wound up and punched a blonde in the face.

Liberty stood in the center of the chaos, her eyes round and terrified. A boy fell into her. She helped him up, and then planted her feet and her hands around her mouth.

"Stop it!" she screamed. "Enough with the killing. Can we just … just stop for a minute? Please?"

Eyes swollen and cheeks wet, she wiped her nose and took a deep breath. "If you were so 'free' under the Progression, why are you guys acting like this now that the major is dead?" she asked.

The auditorium remained quiet.

"This is your first taste of freedom and you're wasting it!" Liberty pointed at one of the younger soldiers. "You. What's your name?"

He didn't answer.

She swallowed and wiped her eyes. "Please. How old are you?"

"His name's Liam, and he's twelve," someone said from the corner.

Connor searched for the speaker and found a small group of kids doctoring the two soldiers he'd shot. They worked in the limited light from the hall, so he picked up the flashlight the major had dropped and walked it over to them. He heard adjustments being made in the shadows and wondered how many guns followed him. As he handed the flashlight to one of the kids, he felt Liberty watching him as well. She waited until he stopped moving to continue.

She stared at the ceiling for a few moments. When she looked at the group, more tears glistened in her eyes. "When I was twelve I spent every summer day swimming at the public pool with my friends. Do you guys ever get to swim?"

Silence answered her.

"Liam, do you know how to swim?" she asked.

He shook his head.

A strangled noise escaped from Liberty's lips. "Have you ever ridden a bike?"

Again, he shook his head no.

"Have you ever owned a pet?"

This time his brow furrowed when he shook his head.

"Read a book?"

Kylee stood and crossed her arms. "Get to your point, Liberty."

Liberty turned toward Kylee. "They ripped the joys of childhood from you kids, and created killers. The major called this freedom, and you guys believed him because it's all you've ever known. But this is *not* freedom."

Kylee snorted. "And you can offer us more? In case you haven't noticed, you guys are losing. You're dying. You're practically extinct."

"We're only dying because they convinced you to kill us. Just know that when we do become extinct, so will freedom. Kids will never again swim or ride bikes or play with puppies or read books or play games. You'll forever be enslaved to the Progression, going where they say, and killing who they tell you to kill. Do you really want to live like that?"

Kylee picked up her handgun and aimed it at her. "Shut up, Liberty."

"I know you hate me, but please … just help me rescue these kids. Braden knew the truth. He trusted me and he wanted a better way. Please, just—"

"I said shut up!" Kylee shouted. She raised her aim just above my head and squeezed the trigger, emptying her gun into the wall behind me. Then she threw it on the ground and grabbed the assault rifle from her back. "Yeah, he trusted you, and look how far it got him. You expect us to sign up for that? No thanks. I plan to live."

Kylee looked at her brother's body and shook her head. "Brae asked me not to kill you, so I won't. Not this time. But, next time I see you, you will pay."

She dropped to her knees and kissed her brother on the forehead. Then she stood and projected her voice. "Anyone else sick of listening to this stupid woman who wants to get us all killed?"

A few soldiers nodded.

"Good. Let's get out of here."

Kylee marched past Connor with eleven soldiers following her. She swung open the door. Ashley cowered in the corner, and Kylee didn't even spare the girl a glance as she left.

Connor straightened. He retrieved Ashley from the hall and brought her into the auditorium. Along with the remaining soldiers, they stood and silently watched Liberty.

Silence lingered, adding weight to the situation. Liberty sighed and spun around, looking at the soldiers.

"I'm not lying," she whispered. Then she fell to her knees on the floor beside Braden's corpse. "I'm so sorry, Brae. I thought if I could just tell them the truth, they'd understand we're not the enemy. I just wanted the killing to stop. I never thought you'd ... I never meant for this to happen."

Several soldiers had stayed behind. In the darkness, Connor couldn't make out the exact number, but it seemed like more stayed than left. They were interested in the offer Liberty had made.

Connor tugged on Ashley's hand, and the two joined Liberty. Connor knelt beside her and draped his arm across her shoulders. "Hey. Braden gave up his life because he believed we could make peace. Let's not let him die in vain."

Liberty's brows furrowed. "Huh?"

Connor looked up, calling her attention to the soldiers that watched her. When she nearly fell over from the shock, Connor steadied her, and then helped her to her feet.

Liberty wiped her eyes and looked around, her eyes growing round. "So many of you stayed! Does this mean you'll come with us? You'll help us put an end to all this killing?"

Nobody replied. Liberty's shoulders slumped. She lowered her head and Connor started to reach for her. Shuffling noises coming from the shadows made him pause. A single soldier stepped into the light, carrying his semi-automatic. He looked maybe fifteen, and had a mop of red-orange hair and cheeks full of freckles. He marched through the silence, stopping in front of Liberty, where he laid his weapon at her feet.

"I will come with you," he said. "If you'll take me."

Liberty choked back a sob. She lunged forward, hugging the boy. "Yes! Yes, of course. What's your name?"

"Sergeant Aiden Greenshaw, Ma'am."

"Thank you, Aiden. Thank you so much."

Liberty continued to squeeze him as young boys and girls materialized from the shadows. They marched in single file and dropped their weapons on top of Aiden's. Liberty released the redhead only to hug a blonde girl who dimpled when she smiled. Next, came a blond boy with a scar on his cheek. Liberty hugged each, getting their names and thanking them. As they continued to come, Connor took a step back and counted heads.

Thirty-four plus two wounded.

Wow.

Tears rolling down her face, Liberty looked down at Braden. "You were the most courageous person I ever met, and because of that, your death will not be in vain. I promise you that we will take care of your brothers and sisters. Thank you, Brae. Rest in peace."

She leaned over and kissed his cheek.

CHAPTER THIRTY-TWO

Liberty

CONNOR WHISPERED MY name. Fearing that some new terror was upon us, I opened my eyes.

He smiled at me. "There you are. Come on. I need to show you something." He stood and offered me his hand.

Moonlight filtered in through the windows, highlighting the lumpy sleeping bags that covered the floor. The soft snoring of sleeping children sounded like a beautiful symphony to my ears. I glanced around, shocked once again at how many of them there were. Truthfully, I'd been afraid to fall asleep—terrified that they'd all change their minds and sneak off in the night—but there seemed to be even more than I remembered.

"Is it my imagination, or have they multiplied?" I asked Connor.

He grinned. "We'll talk about that later. Come on. We're gonna miss it."

Smiling at his infectious excitement, I gave him my hand and let him pull me to my feet. "What are we going to miss?"

"Shh. Don't wake the kids."

He tugged me along, through the large living room of his old client's unfinished house. We crept out the front door and into the yard, which had been overtaken by horses. Beyond the horses, several soldiers kept watch from shallow holes in the ground, scanning the surrounding area with assault rifles.

"What are they doing?" I asked Connor.

"Pulling security. I'm teaching them how to do it the right way."

I nodded and went back to the horses. "There has to be at least thirty horses here. And is that ... oh gosh, it's Cinnamon!" I could swear she winked at me, so I stepped toward her.

"No time," Connor said, pulling me back. "You can catch up with Cinnamon afterward."

"After what?"

He ignored the question and towed me to the side of the house where a small, wooden gazebo stood. Wildflowers of every color threaded the lattices on the sides of the structure. They smelled like summer, and their vibrant colors stood out in contrast to the wood.

"Did you do this?" I asked.

He shrugged, grinning. "I had a lot of help."

I stopped to admire the flowers, but Connor tugged me inside the gazebo.

"What are we doing?" I asked. "Why the hurry?"

Once we were inside, he turned and hooked his fingers through my front belt loops, pulling me closer to him. "I wanted to share this with you."

I looked around. "The gazebo? You wouldn't even let me stop to look at it."

"Nope." Connor's grin widened as he pointed toward the east. "That."

The sun peeked over the distant mount range, spreading a warm glow over the earth. I leaned against Connor and watched as the sun crept upward, brightening the sky as it brought us a new day.

"It looks different, doesn't it?" Connor asked.

"What do you mean?"

"Everything. It smells so fresh in here. And the sky ... the sky looks like change. Everything just feels so hopeful. This is ... this is God, isn't it? This is what allows you to stumble into hostile situations and survive. This is what you feel protecting you?"

The day hadn't changed, Connor had. Unable to speak, I nodded.

"Look around!" he exclaimed. "It's so beautiful!"

Everything from the tall evergreens to the distant, snow-covered mountaintops was indeed, beautiful. But, my gaze lingered on the ground. Sleeping bags lay scattered everywhere. I didn't know where they'd all come from, but the sight of them brought tears to my eyes. "How many are there?" I asked.

"What?" He followed my gaze and grinned. "Oh. Eighty-three."

"What?!"My dreams collided with reality, sending my head spinning. Once again I counted eighty-three dead children and eighty-three flames of fire. Goose bumps sprouted across my flesh, and understanding made my legs wobbly. Thankful Connor stood so close, I grabbed a fistful of his t-shirt and held on, waiting for the dizziness to pass.

"What's wrong? All the color just drained from your face."

"How certain are you of that number?" I asked.

"We can take another headcount, but I'm pretty sure. We had to keep a tally, because they trickled in all night."

I glanced around at the sleeping bags and the horses. "How did they find us?"

"After you passed out, several kids asked if they could go tell the others, the ones on patrol around the town. I honestly thought they'd changed their minds and were running out on us, but my gut told me to let them go. They multiplied and came back."

"Wow. This keeps getting crazier. There were eighty-three in my dreams too."

"In your dreams?" he asked. "The dreams that told you to go in there?"

"They didn't exactly come out and say that, but yes." I rubbed at goose bumps on my arms. "Bizarre, huh? It feels ... humbling."

"Why do you say that?"

"It's like God's trying to do this huge thing through me and I'm just ... I can't ..." I looked away. "The reason I never told you about my dad is because it's embarrassing."

"Your parents loved each other and your dad died in the service. What's embarrassing about that?"

"I didn't get to the embarrassing part yet. I'm surprised you haven't figured it out."

His brows furrowed.

"My name, Connor. My dad was in the Navy and on ... leave when I was conceived."

His eyes brightened with understanding and he chuckled. 'Liberty call.' That's what the sailor's call it, right?"

I rolled my eyes. "Worst naming ever."

He only laughed harder.

"You're kind of a jerk, you know that?" I asked, struggling to maintain my frown.

"That's funny, and you know it. I'm never going to look at you the same way again."

I shook my head, still trying not to smile. "It's horrid, and so are you for laughing."

"You're laughing too!"

"I am not. I'm just in shock that I told you. I had planned to take that secret to my grave."

Connor's laughter died down and his eyes focused on mine. "I'm glad you told me," he whispered. "I want to know all your secrets. You have nothing to be embarrassed about. You're beautiful and kind and courageous and funny, and I can completely understand why God would choose to use you. I would choose you."

His eyes took on an intensity that made my heart skip a beat. I didn't know how to respond, so I didn't.

"Now tell me about these dreams," he said. "What did you dream about? Eighty-three diamonds?"

I eyed him, suspicious about the abrupt subject change. "No, why?"

"You said I had to buy you enough time for a fat rock. I bought you enough time to win eighty-three precious diamonds."

He pulled his fingers out of my belt loops and slid one under my hand. He slipped the other into his pocket, and then he got down on one knee and looked up at me.

"I'd like to give you one more. Marry me?" Connor asked.

Thrown completely off guard, I chewed on my lip as fear, love, hope, and doubt waged war inside me.

"I don't want some Princess Buttercup who stands by, waiting for me to save the world. I want the fiery redhead so full of passion and hope that she breaks down the enemy's door to free kids. I want you."

My heart melted by his words, he pulled a ring out of his pocket and held it up for me to see. A round, brilliant-cut diamond, encircled by bezel-framed sapphires, sat atop a delicate platinum band. It was beautiful, antique-looking and completely unique.

"That is gorgeous," I whispered. "Where did you get it?"

"My secret." He leaned closer. "Can I put it on you?"

I stared at the ring, mesmerized by the sentiment it represented. *Forever*, it seemed to whisper. This handsome, dangerous man who trusted and loved me wanted to make a lifelong commitment to me. How could I say no? "Yes. Yes, Connor. I'll marry you."

He slid the ring up my finger, over my knuckle and stood, pulling me against him. "I love you," he whispered before covering my lips with his.

An equal number of "awws" and "ewws" could be heard behind us as he kissed me deeply. He tasted of promise and hope, making me realize how much the morning sun had changed. That day, eighty-three kids traveled beside Connor, Jeff, Ashley and me as we left Granite Falls, hurrying to catch up with Boom. We had won this battle, but the war was about to begin.

"That is why we never give up. Though our bodies are dying, our spirits are being renewed every day. For our present troubles are small and won't last very long. Yet they produce for us a glory that vastly outweighs them and will last forever! So we don't look at the troubles we can see now; rather, we fix our gaze on things that cannot be seen. For the things we see now will soon be gone, but the things we cannot see will last forever." 2 Corinthians 4:16-18

Amanda Washington first put her dreams to paper in 1999. She divides her writing time between two series: Perseverance and Chronicles of the Broken. When she's not writing, she's usually busy with her husband, Meltarrus, and their five boys.

I hope you've enjoyed **Liberty's Hope**

Please visit:
http://www.amandawashington.net

Find me on Facebook, too!
https://www.facebook.com/AmandaWashington.Author

Other books by Amanda Washington

Rescuing Liberty: Perseverance Book 1
Chronicles of the Broken Book 1: Deadly Fall
Chronicles of the Broken Book 2: Blood, Fear and Pain

Made in the USA
Charleston, SC
22 February 2014